MW01128443

How Long, O Lord

Stories of
Twentieth Century Korea

GEORGE EWING OGLE

To order additional copies of this book, contact:
Xlibris Corporation
1-888-795-4274
www.Xlibris.com
Orders@Xlibris.com

CONTENTS

Preface

This collection of stories, *How Long, O Lord?* reflects the on-going prayer of the Korean people for justice. Throughout the twentieth century, oppressions of one kind or another have been inflicted upon them. First it was Japanese imperialism. Then, just as they were anticipating liberation and independence after World War II, the United States and USSR divided the country, and the cold war policies resulted in a devastating civil war that permanently separated ten million family members. Technically the war continues. No peace treaty has ever been signed. Both sides continue to maintain large military forces. The "threat from the other side" has allowed the communist dictator in the north and the military dictators in the capitalist south to justify oppression of their own people.

The title of this book comes from phrases in a prayer written by church leaders from North and South Korea in 1988. The prayer was used by churches around the world in 1995, fifty years after the division of Korea.

This book is a history book written in a different way. While it will acquaint the reader with major events of twentieth century Korea, it tells history as stories about peasants, industrial workers, and ordinary citizens as they have endured and reacted to the various oppressions that have come their way. They are stories that speak not only of the unnecessary suffering of people, but also of their faith in their religion and traditions from which comes their dignity and their search for justice. Their courageous witness has helped to shape the course of the nation.

The names in all the stories are written in the usual Korean order with the family names first. Only the name of South Korea's first President is written with the family name last. He

is much better known among English speakers as Syngman
Rhee.

The first story is one that is not often told. *Father and Son*
spans the years from 1919 to the mid-1970's. It is a story of
two generations of peasants from Korea's poorest farming area
in Cholla Namdo who endured and dreamed under the burdens of the Japanese. It is also about the interaction of wider,
stronger forces that sweep away the peoples' dream for land
and freedom; and yet cannot destroy their dignity.

Until recent years I probably would not have written this
story. I arrived in South Korea in 1954, the year after the Armi-
stice was signed. The destruction of the war could still be seen
everywhere. Homes, churches, schools, industries were yet to
be rebuilt. Millions had been killed. Assassinations and massacres had been committed on both sides. As a missionary, I was
working closely with church people. Many of them were refugees from the north who had escaped from communist perse-
cution. They would not have had much sympathy for some of
the characters in *Father and Son*.

Now things have changed dramatically. In 1987 the Korean people won democratic reforms by showing the military
dictators that they could no longer control them by making
them afraid of the north. Koreans see that the perpetuation of
the division has resulted in decades of military build-up, making the Korean peninsula one of the most dangerous places in
the world.

The change in mindset is best described by the following
excerpts from an address presented by Suh Kwang-sun from
Ewha Women's University at the Fourth Korean—North American Church Consultation in Honolulu in 1986:

> Most Christians in the south and the north seem to
> identify themselves with the sons and daughters of Abel
> and would ask the same question: How can the sons

and daughters of Abel make peace with Cain? The Godless Cain is the one who murdered Abel. Cain is the one who divided the country. Cain is strong and has powerful weapons: Cain should not be trusted, and God should destroy him.

But now, at the same time, more and more Korean Christians have come to realize that the sons and daughters of Abel will have to live with the Cains, the sons and daughters of Cain, together, side by side, in peace, in order for them to survive and to live a meaningful life without fear of death and annihilation.

The next two stories, *Strange Things Happen* and *We Won't Go Back,* are written out of my own personal experience in Urban Industrial Mission (UIM). As the peasants did earlier, workers in industry also sought dignity and justice, but they too found their dreams blocked by stronger powers. Military governments in cooperation with large industrial conglomerates refused to accept worker demands for participation.

When my wife Dorothy and I returned to Korea in 1960, industrialization and economic development were beginning to take hold. The mood of the people had changed from one of despondency to one of hope for the future.

In 1961 the bishop of the Korean Methodist Church sent me to Inchun to begin a new ministry. For ten years I worked as a staff member helping to carry out education programs and a variety of support ministries for Inchun's factory and dock workers. My Korean colleagues began their probationary period at UIM by doing labor in one or the other of Inchun's many factories. I was assigned to be factory chaplain. Each week my routine was to visit factories to talk with workers or hold lunchtime rap sessions, to call upon union leaders and company managers, and to make pastoral visits to homes and hospitals.

Through the years we at UIM became very close to Korea's industrial workers. At first, because there was a democratic constitution and labor laws that defended workers' rights, UIM also had good relationships with the government and company management.

When in the 1970's and 1980's the military government and economic planners decided to stamp out the rights of working people in order to achieve their ambitious economic development plans, the UIM staff was put under constant police surveillance. Several were arrested, imprisoned and beaten by the Korean Central Intelligence Agency (KCIA).

I left UIM for an extended furlough from 1971-1973 to complete my PhD in International Industrial Relations at the University of Wisconsin. About the time I was finishing my dissertation I received an invitation to teach at Seoul National University. When I agreed to that offer, I did not realize how different things had become in Korea.

By 1973 the new *Yushin Constitution* had been promulgated. It allowed no criticism of the government and called for secret military trials and long prison sentences. The Korean CIA had invaded almost every area of Korean life. Even in the church there were spies who came and wrote down what was said in prayers and sermons. Many pastors and other Christian friends were put in prison. I attended weekly prayer meetings for them. The wives of the Christian prisoners introduced me to the wives of eight men who had been given the death sentence.

Prayer for the Innocents, My Body and *Tearoom,* tell of the torture and execution of these eight men who were falsely accused of being part of a conspiracy to overthrow South Korea's military dictatorship. The central characters in these stories are not dreamers, nor are they crusaders for justice. They are men and women who just want to live an ordinary life. They are victims of a military power gone amuck. Though they are not heroes, they belong to the "innocents" of this world who should be remembered. Because I prayed for these men I was deported from South Korea in December 1974. My family followed me to the United States in 1975. As my wife was leaving Korea, friends commissioned her with the words, "Go tell our story".

In 1975 I wrote my first book about Korea. *Liberty to the Captives: The struggle against oppression in South Korea. It* documented my years as a missionary in Korea.

In the following years, South Korea's movement for human rights and democracy became more and more organized. There was a broad coalition of groups—students, educators, farmers, laborers, church and civic leaders. The military government responded with more arrests, long prison sentences and torture.

In 1980 South Korean troops attacked protesting civilians in KwangJu killing hundreds. One of Korea's main dissidents, Kim Dae Jung, received the death sentence for allegedly inciting the people to riot. The tide turned against the military government. More and more ordinary citizens participated in the movement for democracy. When the government tried to justify its actions by saying it was necessary because of the communist threat from the north the people answered with cries for democracy and unification.

By June of 1987 protests by citizens had spread to all the major cities of South Korea. There was not enough tear gas to stop them. The President who had hand picked his successor agreed to hold democratic elections.

In 1989 I spent three months in South Korea doing research for my second book, *South Korea: Dissent within the Economic Miracle.* The book tells the story of the long struggle of Korean workers for human decency and democratic rights. It highlights the revolt that began in the summer of 1987. Within six months thousands of new unions and tens of thousands of workers were organized into a democratic labor movement. For several years there were massive work stoppages, some involving ten to twenty thousand people. *Unfinished Conflict*, the fourth story in this collection, reflects the events of this period.

The last story was inspired by interviews I had with North Korean refugees in Russia. *Escape into Bondage* tells of two men who because of circumstances cannot return home. They become "brothers" as their lives are joined in a perilous odyssey in Russia where they have no legal status. One finds haven in South Korea. Through his experiences and interactions with his new friends we gain insight into the complexities faced by those struggling for peace and reunification of Korea.

For Dorothy and me the issue of peace and reconciliation in Korea has been one of our major concerns since 1984. That year Dorothy had an amazing opportunity to visit North Korea as a member of an American Friends Service Committee peace delegation. This was a life changing experience. Her biggest impression was the oneness of the Korean people. Even though they had lived for nearly forty years under different systems their common roots were evident. The tragic division forced upon Koreans had hurt North Koreans in the same way as it had South Koreans. There was the same pain of separated families, the same fear of war, repression in the name of national security and waste of resources on preparation for war. Koreans on both sides were ignorant about life on the other side.

After Dorothy's North Korea trip she traveled around the U.S. talking to church and secular groups about Korea. It was interesting to find that many Korean-Americans had already made trips to North Korea to visit their families—something that was illegal for South Koreans to do. But these Korean whispered to her about their trips. They had been afraid to share this experience with their friends in the U.S. because they would have been considered pro-communist.

After one New York Korean church invited Dorothy to speak, the pastor called to say there was a conflict at their church. Instead of holding the meeting at the Korean church, some of the church members would attend the scheduled meeting at a nearby American church. Seventy-five Koreans attended the American service. They poured through the books from North Korea and stayed for hours asking questions. But amazing changes were around the corner.

In the early 1980's church and secular groups in South Korea tried to discuss the issue of north/south reconciliation but were repeatedly frustrated by the government. To deal openly with this crucial issue, the Korean churches called for international, ecumenical cooperation at a historic consultation held in Tozanzo, Japan in 1984.

The World Council of Churches responded by visiting the north and south and sponsoring meetings of Christians from the north and south. The National Council of Churches of Christ—USA also visited the north and south. In 1986 they prepared a Policy Statement, *Peace and the Reunification of Korea*. This policy statement, though controversial, opened the door for discussion of north/south issues in the United States. And in South Korea, with the democratic reforms of 1987 there was an explosion of interest in reunification.

In 1988, for the first time, an international conference on reunification was held on South Korean soil. Unfortunately no North Koreans were able to attend. At one worship service over three thousand people were praying aloud for reunification.

In 1989 Dorothy and I attended a reunification conference in Washington DC. The highlight of the meeting was a symbolic ending of the division. On the floor was a huge map of the entire Korean peninsula with a straw rope across the 38th parallel. Church leaders from the north and south lit fire to opposite ends of the straw rope. When the rope was completely burned the crowd danced and sang together with new hope.

Unfortunately little progress was made in improving north-south relations until former dissident Kim Dae Jung became President in 1998. By this time floods and drought had taken its toll on North Korea. The North Korean economy was devastated. Millions were dying of starvation

In 1998 I had the privilege of attending the inauguration of President Kim Dae Jung where he put forth his "Sunshine Policy" toward North Korea. Following this path he went to North Korea and stated clearly his goal that seventy million Koreans should be free of the fear of war. He embraced the leader of North Korea, Kim Jong Il. They held hands and sang together, *Our Hope is Unification.* For this breakthrough President Kim Dae Jung was awarded the Nobel Peace Prize.

Though there were some family exchanges and some progress in joint projects, things have stalled again and again. First of all South Koreans who have been suffering from economic recession are very concerned about the financial cost of reunification. Lack of progress in U.S.-North Korea relationships also slowed down the process. Kim Dae Jung is in political trouble on the domestic front and is nearing the end of his term without accomplishing his goals.

Events and people in this land that I greatly love and respect have influenced most of my life, over a period of a half-century. Because of many unique experiences that have come my way, I find it incumbent upon me to tell the stories in this book. I am, however, an American writing about people and events in Korean history. If I am mistaken in some of the details of my stories, I hope it will not detract from the bigger story.

History books will make little, or no, mention of these events, or these people, but I believe their stories, their traditions, their dignity are the very values that we wish to pass on to the future. We can only be grateful for their lives.

Foreword

By Dorothy Ogle

Looking at options for the cover design for this book we were immediately attracted to a background called "Golden Sun". This background inspired a vivid flashback for me.

It was a day in January 1975, only a few weeks after my husband had been deported from Korea. The sky was overcast and a cold wind was blowing. I had been to the Shinchon Market and was walking quickly along the winding, wooded road to our home on the Yonsei University campus.

My heart was heavy as I contemplated the decisions that we would soon have to make. Korea was our home. The children were so happy attending the Seoul Foreign School within walking distance of our house. Korean friends were encouraging the children and me to stay in Korea, but I knew that we would have to move forward with plans to join George in the United States. Our future seemed so uncertain.

As I approached our house I could see ahead of me an elderly man dressed in Korean long white coat and white baggy pants. When he turned into our driveway, I realized that it had to be "Diamond Mountain Yun", a retired pastor who had become a legend in church circles. A few months earlier we had been at his house for dinner. We sat together on the *ondol* floor of his Korean-style house while he demonstrated how he was braiding rope to raise money to send missionaries to New Guinea. Of course he was happy to accept our donations for the cause.

I caught up with him as he approached our door, and we went into our living room to visit. He expressed his gratitude for our ministry in Korea and his sadness for the political situ-

15

ation in Korea. I have never forgotten his parting words, "There's a dark cloud in the sky, but some day the bright sun will shine."

My mind jumped to another more famous elderly Korean man who also was known for always wearing Korean clothes. Teacher Ham Sok Hon was a saintly Quaker gentleman with a long white beard. He worked tirelessly for justice, democracy and reunification of Korea. His efforts landed him in prison many times—first under the Japanese and then during the time of the military dictatorships.

The voice of Ham Sok Hon was frequently heard counseling the people of Korea about the essentials for the reunification of their homeland. In a letter written in the 1970's he said the following:

> We must become one, because we are one (people).
> We can live only by becoming one.
> We cannot live in this divided situation, and even though we are alive, we are not living. The South must trust the North, and the North must trust the South. And on this faith let us stand up together. The earlier we stand up, the better . . ."

Korea's current President Kim Dae Jung acted in the spirit of Teacher Ham's words. He broke with the confrontational patterns of the past. Acting out his "Sunshine Policy", he went to North Korea expressing the desire that all seventy million Koreans (north and south) could live free of the fear of war. The sun shone brightly for Korea on the day that the leaders of the two halves of the country held hands and sang "Our Hope is Unification".

Today there is another cloud over Korea. Fears on both sides of Korea have slowed down progress toward reconciliation. A provocative U.S. policy has raised new concerns about war.

It is my prayer that the "Golden Sun" of this book's cover will reflect the wisdom and vision of Teacher Ham and the hope of Rev. Yun that "Someday the bright sun will shine."

FATHER AND SON

Background

When I was in Seoul in February of 1998, I met a Mr. Kim. He had spent more than twenty years in South Korean prisons because he had been considered a communist. While in prison he wrote a book of beautiful, compelling poetry, a copy of which he gave to me. As I read the poetry and recalled our conversation, I was inspired to try my hand at writing a story that would reflect something of the history that Mr. Kim and many others had suffered through.

This is not a biography of Mr. Kim, though several incidents in my story are parallel to or borrowed from his life. My story is fiction based on what I know of Korean history. The actors are, I think, believable characters who could have lived and undergone the experiences depicted in my story.

I have used actual names of well-known cities and historical figures, but the names of other characters and their home village (Sooncho) are fiction.

When the story begins, Koreans are seeking independence from oppressive Japanese colonialism. By 1910 Japan had formally annexed Korea into its imperial empire. Japanese occupation meant two things to Korea: a forced march into the modern world of education and industry; and humiliation at the hands of an ancient, brutal enemy. Japan had first earned the hatred of the Korean people when it devastated the land back in the sixteenth century. The twentieth century takeover only

19

aggravated the ancient hatred that had persisted through the centuries.

When Japan began its rule over Korea, eighty percent of the population still lived in rural villages, earning their livelihoods through small-scale farming. Japan demanded that Korea start on the road to industrialization. Peasants were forced off the land into the cities to work in newly developed textile, chemical and metal industries. Japanese, and some rich Korean collaborators, took possession of the farmland.

On March 1, 1919 Korean patriots in Seoul and around the nation publicly read a Declaration of Independence. The leaders of the movement were unmercifully suppressed, but opposition to the Japanese never died out. In the 1920s communists began to organize underground cells among industrial workers and peasants, preparing for the day when Japan would be ousted and a "Peoples' Republic" would take over.

The peasants who remained on the farms harbored the dream of freedom and land. As World War II drew to an end, agents of the underground communist party encouraged that dream. Though most peasants had no idea of what communism meant, they were carried away by their own dreams.

World War II ended in 1945. Koreans thought the Japanese defeat would mean freedom for the nation and land for the peasants. This dream of independence, however, was short-lived. The victors in World War II, the United States and The Union of Soviet Socialist Republics, divided the Korean peninsula into two parts. North of the 38th parallel USSR would hold sway; south of that line, the USA would be in control. For three years the American War Department governed South Korea. Unfortunately it had little expertise with which to handle this responsibility. When the U.S. military government rejected the beginnings of a popularly based government, great antagonism developed in local areas.

In 1948 the division became formalized. Two governments were created on the peninsula—the Peoples' Republic of Korea in the north and the Republic of Korea in the south. The United States turned power over to the right wing party of Syngman Rhee. The land situation became even more confused. Rhee feared the peasant's cry for land, interpreting it as communist subversion. In both north and south ideological extremes destroyed the middle ground. Many people were imprisoned or assassinated.

Few Koreans, north or south, wanted the nation divided. Consequently a great civil war was waged from 1950 to 1953. Northern forces occupied most of the south for three months. In that short time an unspeakable wave of executions and massacres took place. Hatred between north and south deepened and would dominate all subsequent attempts to reconcile the two halves of the country. The land on both sides of the parallel was destroyed, millions died, but the division remained. For ten years after the truce was signed in 1953, the communist north and the capitalist south both struggled to maintain themselves, repair war damages and defend against the other side. Both north and south began unprecedented military build-up, and in addition, a contest arose as to which side could create the quickest economic development.

Not long after President Syngman Rhee was ousted by a student revolution, there was a military coup. The South Korean government evolved into an oppressive military dictatorship that justified abuse of human rights because of an alleged threat from the north.

"Father and Son" is a story of two generations of peasants as they seek freedom and justice in the midst of all this international imperialism and internal conflict.

Chapter 1

THIRTY OLD MEN

The thirty old men sat in the hot sun and waited. They were dressed in traditional Korean style—black, broad rimmed, horsehair hats; white, loosely fitting pants and jackets. What they had been planning for a year had been accomplished. Only the consequences now had to be faced. The crowd of men who frequented Pagoda Park was stunned by what they had heard. They pressed in on the thirty old men shouting, "Who are you? You mean we are now free from Japan? The Japanese are going home? You're insane! You'll get us all killed!" Then fearful of reprisal for what they had just heard, the crowd retreated to its former postures, playing chess, hunched in little groups talking, or sitting around the periphery of the park staring straight ahead.

The thirty old men maintained a posture of ancient dignity. They kept their peace and waited. The police, it seemed, were taking a long time. It had been just two o'clock when Son Pyung Hi had stood up and begun to read the Declaration of Independence. He read in the deep-voiced, chanting manner of ancient Korean rhetoric:

> We herewith proclaim the independence of
> Korea and the liberty of the Korean people. We tell it
> to the world in witness of the equality of all nations,
> and we pass it on to our posterity as their inherent
> right . . .

The thirty-three elders who signed the proclamation came

from all parts of the country and represented Korea's three major religions.[1] It had taken them a year of secrecy to compose the Declaration and organize for this day, March 1, 1919. The Japanese police, so ubiquitous in everything else, had gained not a hint of the conspiracy. After Son Pyung Hi had finished reading the proclamation, a young man went to a telephone booth and according to plan alerted the police as to what had happened.

At first the police paid no attention to the phone call, thinking it was some crank. "Korean independence! Absurd!" They laughed. But when a detective came running in with a copy of the Declaration, the attitude changed. If it were true, the heads of the police chief and others would certainly roll. Within seconds a squad was out the door and a general call went out for backups to converge on Pagoda Park.

By the time the police arrived at the park, their humiliation at having been out-maneuvered by Koreans had turned to deep fury. They waded into the crowd swinging their clubs. When they did not scatter quickly enough, the police opened fire killing several. The thirty old men remained seated on the ground. The police beat them on the head and shoulders, dragged them out of the park and threw them into a police wagon. They spent their remaining years in prison where they suffered many indignities. Son Pyung Hi, as spokesman for the group, suffered most. He was severely beaten. After two years, Son could endure no more. He died in prison.

The surprise for the Japanese was not yet over. Copies of the signed Declaration of Independence had been secretly dispatched over the entire Korean peninsula. On the very same day, March 1, crowds of people gathered in more than 200 cities and villages to hear the Declaration. The Japanese reprisal was first hesitant and then savage. Men, women and children were beaten. Thousands were killed. Leaders were imprisoned and tortured. In one village members of the Christian Church and the followers of the *Chundokyo* (the Heavenly Way)

1 Buddhism, *Chundokyo* and Christianity

were herded into a church building. The church was then burned
down around them. The consequences of the old men's action
were more severe than they ever expected.

On March 1 of that year, 1919, the villagers of Sooncho in
the Province of Cholla Nam Do gathered under the protection
of an ancient and sacred oak tree, where the peoples' prayers
were sent up to the Great Spirit. They listened to Kim Kyung Sil
read the Declaration of Independence. Kim's family had lived
in Sooncho from time immemorial. He was a member of the
Chundokyo religion,[2] strongly committed to independence and
justice.

Kim's father had been part of the great *Tong Hak* Rebellion
of the earlier century that attempted to drive out domestic and
foreign oppressors.

Kim had only finished the Declaration when the Japanese
police moved in. With their truncheons they beat the villagers
gathered under the sacred oak until all had fled or were unconscious. Kim Kyung Sil, they dragged off to the provincial police station.

Seven days later Kim was found in the middle of a rice
paddy not far from the tree. Both his legs had been broken, his
face hideously disfigured. He had been thrown into the rice
paddy to die, but Kim Kyung Sil refused to cooperate.

---

2 *Chundokyo*, Path of the Heavenly Way, was a Korean religion that
   combined Confucian, Christian and Buddhist teachings. It had its
   origins in what was called the Tong Hak Rebellion of the mid and
   latter-nineteenth century when Korean peasants rebelled against the
   interventions of China, Japan and other foreign governments in Korean affairs.

Chapter 2

LAND REFORM

Kim Kyung Sil lay in a coma for six months. Then a loud knocking on the gate awakened him. "*Yobo, nugoo oshuttda. Moon yuro.*" — "Wife, someone has come. Open the gate"— were his first words. He tried to sit up, but found that he was too weak to do so. He lay back down. "Bring the guest into see me." He directed his wife.

The guest, however, would not enter the house. Instead he stood in the small courtyard and proclaimed his business in a loud, insulting tone. "Kim Kyung Sil, you must vacate this house and property by September fifteen or sign a contract of tenancy with Hong Tak June by that date. Otherwise you will be evicted by force." The messenger put the written proclamation on the step, turned and went out the gate without further word.

"Wife, who was that? What does it mean?"

"Husband, you have been asleep for half a year. The Japanese have announced that all land is now the possession of their emperor. They have surveyed the whole valley and drawn new property lines. They are selling the land off acre by acre."

"They are selling my land, my father's land? They can't do that! This land has been ours going back ten generations. There must be a mistake. I must go and tell them."

"Husband, the Japanese do what they want. Our whole village is being bought by the Japanese—or by Korean collaborators. Besides, you are too weak to stand up. How will you go anywhere?

Nevertheless, within a few days Kim Kyung Sil was on his feet. His broken legs had not fully healed and his muscles had atrophied from being six months in bed, but with the support of his wife he dragged himself to the village office. The sign over the door was now written in Japanese. Inside, a Japanese officer sat behind a desk. On either side stood Koreans in Japanese police uniforms.

"Man, what are you doing here?" One of the Koreans asked in a low, insulting tone.

Kim was taken aback. Since when did young men speak to older men in low language? His temper flared. "Have you no manners? To talk to me that way?"

The young Korean laughed at him. "You should go back to sleep. You're already an old man. Your day is over. We are making a new, modern Korea."

Speaking with the Korean as interpreter, the Japanese took over the conversation. "Old man, we know who you are. You tried to mislead your people and oppose Imperial Japan. You are responsible for much suffering. You have been kept alive only by the grace of our emperor. Now go back to your house and prepare to move. Do not come back here unless I send for you. Do you understand?"

Kim Kyung Sil was too humiliated to reply. These men were unreal. This couldn't be happening. Perhaps he was still in a coma. But a shout of, "Get out!" broke into his consciousness. His wife carried him back home.

The very next day an automobile drove into the village. Two men got out and headed straight to Kim's house. His wife saw them and gave warning. "Two men are coming. I do not know them. They look angry. Better go out to meet them."

Before Kim could get on his crooked legs, they were upon him. First came the discourteous pounding on the gate. Then the loud shout, "You in there, open the gate! The landlord has arrived."

As the wife opened the gate, the first stranger pushed it in almost knocking her to the ground. After him came a Korean man dressed in western clothes. He, like everybody else these days, spoke low, demeaning language. His every word offended Kim Kyung Sil, who nevertheless remained silent.

"I am Hong Tak June, your new landlord. You, Kim Kyung Sil, I should not allow some one like you to work on my land after your behavior on March 1. However, I am a generous man and I will let you stay. You may work one half acre of rice land and two of mountain land. Mr. Lee, here will act as your foreman and tell you what to plant and where. Do you understand?"

Kim could not make his mouth work. He had never met Hong, but he knew all about him and his class of rich people who sold his country out to the Japanese. Anger raged within him, but he dare not speak. If he opened his mouth, he was sure his anger would explode. He wanted to throw his broken body against this hyena. Through his mind went the question: "What can I tell my father and grandfather, my ancestors? I have lost their land. I shall never be able to face them."

"And one more thing," the landlord went on, "We will share the harvest fifty-fifty. In most cases I allow sixty-forty, but since you are a cripple, your production will be less than that of a healthy man. Do you understand?"

Kim managed to say, "Yes, I understand."

"Good. Then sign these papers," ordered Mr. Lee, taking three sheets of paper out of a bag he was carrying. The contract was written in Chinese characters. Kim could not read Chinese, but he signed. It was futile to resist. Lee did not bother to explain that the contract also bound Kim to pay for fertilizers and transportation costs. There was also a land tax that Kim would have to pay.

Lee took the signed sheets, put them into his satchel and concluded, "Tomorrow morning at six o'clock you and other peasants contracted to landlord Hong will meet in front of the big house where I now live. I will give you your work instructions then. Do you understand?"

"Yes, I understand."

Thus began twenty-five years of serfdom. Each year Hong would come to see that he received his fifty—percent of the rice harvest. Each year the government increased the taxes to help pay for Japan's militaristic ventures. The lives of Kim Kyung Sil and his wife became desperate. Often Kim found his wife going hungry, giving him the very last sweet potato. During these long years of suffering Kim Kyung Sil was thankful for only two things: he did not have to see his children suffer since he had no children; and secondly he was glad his wife did not have a pretty face. She did not have to answer summons to the big house like the more attractive women had to do.

Chapter 3

STRANGER BY NIGHT

In the year 1929 two events of consequence occurred. The first was the birth of Kim Kyung Sil's son. Kim had not desired a child, but he was happy when a son was born. Though he was forever ashamed before his ancestors because of the loss of their land, at least he now had a son who would continue their name. The boy's birth date, however, was not a happy one. He was born on March 1, just ten years after the events that led to his father's humiliation.

A name had to be found that would counter whatever bad omen "March 1" might carry. The village fortune-teller was sent for. The date and exact time of birth, markings on the child's body, the names of his ancestors and the exact juncture of the stars had to be ascertained. After that the fortune-teller would analyze the ancient books to create a name worthy of the child and his family. In this case with the birth falling on March 1, with all it's meaning, it would take much time before an efficacious name could be discovered.

Two weeks later the fortune-teller returned to the Kim house. "I have discerned a name that will provide courage and hope. With a name like this he will grow into a man of whom you and your ancestors will be proud. His first name will be "Myung" meaning "bright and clear as a newborn day". His second name shall be "Gul" meaning "hero" or "one who leads his people. Kim Myung Gul." Perhaps, thought his father, he will lead our people to freedom; even restore the lands of our ancestors. Perhaps, thought his mother, he will be strong of body and help his father in the fields.

Myung Gul was spoiled as the first born usually is. He

32-OGLE

nursed until he was two and ruled the house as his private domain, but by the age of five he began to take on responsibilities. He ran errands, gathered wood from the hillside, carried water and took food to his father in the fields so that he would not lose work time by walking back to the house. At the age of six, he went off to the public school where his Japanese teachers taught him how to read, write and speak Japanese. At home, he learned to master his own language and to revere his native land. Quickly he learned the stories of his ancestors and memorized the slogan of the *Tong Hak* Rebellion: "Freedom, Equality and Land for the Peasants." Over and over he heard about March 1 and his father's legs. The Japanese failed in their attempts to make him Japanese. The coals of liberty were stoked red hot in his stomach.

The other significant event of 1929 was the appearance of a stranger who came by night. A neighbor, who lived next door to Kim Kyung Sil, greeted him one afternoon with the usual inquiry about the growth of his rice, but as he passed by, quietly under his breath the neighbor whispered, "Come to my place at midnight."

Kim Kyung Sil did not know what to make of this. He was apprehensive. It sounded like trouble and he could ill afford trouble, especially now with the boy. Nevertheless, a few minutes before twelve he slipped out of bed and made his way to the appointed house. The gate stood open so there was no need to knock or clear his throat. He walked in. His neighbor's wife motioned him to enter the house. Inside, four men he knew were sitting cross-legged on the floor. A stranger sat in the place of honor. A small candle was the only light in the room. No one spoke until another neighbor arrived. Then the master of the house, Song Ma Jong, spoke in low whisper,

"Listen carefully. We dare not speak loud since the other houses are near by. Others must not know of this meeting and what we say must be kept secret. This could be very dangerous, so if anyone wants to leave, please do it now."

He waited. Kim Kyung Sil shivered. He did not want to be here, but he did not move.

Song Ma Jong spoke further. "Our guest has news for us. You do not need to know his name." Song motioned with his hand and the guest started to speak. He was a little man, dressed western style. His voice was deep and urgent. "Comrades, I have come to bring you hope. A great revolution has taken place in Russia to the north of us. The government has been taken over by workers and farmers. Landowners and other exploiters have been driven out. Land has been returned to the peasants."

One of the men interrupted, "Did Japan not defeat Russia in war just a few years ago? How can they help us against the Japanese?"

"That was before the revolution. The decadent Russian ruling class has been swept away. Japan now fears Russia."

"What has that to do with us?"

"They will help us gain our freedom from Japan. When the time comes, they will send troops to our rescue. In the mean time we have to prepare. Already we are organizing in the textile mills and other factories. Just a few days ago over 300 women working in a spinning mill in Taegu were arrested for distributing handbills calling for resistance to the Japanese. We are organizing quietly in factories all over the country. Peasants must be in the forefront of the revolution when it comes. We have to organize cells among the peasants and factory workers so that we will be ready for the day when the revolution comes."

One of the men interrupted, "Spies of the landlord or the police will find out and we will be arrested or put off the land. It can not be done."

"You remember March 1, don't you? All that planning escaped the Japanese. We can do it again and this time the results will be different. You remember the Tong Hak Rebellion! We are of the same spirit and purpose. This time we will drive the little bastards back across the sea."

Kim Kyung Sil entered the conversation. "You see what the "dwarfs"[3] have done to me. I am afraid for my son. But, I am with you. Our lives have been reduced to slavery. What do you want us to do?"

"I have brought two pamphlets for you to read and study together. They are about the world revolution and the communist party that leads the working classes to victory. I give them to you." He handed the two pamphlets to Kim Kyung Sil.

"What shall I do with them?

"Take turns reading them and then study them together. Commit yourselves to the party and the revolution. Do not copy them. Always keep them hidden. No one must be told about this meeting, or the pamphlets. Warn your wives that they must say nothing. You six men are the hope of the revolution. Now I must leave. I will be back in a couple months. Long live the revolution!"

He went out the door. The other six men sat in silence for a while. Slowly, quietly they stood up and left one at a time.

As Kim Kyung Sil returned to his own house, a suspicion rose up in his mind. He had lived in the same village with Song Ma Jong forever, but he knew very little about him except that he was a good worker, someone to depend on. Now, however, it dawned on Kim that recently Song had been mysteriously absent on a couple of occasions. His wife always said it was because of stomach trouble—which was believable since most everyone had some kind of stomach sickness.

A few days after the midnight gathering, Kim met Song in the fields. "Come to my house this time," said Kim Kyung Sil. "Like last time. Twelve o'clock, tonight." Without hesitation Song agreed.

They spoke quietly in the room lighted only by a small candle. Seated on the floor so close that their knees touched, Kim began the questioning. "How do you know this man? What

3 A derogatory term that Koreans use for Japanese

do you intend to do with the pamphlets he gave us? Where is this all going to lead us?"

"I had hoped you would not be asking those questions. The fewer of us who know what is going on the better and the safer for those who do not know. Are you sure you want to hear? Once you learn, you are in deeper and if ever arrested, you're more likely to be tortured."

"I understand that much. They cannot do much more to me than what they already have. What's going on?"

Okay, here we go. A few years ago on New Years day I went to the cemetery to pay homage to my father and family ancestors. We had just finished the dedication of rice and wine. My brother and I were sitting at the foot of my father's grave when a man from his village came up and sat down beside us. My brother introduced us and said that he and the man wanted me to join them in the resurrection of a movement like the *Tong Hak*. It was, of course, secrete. If the police found out, it could mean torture and death.

They gave me a pamphlet like the one our visitor gave you and asked me to think about it. They said they would contact me in a week or so. I could decline, but in any case I could tell no one about our meeting.

About a month later my brother made an unexpected visit. I had read the pamphlet and understood that the movement they spoke of was anti-Japanese and led by a group called communists. I did not know what the communists were, but the language of the pamphlet clearly showed them to be on side of liberty and land for the peasants. I asked my brother what I would be required to do. What they

wanted, he said, was for someone who would recruit
people from adjoining villages into the movement.
You may have noticed that I was sick several times
last year. Actually I was off recruiting people into the
cause. I have been active now for almost two years.

Kim Kyung Sil sat in the darkness pondering. His father
and grandfather had been part of the great *Tong Hak* movement. Now he was being given the chance to be part of another
movement that would stand for the people. "How many people
are involved in the movement?"

"I am not sure how many members there are actually. No
one would know the answer to that, but we know that there are
cells in almost every province of the country. There is an organization called the Korean Federation of Farmers and Laborers.
It is legal and operates openly according to Japanese rules, but
underneath, it is used as a meeting place for revolutionaries
from around the country."

"Song, I am willing to join with you. What do you want me
to do?"

"We, of course, know how you have already suffered. We
ask only that you stay alert to what goes on in this village and
when the time comes that you lead the people to support the
revolution."

There was nothing more to say right then so Song got up to
leave. " Please warn your wife to not ask questions and to re-
frain from speaking to others about any strange behavior she
might see. Some time soon the man who came to my house
will be in contact with you. You and I will not talk about these
matters again." He put his shoes on and left.

Chapter 4

A MARRIAGE

After that night, a knot of fear in the belly and a shaft of hope in his heart were added to Kim Kyung Sil's existence. The little stranger appeared only now and then over the next five years. On his last visit he told of a meeting that took place in Vladivostok, Russia where underground agents from Korea and Russia were already setting up plans in preparation for the revolution. Workers in factories and peasants in all corners of the peninsula were being organized he insisted. "War with America is coming. Already Japan is at war with China. After it has bled itself fighting these two enemies, the time will come for revolution from inside and outside. Bear your sufferings just a little longer."

For Kim Kyung Sil and the other farmers of the valley the increased suffering came on quickly. The village chief announced "In order to support the motherland during these times of holy war, production of rice must be increased. In addition a small sacrifice of a one percent increase in land tax will be required of each household."

Kim Kyung Sil and his wife sat dejectedly looking at each other. Kim's body was old beyond his years. He had no extra energies left. Already his wife did most of the heavy work. She too was at the breaking point. There was only one solution. Myung Gul would have to stop school and work full time. Kim Kyung Sil called his son into the house.

"Myung Gul, I had hoped that you could finish your education, but now I know you must stop and work with me. Your labor must be added to mine to meet the new demands. I am sorry. I feel guilty for losing our ancestors' land and now I must ask you to sacrifice your future. I apologize, my son."

"Father, please do not think that way. I will be honored to work in the fields with you. You did not lose the land. It was stolen. Our ancestors understand. I will begin working tomorrow."

Kim Kyung Sil sat in silence. How blessed he was to have such a son. Indeed, his ancestors would be proud of him. "My son, there is also one other thing that we must talk about. Your mother is getting old and needs help in the kitchen. You are now fourteen years of age. It is time for you to marry. Your mother has begun to make inquiry. It will not happen for a while yet, but we want you to know that we have not forgotten."

"Father, I understand. Then, sometime soon I must cut off my long hair. It will seem strange having short hair, but I look forward to it."

Father, son and mother worked together and managed to meet the new quotas set by the Japanese rulers, but one afternoon in the heat of the sun Myung Gul's mother collapsed and had to be carried back to the house. She was on her feet again the next day, but her strength began to noticeably decline. She was the daughter of a peasant from a near-by village. Unlike most women she knew how to read. Her father had taught her. When there was a free moment she liked to read stories of ancient times. Her mother had made the marriage match with Kim Kyung Sil's parents. But even before the match was announced she had seen and fallen in love with Kim Kyung Sil. Being as plain as she was, she never dreamed that she would qualify as his wife. Her crowning glory came when she gave birth to his son. Now she had spent her all. She was near the end of the path.

Walking back home one evening Kim Kyung Sil spoke to his son. "The time has come for you to marry. Your mother's health is not good. She has looked over the young women of the village and has found one person whom she thinks will be a good mate for you. Her family is Christian, but Christian teachings do not differ much from our Chundokyo religion. Many of them have been leaders in the independence movement. We would like to have the engagement ceremony next week and the wedding as soon as possible."

"I understand. If my mother has selected someone for me, I am sure she will be a good wife. I am willing to marry when my mother wishes."

So it was that Kim Myung Gul was married. The two houses were too desperately poor to hold a traditional ceremony. The fathers of the bride and groom held the official engagement between them. A toast was made to the health of the newly weds and to the prosperity of the families. Custom dictated that the groom's family presents a gift to the bride's household, and the bride was to provide a dowry to the groom's family, but neither household was able to do as tradition dictated. The toast had to suffice.

On the wedding day, Kim Myung Gul walked to the house of his bride and bowed to her father and mother. Then the bride and groom were carried back to the groom's house where a Christian ceremony was held.

After all the guests departed, the two young people went into a room by themselves. It was their first opportunity to look at one another. Grins lightened up both faces and they knew instinctively that something good had been done to them.

Myung Gul ventured the first words. "I've seen you at the well."

"And I have seen you in the fields. Last harvest time you and your father worked with my father."

"I like your name, Soon Ae. It means pure love, doesn't it?"

"Yes, it was my father's choice."

A silence came upon them as Soon Ae picked up the bed mat and cover that Myung Gull's mother had prepared for them.

She laid them out on the floor. They both took off their outer garments and lay down conscious of Myung Gull's father and mother on the other side of the paper door, trying to interpret the sounds that came, or did not come, from the young couple. Only after several hours did the deep breathing of mother and the loud snores of Kim Kyung Sil liberate the bride and groom. The inner garments came off slowly. After a few fumbles, the connection was made, and once made, they were lost in each other forever. That morning their first child was conceived.

Chapter 5

JAPAN OUT, USA IN

War between Japan and America did come. With it, came eruptions in Korea that Imperial Japan had not expected. Underground organizations of peasants and industrial workers took every opportunity to interfere with production. Armed guerrillas had also been organized in the mountains. Peasants who refused to endure the increased oppressions fled to the mountains where communist cadre trained them in military tactics. The numbers were not large enough for direct attack, but they were enough to strike a Japanese police box or a take over a trainload of rice or burn a field of wheat. To the peasants these military strikes were a foretelling that the time for revolution was near at hand.

Japan bragged of its invincibility during the first two years of war against America, but gradually the attitude changed and after Hiroshima, the empire quickly collapsed. Freedom for Korea was near at hand. Immediately upon the surrender of the Japanese, Russian troops swept into the north and established a Korean-led government. The people of Sooncho expected them to sweep on south and make the revolution complete, but the Russians reneged on their promise. They had made a secret pact with the Americans not to go below the 38th parallel. They kept that promise rather than the one they had made earlier with the villagers.

The Americans, for their part, did not even show up until a month after the Japanese collapse. The Japanese governor-general for Korea, fearing that Japanese citizens in Korea would be massacred unless order were kept, arranged to have government authority turned over to a popular, Korean patriot named

39

Lyuh Woon Hyung. Lyuh was a progressive who held the respect of people from all sides of the political spectrum. Under
his guidance the Japanese were evacuated without incident,
but more importantly Lyuh and his comrades organized villages, towns and industries throughout the country into
"peoples' committees." The committees were the grass roots
for a temporary government structure called the "Peoples' Republic."

Lyuh, however, misread the Americans' intentions. He
thought they would welcome a democratically structured government that was in place ready to operate. In this he was mistaken. The American military knew little of Korea and even
less of its politics. The general in charge of the American forces
that finally arrived on September 9, 1945 had orders from
Washington that South Korea was to be run as a military government. No political party was to be recognized. He, General
James Hodge, alone was to rule the country.

Lyuh sent his brother and three English-speaking assistants
to Inchun to welcome Hodge. Knowing nothing of Hodge's
orders or his anti-communist mind-set, Lyuh prepared docu-
ments outlining the history, organization and location of the
Peoples' Committees and included a brief statement of the policies proposed by the Peoples' Republic. He hoped that Hodge
would recognize the good work they had done in preventing
chaos and in providing a peaceful transition to a civilian government. At the meeting scheduled for the next day Lyuh intended to offer the services of the entire Peoples' Republic to
the American general.

Chapter 6

BROKEN PROMISE

"Why have they not come," my father, Kim Kyung Sil, asked over and over during that month of August in 1945? "We believed them. They promised. If they do not come, all is lost."

We were all baffled by Russian inaction. They had promised us a revolution. They could have come easily at any time during the month of August. They would have been welcomed. Expectations for the revolution had been built up for years. Now was the time. The hated Japanese were gone. The land could be restored to the farmers. Now was the time to set up a government of the people. That is what we had heard from the time of the little man's first visit in 1929. But the Russians broke their promise. They did not come.

"But Lyuh Woon Hyung is a good man, well respected by everyone." I answered to my father's despondency. "His coalition works for many of the same goals as the revolution. Until something else develops we have to support him. When he meets the American army general tomorrow, he will be able to persuade him of the rightness of our cause. We have to support him."

"You are right, and I will do that. Even at the village meeting tonight I will encourage everyone to rally around Lyuh. But my instincts tell me we are facing disaster."

My wife, Soon Ae, moved over to father and put her hand in his. "Father, we will still be here. We'll have our land to work. We have your grandson to raise. Don't be discouraged."

Father loved Soon Ae as much as I did. Her words made him proud and he smiled.

"Soon Ae is right," I said. "We have worked for the revolu-

tion for many years. We will not turn back now." My words
sounded brave, but my heart trembled like that of my father,
only I did not understand the consequences of a failed revolution with the same clarity as did his old broken body. I had
learned of the revolution several years previously. I had been
awakened one night by voices in my father's room. Early in the
morning before sunrise several men were talking. Then I heard
of the Russian promise to bring a revolution to Korea. I heard
the men tell of how they were risking their lives to organize
others so as to be ready when the time came. The next morning
I told my father what I had overheard. I told him I wanted to
work with him to bring that revolution.

" I had not intended to bring you into this yet. You are still
young, but if you are of a mind to join your destiny to that of
the revolution, I welcome you gladly. The revolution will bring
honor to our ancient traditions and the teachings of *Chundokyo*
and Christianity."

That evening there was a large rally of the village people.
Speaker after speaker led cheers for the revolution. When it
came time for my father to speak, he did so quietly and so-
berly: "Comrades, it has been a whole month since the Russian
forces came into the northern part of our country. The Americans will not arrive until tomorrow. Yet the Russians have delayed. They have not come to complete the revolution as they
promised."

Many in the crowd objected noisily to father's words, but
most knew he was telling the truth. He went on. "Our only
hope lies now with Lyuh Woon Hyung. Tomorrow the American general in charge of South Korea arrives at Inchun. Dr.
Lyuh will go to welcome him and present to him our plan for
the Peoples' Republic. Dr. Lyuh has worked with many comrades to put together a democratic constitution for our people.
Let us pray that the American will have the wisdom to cooperate with him. Then we might still be able to achieve something
of the revolution's dream."

When father finished, the crowd cheered and shouted, "*Mansai, Mansai!*—Long life, Long life!— for Dr. Lyuh."

It was two days later that we heard news of what had happened in Inchun. The American general had insulted Doctor Lyuh. Had refused even to meet with him. Hodge had sent word to Lyuh that he and he alone was in command of South Korea, and he would have nothing to do with an organization called the "Peoples' Republic." We were outraged. How dare he insult the honored representative of the people? Inside our rage, however, was fear. We knew very well that Hodge would have to depend on one or the other Korean political parties. His rejection of Lyuh left him with only one option: Syngman Rhee. Rhee had lived in America for a long time and had a foreign wife. He was known as a fanatical anti-communist. Chief among his followers were the former collaborators with the Japanese. Many of the hated absentee landlords in our own village were Rhee's financial supporters.

That night we had another mass meeting of the villagers. The attitude was somber. Faces reflected bewilderment, anxiety. My father again took the lead as the people formed a circle around where he stood. At last he started to talk. "Friends and neighbors, we must be honest with each other. The revolution must be put off. The Americans' way of thinking is against Lyuh Woon Hyung. They are likely to turn to one they know, Syngman Rhee. He has worked in the United States for two decades for Korean independence, but he has sold himself to the wealthy classes. He stands against the revolution.

If the marriage between Rhee and the Americans takes place, we will be in great jeopardy. We may again come under harsh oppression."

A voice from the crowd rang out, "But surely the Russians will not stand by and allow its allies to be destroyed by the Americans. War will come and the Russians will triumph. The revolution has been postponed, but not defeated."

A young man, my age, spoke up. "We, who are able, should

join the military cadre in Mt. Chirisan. We must not again submit to oppression by foreigners and wealthy collaborators."

That night after the rally, I sat with father and Soon Ae quietly reviewing all that had happened. "I would like to go to Chirisan," I said. "It seems like the only way to defend ourselves."

Father said nothing. He seemed to be musing on what I had said. After a quiet pause, Soon Ae rejoined, "I also had the thought that you should go to the mountain." She gripped my hand tightly. "But I think your place is to be near father. Father has become known as a leader of the revolution. If the bad men come, he will need your help more than ever." She spoke the words firmly, but her voice gave way to quiet weeping.

I knew she was right. The danger to my father had not until that moment hit me with such clarity. Perhaps he should be the one to go to the mountains! Impossible! He is crippled, and old. Soon Ae's weeping spoke our common fear.

Chapter 7

ARRESTS

I had just finished my application for a ration of fertilizer at the village office when our neighbor, Song came rushing in. "Myung Gul, quick! It is your father. The police have taken him."

As I ran into the house, I saw Soon Ae lying on the floor with blood coming from her left cheek. I knelt and embraced her. One of the neighbors brought water. I washed away the blood and saw the heavy bruise around her eye. "Soon Ae, what happened?

"The police. They beat Father. When I tried to protect him, one fellow hit me with his gun."

"Where have they taken him? What are they going to do to him?"

"I do not know. I do not know. But they were very cruel. Poor father. He has suffered so much."

I went immediately to the local police box. Though the Japanese had been defeated, many Japanese police were still retained and the Korean police were the same ones who had served under them. Little had changed.

"Where is my father? What have you done to him?" I shouted in my anger."

"Don't come in here shouting at us. Who are you? Speak with respect."

"My father is Kim Kyung Sil. You arrested him a little while ago. On what charges? Where is he? I want to see him."

"Kim Kyung Sil? The traitor? Better for you if you were not his son. He has betrayed his nation."

"Are you mad? My father was one of the readers of the

March 1 Declaration. He has always been a patriot."

"Until he sold out to the communists and started advocating revolution. He has betrayed the spirit of March 1."

Knowing that it was useless to argue with the scum that stood before me, I lowered my voice and meekly asked, "Where is he? May I see him?"

"He is on his way to Mokpo prison. You may not see him. Now get out of here and learn from your old man's mistakes."

I never saw my father again. I made countless trips to the Mokpo prison, but they were all fruitless. Many years later, when I myself was in prison, I heard a rumor that Father had died under torture a year after he was arrested. When I heard the news, I closed my eyes and let the darkness shudder through me. A giant, an honorable man, had fallen. I prayed that I could be faithful to the same destiny that had nourished him. Would that I could but see the ground where he lay. Oh, Father, Father, how I wish I could have saved you from your sufferings!

After Father was taken, Soon Ae and I were left to work the fields and care for our son. We did our best, but the world came apart all around us. The Japanese had been defeated, but their system still held firm. Indeed it became even harsher. In addition to our rents and taxes, those now in charge demanded that we sell our rice to the government. The price they paid was less than what it cost us to raise it. The village children did not have enough to eat. Their eyes were sunk in their heads and their little bellies bloated out like balloons. Finally people revolted. The first one began in Kyung Sang Province to the east of us, but it quickly spread over to us. Peasants refused to work; they would not sell their rice; and they attacked police boxes killing many policemen. The American military regime had brought destruction to our land.

Then it was announced that there was to be an election. The Americans intended to turn the governing of South Korea over to South Koreans. An election was to select delegates to a national assembly and then later another election would choose a president.

We all knew that such elections meant the permanent division for our country. Certainly the government in the North would not defer to the one in the South, nor vice versa. Our village rallied against the election. We did not want the country split in two. As speaker after speaker denounced the elections, eyes began to turn my way. I was the son of Kim Kyung Sil. Where did I stand? I looked at Soon Ae, saw the anguish and love in her eyes, and stood up.

> Thirty years ago, under the old oak tree my
> father read to this village the March 1 Declaration.
> For that act he was tortured and his legs broken. But
> he endured. He worked for his family and village all
> his life and for liberation from the Japanese. He
> worked for a revolution that would bring us all
> justice and land. Now the Americans and their
> collaborators call him a traitor. They want to divide
> our peninsula. They want the South to be ruled by
> landlords and other oppressors. We must not accept
> this election. It is worse than defeat by the Japanese.

I had never spoken in public before. The applause and cheers surprised me, but at the end of the rally, I was also surprised that most people seemed to shun me. Only a few shook my hand. As Soon Ae and I walked home, neighbor Song passed us. Looking straight ahead without indication he was talking to me, he said, "Myung Gul, you must go to the mountains. There were many informers at the meeting. Go quickly."

"Yes," said Soon Ae. "Now is the time." She took my hand and urged me to run to the house, get some things and flee. But it was too late. They were waiting for me at the gate. "You traitor bastard! Just like your father. Now you will get what all communists deserve." Two stout fellows tied my arms behind my back and pushed me out the gate.

I heard Soon Ae wail, "My husband! My love!" The police pushed me into a black jeep. It took me to a police station and then to a prison from which I would not escape for many years.

Chapter 8

NUMBER 1300

The next day was market day for our village. People, mostly women, brought foodstuffs, clothes, bowls, chickens, dogs or whatever to a central market place to sell. From morning to night the market was a busy, crowded and very noise place as each salesman tried to bring her product to the attention of the buyer. The wares were poor but the enthusiasm was rich.

In the middle of market bedlam, five young men set up a large signboard. It said, "Farmers' Association. Join now! Work for Land and Justice." Two months after Hodge had refused to meet with Lyuh Woon Hyun, he had outlawed the Peoples' Republic. And a few days later, Lyuh Woon Hyun was assassinated on the streets of Seoul in broad daylight. In response to that outrage, some members of the outlawed Peoples' Republic began a new organization called the Farmers' Association. The signboard reminded people of the American insult and at the same time declared a new organization to protect the farmers' rights.

Few people paid much attention despite the efforts of the young men to talk above the drone of the market. The chief of the local police, however, read the sign and was frightened. He had just recently come from North Korea and immediately interpreted the sign as the work of communists. He drew his fellow officers off the streets into the safety of the local station. He called for reinforcements. In a short while a truck with a score of armed national police arrived on the scene. The five youth were arrested and put on the truck. Then a search was carried out in the market and the village streets. When the truck was finally full of young men, it slowly drove away. That night

49

quiet, ghostly searches went on throughout villages of the whole area. When daylight came, the valley was bereft of young men. They had been arrested and charged with taking part in a communist plot to overthrow the government.

Many of them ended up at the Mokpo prison just as I did. The night I was dragged away from Soon Ae I spent at a local station where the police took turns beating and insulting me.

By the time I arrived at the gates of Mokpo prison, I was already half dead. I was placed in a cell with nineteen other young men, most of them from Sooncho. We were made to sit with our knees up close to our chins. Our heads rested on our knees. One could not lean against the back or side of the cell, or each other. Movement of any kind was forbidden. A sharp whack on the head or back was the penalty. For several days we sat in that position. Our food was thrown at us and water was rationed to us once a day if you had a shoe from which to drink.

I grew delirious. I tried to focus attention on Father, Soon Ae, Mother, my childhood, the ideals that I stood for, but it would last for only a brief time and I would lose consciousness and move or groan. On the fourth or fifth or tenth day, I cannot tell, the warden came by to inspect us. "Have mercy. Save us. We are going insane." I instinctively yelled. The pain was too much.

"Who said that?" asked the warden.

I raised my hand and without looking at him said, "Kim Myung Gul. Please have mercy upon us."

"Get that man out of there!" came the warden's command.

I stood up. The change of posture shot pain throughout my back, but it was such pleasurable pain. As I stepped out of the cell, a guard hit me hard with the butt of his gun. I went down. But oh how good to lay stretched out and unconscious.

I awoke into darkness, in a concrete cell—not quite as tall as I—not quite wide enough to extend my arms. It was dark, terribly dark. I lay on the cement floor curled up like a baby, listening to the pain throbbing through my head. I stood up, but not quite. The ceiling was too low to stretch my legs. I turned around. The walls were just wide enough to allow that. I sat down. There was no light, no sound. My eyes could see nothing. My ears were of no use.

My brain, however, would not stop. It reviewed my whole life. My father, mother, Soon Ae faded on and off the screen of recollection. I tried to focus, to hold on to the picture of Soon Ae's lovely face, but I could not. She disappeared and her weeping would flood over me. I wanted to hold on to Father, but in an instant his image gave way to the impact of a gun hitting my skull. I began to talk back to the images that filled up my mind. I began to jabber, talk foolishly. I screamed and cried. It was terribly dark.

How long I lay in that dark, lonely cell, I do not know. It seemed like eons. I may well have gone insane, but suddenly a faint sound and a dim light. A small slit in the door was opened and a dish of barley and turnips was pushed through. No word was spoken, but I felt the presence of another person. I heard. I saw. What a great joy! I took a deep breath of the foul air and devoured the food.

After that, my life became a hateful routine without regularity. I was interrogated, fed, and exercised, but without a regular rhythm. Sometimes it was light, sometimes dark when I was allowed outside to stretch. Sometimes I was permitted thirty minutes, other times, only five. Some times I got food, sometimes not. Even the cleaning of my slop jar was at the whim of the guard.

"Number 1300." I would hear as the door to my cell slid open. 1300 was me. My name was canceled. I now became a number, 1300. "1300, clean out your slop jar." "1300 come out for exercise." "1300, time for interrogation." "March, one, two, three, four . . . one, two, three, four . . ."

The interrogations followed a certain routine: Always I suffered a tirade of dirty names. I was called a traitor, a scum beneath their dignity to even talk with. "Your mother must be ashamed to have borne a scum like you." "Your father was a traitorous rat who sold out his people." "You communist dog. You should die, but we are generous to keep you alive. But you don't know how to even say thank you. You son of a lousy dog."

The verbal attack came along with question after question about my father and the revolution followed by demands that I confess to being a communist, a traitor to the motherland. They demanded the names of my fellow conspirators. Interrogations took place in the "torture room." Intermittent with the questions were beatings, electric shock and the forced injection of foul water into my mouth or anus. In all this time I saw no one other than the guard and the interrogators-torturers.

As I walked the corridors to interrogation or exercise, I was ordered to keep my head bowed, to look neither left nor right, but I could tell that the corridors were lined with cells like mine. The only opening was a narrow hole that the prisoner had to crawl through.

The beatings, the lack of nourishing food, and the bad air quickly reduced my body to a skeleton that ached at every point. Long hours of silence and darkness "ate at my liver," sucked at my life energies. How I longed to talk to someone, to touch someone, hear something. Thinking that there was probably another human being in the cell beside me I tried knocking and scratching on the wall. Even a return scratch would have been a joy, but it was useless. My fist, and fingernails, made no sound against the concrete. I waited longingly for a sound even if it was the sound of torture.

But strangely enough I did not again slide into panic and desperation as I had previously. I did not jabber at imagined memories. Rather, I began to calm myself in the recall of my father's voice, my mother's face and Soon Ae's eyes, brown as the wings of a thrush. And ironically the guards and torturers contributed to my sanity. They were real physical evidence that the world still was there. My hatred of them centered my thoughts and soothed my nerves.

One day I heard my number, 1300. I was taken for interrogation. When I entered the torture cell, one of the torturers exclaimed, "We have good news for the whole land of Korea. Your father is dead! Is that not indeed good to hear?"

With that he boxed me on the ear knocking me to the floor. I had already heard of my father's death so what he said did not disturb me. I had often had nightmares of Father at the mercy of men like these, but now I knew he was free with our ancestors. My mind was at rest. I thanked my tormentor for the news.

Then one morning a new sound was heard. We were told to bring all our belongings, of which I had none. We were to be transferred to Seoul, West Gate Prison. There we would receive our final judgment and probably our execution.

My hands were tied behind me. A rope that encircled my waist was tied to the man in front of me. "Keep your heads down. Do not look right or left. Absolutely no talking." These were the orders as we were all marched into the waiting buses.

I ventured a few glances at the other men as we sat down on the bus. Many I recognized as from my home village. We stopped one night at the prison in Taejon. The next day we arrived at Seoul and were marched into West Gate Prison, built by the Japanese to incarcerate and execute Korean freedom fighters. The date of our arrival, we learned later, was June 24, 1950—the day before North Korean forces invaded the South.

We were told nothing, but instinct told us that something had happened. The guards were distracted. There was an air of anxiety among them. Then three days later we could hear a faint sound of gunfire. The guards put on helmets and carried their carbines as they marched up and down the corridors. They were quiet, as before, but their quietness was that of caged rats rather than that of their normally arrogant selves.

On the fourth day—a Wednesday— the guards were missing. The gunfire had ceased. Silence. And then, we heard the clanging of the front gate of the old prison being opened. Our hearts stood still. We dared not breathe. Then a volcanic explosion struck our bewildered brains: "*Mansai*! Mansai! Long live the revolution! Comrades you are free! The Peoples' Army of North Korea has set you free."

My spirit soared. My hope was reborn. The revolution my father had worked for had finally come. As I crawled out the opening of my cell, I wept. I stood up. I breathed the clear air and I thanked the gods, and the Peoples' Army. The war cry of revolution and liberty was once more heard over the motherland. Long may it be so.

Chapter 9

WAR

We were marched into the auditorium of a former high school. The exhilaration was almost too much for our beaten, starved bodies. How much I had wanted to talk to someone, to touch another person, but now I was in such ecstasy that I could hardly say a word. A grin had frozen itself on my tired, old face. The soldier standing in front of us clapped his hands three times and everyone grew quiet.

"Comrades, congratulations on your release. You have been freed to help the Peoples' Army complete the liberation of our glorious motherland. Even now our soldiers are in the process of driving the imperialistic army of the United States into the sea. We need you to help us. Every man and woman will be assigned to a place of duty. As the guards instruct, each of you is to come forward and identify yourself. I am Captain Choe Yong Hoon. I will assign you to your place of service. Do you understand?"

A loud roar of, "Yes, we understand" was the answer.

After several hours of waiting, I was told to go forward. "Identify yourself!" commanded captain Choe.

Seeing that he had the prison records before him, I responded, "I am number 1300." Strange, but I felt comfortable with that as my identity.

"Comrade! You are free! No numbers! What are your family and given names?" the captain shouted.

"I am Kim Myung Gul."

"The captain looked into another book he had in front of him. "Oh yes, we have heard of you comrade and of your father. Are you ready to fight for the revolution?"

"Yes, comrade I am, but I am no soldier and as you see my body has been wasted by torture and imprisonment. But send me where you will. I am ready to act."

"Report immediately to the cultural commissar for the Fourth Division. The comrade standing behind me will tell you where to go."

I was issued a uniform, a pair of boots and a blanket. I was given a bowl of rice. The marvel of once more tasting rice was too great. I wept. That first night of freedom I slept out of doors with the other men and women attached to our commissar. Life again seemed worth living. My heart filled with thoughts of my Soon Ae. We would be together again. I fell asleep and in a dream I sat with Soon Ae under the old oak tree of our village.

In the morning we started south. The assistant commissar rode in the truck with us and explained our mission. The American forces were locked in a narrow perimeter around Pusan. They were surrounded and had no way out. In a few days the Fourth Division of the Peoples' Army would drive across the Naktong River, cut the American forces in two and then drive them into the sea. General Pang Wei, himself, had proudly declared, "The enemy is demoralized. It is given to us to annihilate the remnants of his forces." We were jubilant. Only a few days were left now before complete victory.

Our task was to follow the army across the river and begin to organize the villagers in support of the revolution. "When you get into the villages and towns you will quickly identify our agents who are already there. You will know them by a white spotted bandage that they will wear on their left hand, or by the black blouse they will be wearing if the agent is female. You are to follow their lead."

"Comrade commissar, what shall we do if there is no agent?"

"You will proceed to identify the enemies and quickly eliminate them. There is no time. Do not hesitate to kill. Simultaneously, you will gather the citizens together and begin to educate them about socialist life."

By the time we arrived at the appointed place, the Fourth Division had already begun the attack. The river was wide, perhaps half a mile, and was eight feet or so deep. On both sides it was commanded by high mountain ranges. Our glorious army overcame those obstacles. Suffering only a few casualties, it moved quickly across pontoon bridges, and gained control of the east side of the river. The Americans could not hold. They fell back. Slowly but surely our troops moved forward. The forces of the imperialists could not stop the victorious army of the people. The road linking the enemy troops in Taegu to the north with those in Pusan to the south was only twenty-five miles away. One or two days more and the American armies would be obliterated.

Our contingent was scheduled to cross the Naktong the next morning. All was ready. We were prepared to win the minds of the town folk like the army was winning on the battlefield. The sun came up bright and beautiful—not a cloud in the sky. Orders came for us to move, to cross the river.

All of a sudden, the beautiful sky exploded. An unimaginable roar paralyzed us in our tracks. Fighter planes swooped down upon us gunning hundreds of us down as we tried to cross the bridge. They came again and again. Bombs dropped like a deadly rain. In seconds our vehicles, buildings and the bridge were in flaming wreckage. Bombs of fire turned the earth to ashes. Comrades died horrible deaths.

The beautiful blue sky had become our greatest enemy. The airplanes came over and over again, making it impossible for us to cross the river. At the same time other warplanes were pounding away at our forces heading toward the coveted north-south highway. Our troops had no defense against the air attacks, and to make things worse American ground forces had received reinforcements. Fresh Marine units were now in combat with the fatigued soldiers of the Fourth Division. Our offensive came to a stop. Gradually our troops were pushed back to the Naktong. When they tried to gain the west side of the river, the American planes were like savage bees. Thousands of our comrades were slaughtered.

The Americans, however, did not have the strength to advance across the river. Our generals licked their wounds and prepared for another assault. The Americans seemed to be doing the same, waiting to see what our next move would be.

We stayed in deadlock for several weeks, and then a terrible rumor began to circulate: American and South Korean troops had landed in Inchun some one hundred miles behind our lines. They were moving rapidly across the peninsula. Our army could be cut off from supplies and leadership. We were caught between two blades of a large pincers movement. At first the rumor was disbelieved, but quickly the unease turned into panic. The officers tried to keep the forces under command, but large numbers fled northward in disarray. These comrades were easily eliminated by enemy troops moving south. It was a terrible debacle.

I made my decision without hesitation. I would not go north. I would go south. I had to see Soon Ae. After that, I would join the guerrilla forces in Mt. Chirisan. Our village, Sooncho, was not so far away, but the land was filled with retreating North Korean soldiers and advance scouting parties of the enemy. To be caught by either meant death. I traveled by night. Kept to the back paths and hills. I made it without being discovered.

It was evening when I got to Sooncho. The sun was beginning its descent. The old oak tree still stood on the outskirts of the village. I climbed up into its friendly arms and waited. She came from the fields, went into the house and immediately came out again carrying her water jug on her head. She went to the well where I had first seen her so many eons ago. I waited some more. All the lights went out and I waited a little longer. Then I walked slowly to our house. I feared to knock or make a sound, but to my astonishment the gate was open. I pushed it in. It gave. I heard Soon Ae's soft voice, "My husband, you have come." She was in my arms. Silently we embraced and kissed. "Come," she whispered, taking my hand, leading into me into the house. "Eat. I have prepared rice and turnip soup."

"But how did you know I would come?

"Several nights ago I dreamed a dream. You and I stood under the old oak tree. Last night I had the same dream, and I knew you would come. My heart felt your love coming to me. Now eat, and let us not talk. The boy must not awake."

"The boy?"

"You remember? Your son?"

"I had almost forgotten. May I see him?"

"Of course, but first eat."

The boy was a beautiful lad of four. His mother said that he was a good child. She often told him stories about his grandfather and me so that he would grow into manhood with a right mind. Again she took my hand, and led me into the side room. The bed was laid ready for us. At first we were awkward even as on our wedding night, but then the connection was again made and we were lost in each other— forever.

I had been asleep for only a short time, when Soon Ae woke me. "Our son must not find you here. There are informants everywhere. He will awaken soon. I have prepared a place in the storage room. Stay there until the boy and I leave. At mid-day I will leave him with one of the other women and come back for a few moments. In the meantime we must make plans. What can we do? You can not stay here." With that she again came into my arms and quietly we wept together.

By the time Soon Ae returned, I had decided what to do. The revolution was a shambles, finished. There was no future now to hope for, and no past to go back to.

"My only option," I told Soon Ae, "is to spend some years hiding in the mountains. Maybe after a while, things will quiet down and I can find a new identity. Otherwise I go back to prison, or worse."

Soon Ae listened to my words, nodded her head, and returned to the fields.

Early the next morning I left.

Finding my way to Mt. Chirisan was easy enough. Before the sun came up I had located a hollow under a rock at the foot of the mountain. I crawled in and went soundly to sleep. Unfortunately, others before me had used that same hiding place. I felt the sharp bite of a bayonet into my leg. "Out of there and on your feet, you son of a dog!"

Chapter 10

BACK TO PRISON

Party officials and military men caught out of uniform were executed. I was sentenced to life in prison. Solitary confinement once more became my life style, this time in Pusan's oldest prison. The air in my cell was rotten, its smell, sickening. Sufficient oxygen remained to support life, but my lungs protested with fits and spasms.

The routine I had endured in Mokpo was repeated in Pusan. My cell was a little smaller. Again I slept on the concrete floor. I lived in darkness except for the irregular times when I was allowed out side for exercise. Again the great urge to see some one, talk to some one, feel another person began to overwhelm me. I fell in love with my guard for though I never saw him or his face, he would make a loud noise as he slid my food in through the small slit in the door, and at times he cleared his throat as though trying to say something to me.

For ten years I lived in that dark pollution. I stayed alive only because I willed it so. I came to gain control over my brain. For protracted periods I sat unconscious, emptied of thought or feeling. At other times I could re-run my life as though it were a movie. I sat entranced by the replay of my father and mother, of Soon Ae. Time no longer became a dimension of my consciousness.

A frightening sound woke me from reverie. The rusted door to my cell creaked open. A human voice commanded, "Come out!" I hesitated. The voice got louder. I crawled out on all fours like a dog and lay there at his feet. "Stand up!" growled the guard. I stood up. "Follow me." I followed. I knew better than to ask questions. I bowed my head and shuffled down the corridor. We went up stairs and light hit me like the butt of a rifle. It was too much. I fell to my knees, groaning, protecting my eyes with my hands. He waited. After a few minutes, he again ordered me to get on my feet. I stood. With my hands shadowing my eyes I followed. I was aware of the presence of other people, but I looked neither to the left nor to the right.

I was told to sit down. I groped for the chair, finally found it and sat with my head still bowed.

"You are number 1300, Mr. Kim Myung Gul?"

"Yes."

"You are a communist. You served under the political commissar of the Fourth Division of the North Korean Army. Is that correct?"

"It is correct."

"You are a traitor and deserve to die don't you think?"

"I wish to die."

"But we have decided to be generous and allow you to rejoin society. You will be removed from solitary confinement and assigned to work duty in the lumber mill. You will receive classes in social and political education. When the time comes that you are willing to sign an apology for your traitorous acts of the past and pledge allegiance to the government of South Korea, you will be released. Do you understand?"

"Yes. I understand," I responded, but it was the response of habit, not of understanding. His voice so jarred on my ears I could barely distinguish one word from another.

Three of us political prisoners were put in one cell. Though I had longed for human companionship for ten years, now I found it difficult to relate. My brain was rattled. It had lived within itself for so long that the presence of others seemed to be unreal. My responses to others' words or acts often did not match. Entering into discussion at the political education classes was beyond my capacity. My words came out jumbled. I could think to myself, but my abilities to cipher and respond to others had degenerated.

The guards, teachers and even some of my cellmates interpreted my handicap as surliness and "hard core communist attitude." Consequently, I received many an undeserved beating. I functioned best at work. Each day I labored in a lumber mill where the sawdust was thick as rain in a heavy downpour. I was assigned a job at quality control. As each slice of lumber came past me, I had to inspect it for defects. I worked alone and was responsible only to my foreman. The work was tedious and dirty, but I was fed twice a day and at intervals allowed water to bathe. For me it was a strange, phantom-type of world.

Then I received another jolt. It was maybe a month, maybe two months after my entrance into the new world. Once a month I had a day off from work. I was lying in my cell when I heard the guard yell out, "Number 1300, visitor to see you." Those words broke into my consciousness like the sound of my cell door clanging open. Like a zombie I followed. Her eyes immediately found mine. Those beautiful brown eyes. As when I saw light for the first time, her eyes were too much for me. I fell to my knees and groaned. She had lived within my brain for so long. Now my eyes were seeing her!

The guard picked me up and set me on a chair in front of Soon Ae. I reached out for her, but only then realized there was a thick glass between us. A small hole would have allowed us to talk to one another, but neither of us could speak. Each time I tried my throat would flood with tears. Our five minutes passed in silence. Finally she whispered. "God has answered my prayers. I will return next month," and she was gone. My brain wondered if it had not seen a specter. I did not move until the guard jerked me up by the collar and pushed me back into the bowels of the prison.

For a month I lived in a stupor, half-suspecting that I had hallucinated. Had it really been Soon Ae? When I again heard: "Visitation for number 1300," I raced to the room where she sat waiting.

Her smile was glorious. Beside her stood a young girl, a pretty replica of her mother.

I stammered as I looked at her. " I . . . . didn't know. She's beautiful."

" The night before you left . . . It was also beautiful."

"How did you find me? It's been so long."

"We heard in the village the very next day that you had been captured at the foot of Mt. Chirisan. Rumors told us that you were taken to Pusan. I have known you were here, but they would not let me see you. Then all of a sudden, after so many years, I received word that I could visit you."

"But how do you make the trip from Sooncho to here? It is a long way."

"We no longer live in Sooncho. The children and I have moved to Pusan so that we can be near you."

"But what about the land?"

"There has been another land reform program. It is hard to explain, but other people are now farming our land."

All of this was more than I could digest, but little by little I began to realize that Soon Ae lived in a one-room shanty not far from the prison. Many of her neighbors also had husbands in prison. Some other women from Sooncho were also nearby. She earned her living by selling fruits and vegetables in the market. The two children went to school. Both were good children she said but the boy was sixteen now and beginning to disobey.

My life took on a busy routine measured in months. Every day I labored in the lumber mill. In the evenings my cellmates and I went to political education and for five minutes each month I could look into the eyes of Soon Ae.

Chapter 11

DEATH

My reemergence into the external world was accompanied by a great load of guilt and anxiety. Each month Soon Ae would come. Each month she would bring me clean underwear, books and food. The guards would pass the underwear and books on to me. Most of the food they kept for themselves. For months, and years, I accepted Soon Ae's visits and gifts knowing they were her expressions of love, but at the same time, each month I could see her getting older and more bedraggled. She was so very thin. I wanted so much to be with her, to touch her, to go to the market with her, to help raise the children. Instead of a husband I was a burden, draining the very energy from her bones. I could have relieved her suffering by the mere act of signing a piece of paper.

There was the snag. To get out and be with Soon Ae meant I would have to apologize for my ideals and for those of my father. How could I possibly turn my back on the truths for which we stood? My conscience and the honor of my father were on the line. In addition most of my new comrades were also political prisoners. Some of them I even knew back in Sooncho. Many of them knew that I was Kim Kyung Sil's son. We had fought against the Japanese. We were committed to the socialist revolution that would restore us to our land, rid us of foreign domination and unite our country. This common commitment and the experience of life-together in prison forged us into a profound camaraderie. We would never sign an apology for our part in the revolution. Nor would we ever pledge our allegiance to the government of Pak Chung Hee. From time to time the instructor in our political education groups would ask

32-OGLE

if anyone was ready to sign the pledge. Each time there was stone silence as we all bent our necks and stared at the floor.

We still harbored hopes, more like dreams, that the revolution might come. News of student uprisings seeped in through the prison walls. We went on a hunger strike to support them. We demanded that freedom and democracy be restored to the land. We also wanted better food, and safer work places. Our strike was feeble at best and after a week we had to give up. Our bodies were too weak to sustain a fast. Nevertheless, it made us proud that we acted all together. The bonds that held us together were made even stronger.

Soon Ae knew my dilemma. The prison officials had notified the wives of the conditions under which their husbands could be released. From time to time Soon Ae and I would talk about the bind we were in, but never did she urge, or even suggest, that I apologize or sign a pledge. She knew it was something I had to wrestle through in my own soul.

The dilemma was broken in an unhappy way. I could see Soon Ae's health deteriorating each time she came.

" Please," I begged her. "Do not spend money for books and food for me. Other men get books that they pass around. The guards take most of the food. Use the money to buy food for you and the children. You must eat and stay healthy until I get out."

"I am all right." She would say and continue bringing the gifts. How like my mother! She had sacrificed her own health for the sake of my father.

On one visit we were talking about our son. Soon Ae was much worried. The boy had been brought up in the middle of Pusan's slums. He had no father, or uncle or aunt to help him grow, and his mother was busy earning money in the market. He did go to school, but otherwise roamed around the city with other boys his age. They often got in trouble. Once the police had arrested him. The boy did not know his ancestors and had no land from which to learn true ways of life.

As Soon Ae told me this, she began to cry and the crying turned into a fit of coughing. She bent over but could not bring it under control. After that day, she frequently had to give way to such fits. My load of worry and guilt grew heavier.

Then for two months she did not come. No word. What had happened? Was she too busy? Has she become sick? Had something happened to the kids? My mind was in torment. At work I almost cut off my arm being careless in front of a circular saw.

On the third month, my name was called for visitation. What a relief! She was okay—nothing serious after all. But she was not there. It was my daughter.

"Father, Mother is very sick. It is what the doctor called tuberculosis. She will not be able to come to visit you any more. I must stay with her in the morning and work in the market in the afternoon. I will visit you whenever I can make time."

Her coughing spells had made me suspect TB, but I did not want to admit it. I had seen many of my fellow prisoners die of it.

"Tell your mother that I am coming to her. She must hold on. Make sure she eats and takes her medicine. Take care of her. Tell her I am coming. She must not die!" I chattered in desperation.

Immediately I requested a meeting with the warden. To my surprise my request was granted and I was led, arms tied behind me, into the warden's office. I told him the whole story and begged him to release me.

"You know the conditions under which I can let you go. Those can not be altered."

"But you ask the impossible. How can I apologize for my past? That would be a betrayal of my father. That would be a shame that I could not endure. I will pledge to be loyal to the government and participate in no political actions. Can you not accept that?"

"Are you willing to forswear all allegiance to the communists and the communists' revolution?"

"I am."

"I can not make this decision by my self. I must talk with the Department of National Security. I will present your case to them at our next meeting in September."

"But that is three months. My wife could be dead by then. Please make a special case? Contact them now. Please," I begged.

He shook his head. "It can not be done."

For three months I waited in anguish. Only once did my daughter come. Soon Ae could no longer get up. She kept to the bed.

The warden sent for me. I went in, head bowed. I did not want to look at his face. If the answer was no, I did not want to know it ahead of time.

"Kim Myung Gul, The National Security Office has agreed to accept your terms. You are to be processed for release in two days. You will be given a suit of clothes and fifty dollars. But you must sign this pledge: you agree to be loyal to the government of South Korea in all your acts and words. If on any account it is considered by National Security that you have violated this pledge, you will be imprisoned for the rest of your life."

"I am willing to sign the pledge." They pushed the paper in front of me. I read it, signed my name.

For two days I spoke to no one and no one spoke to me. On the third day my daughter came to get me. My comrades of so many years watched silently as I walked out through the gates.

The place where Soon Ae lived was a shack inside a dirty congested slum close to a sewer ditch. I stooped down to enter the door. It was dark inside, but I immediately saw her, lying on the floor under a thin cover. I knelt quietly beside her. She looked up, and for a moment the light of her beautiful eyes went on.

"I have waited for you. I refused to die until you came.

Now I can go. I have seen you again. God has answered my prayers."

"My love. Now you must not go. You must stay and give me life. Without you I am the same as dead."

"I have prayed to God for you. You will be all right under His care. The time has come." She whispered these last few words, and with a soft smile she passed out of this world into the land of her Jesus.

Chapter 12

ANCESTORS

I wanted nothing more than to go back to prison. Everything I had known or wanted was gone: Soon Ae, Father, Mother, my village, the land. I found myself in a jungle of poverty where people resorted to any device just to stay alive.

I followed my daughter, Mi Kyung, around like a fool, not knowing what to do or how to help. After several days of going to the market with her, she asked me to stay at home.

My son would not talk to me. He blamed all his troubles on me. Because I was a jailbird and a communist he was always discriminated against. His teachers marked him as a subversive; he was not permitted to play on the school soccer team; and colleges would not accept him. I had ruined his life. I could not blame him for his attitude. I had never been a father to him. He knew nothing of me, and I knew nothing of him.

By chance, one day as I was wandering around on the streets I ran into a comrade from prison. His situation paralleled my own. Not long after he had come out, his wife had also died. He was a lost soul without friends or family. We agreed to room together. I moved out of my children's place and into his one room space in a different part of the ghetto. The children were glad I was gone. For several years we went our separate ways seeing each other by chance rather than intention.

Then one Saturday evening things changed. I was sitting in our little shack playing cards with my friend when I heard this voice outside our door yelling, "Old man! Come out! Let's drink." It was my son. Anger swelled up in me. How dare he talk to his father with those words in that tone of voice? He should be reprimanded. But I let it pass and went out side. The boy had been drinking and was already quite drunk.

"Come old man, let me buy you a drink."

I said nothing but walked with him to a wine house. He ordered Korean beer, and then began to berate me for all his troubles. His drunken voice rattled throughout the wine house. A couple of the other patrons yelled at him to shut up. For a while I thought we might have a brawl, but then a young friend of my son's came in. Seeing us he walked over and sat down at our table. He looked at my son and then at me as if to say who is this guy.

My son was in a quandary. He had never let on to any one that I was his father and he had never used the word "father" directly to me. He wrestled in his heart for several agonizing seconds and then blurted out, "This is my long lost father." At the sound of the word "father" the dam broke and he began to cry. The friend thought he was crying for joy. I knew that he was crying tears of humiliation.

The next day my son, Sung Hyuk, came again. This time he knocked on the door and spoke with respect. "Father, Mi Kyung and I would like to have you come back to live with us. Would you do that?" Soon Ae was praying for us I thought. " Yes, I will be happy to come back. Maybe I can now be of help to you and your sister."

We got along well together. I learned from Mi Kyung how to buy and sell in the market place. Sung Hyuk worked with us during the day. In the evening he went to a small local college. He wanted to be an engineer, he said.

But there was something wrong. Working just to live leaves one empty. I felt the absence of my ancestors. The children knew little of their mother and father, and nothing of their grand parents or great grand parents. I planned a pilgrimage home.

We went to Chinju by train and then road a bus to Sooncho. The bus stop was three miles away from the village so we walked over the hills and into the valley that I had been forced to leave twenty years before. As we walked down the path into Sooncho, we passed both the shrine of *Chundokyo* where father had worshipped his ancestors and the Lord of Heaven, and the Christian Church where Soon Ae had learned of the love of Jesus. Our house, in which the children were both born, still stood with its thatched roof and walls of mud and straw. The people inside were strangers. We walked past the well where I had first seen their mother and on to the other side of the village where the majestic old oak still ruled. There we sat. I recalled for them the story of our family. I began by reciting some of the Declaration of Independence of March 1, 1919, which their grandfather had read under this very tree. I showed them the spot where the Japanese had thrown his body after they had tortured him. I told them about how the Japanese had stolen our land and forced their grandfather and grandmother to work like slaves.

> I remember one night a little man came from the North and promised us revolution, but that revolution was betrayed by the Russians. We then put our hope on the Peoples' Party led by Lyuh Woon Hyung, but that was dashed when the Americans insulted him. We then tried to prevent the division of our country, but in that too we failed.
>
> One evening, when I was still a young man, after my father had been arrested, I made a speech to the villagers asking them not to vote for a separate government in the South because it would mean the permanent division of the country. For that they called me a communist and threw me into prison for twenty years.

Mi Kyung and Sung Hyuk could hardly take it all in. They listened intently. Towards the end of my tale, Sung Hyuk quietly muttered, "Father, forgive me. I did not know."

But I did not want to stop. I wanted to tell them about their mother and our love for each other.

"When I was out of prison at the time of the war, I hid myself in the branches of this old tree waiting for your mother to appear. When I went to the house, she had the gate open, ready for me. The night before she had dreamed of me under the tree. Only her dreams and prayers have kept me alive and sane."

"Father, forgive me. I did not know."

"You had no way of knowing, but now you know who you are. Always remember from whom you came. Sung Hyuk, do you know what your name means?"

"Means? No. It is just a name, isn't it?"

"Your grandfather had it created for you. Sung means "victory." Hyuk means "revolution." A name is your future. You grow into it. Your grandfather wanted you to remember the lineage from which you came so that you would have the courage to stand for the right."

"Mi Kyung, do you know the meaning of your name?"

"Yes. Mother once explained it like this: Mi means beautiful; Kyung is a mirror of one's heart."

"Yes, your mother had the elder of our village make this name for you so that you would grow into a beautiful, honorable person."

As we walked back through the village, I felt as though a great crowd of witnesses was surrounding us. I think the children felt that way too. Despite all the tragedies that had over taken us, in my heart I felt no anger or regret. I felt only gratitude for all the villagers that had labored on this land, for my prison comrades, for my father, my mother, my wife and now my children. As we passed the church and *Chundokyo* shrine, I offered up a quiet prayer of thanks.

STRANGE THINGS HAPPEN

Background

Because of blatant election irregularities, South Korea's first President Syngman Rhee was ousted by a student revolution in 1960. After a year of chaos, a military coup brought General Pak Chung Hee to power. In 1963 he was elected President.

Under his policy of "guided capitalism" Korea began to lay the foundations for the rapid economic development that was to come in the seventies and eighties. At first there were good labor laws, and the government left some room for the development of democratic labor unions and citizen participation in politics.

During the sixties Christian churches began their ministry to industrial workers in the city of Inchun. For ten years the author served, along with several Korean colleagues, in this ministry called "Urban Industrial Mission"(UIM). In the early days this project prospered and worked closely with labor, industry and government.

By the late 1960s, however, it became clear that Pak was not about to give up the Presidency. After the constitutional limit of two terms was completed, instead of stepping down, he proceeded to transform his regime into a military dictatorship. All efforts at democratic participation by citizens, laborers and students were harshly suppressed.

In 1972 Pak tightened his control by promulgating a new constitution that allowed him to rule for life and rule by decree. The Korean CIA enforced Pak's decrees by invading all

75

sectors of Korean life. This turn of events brought the UIM, along with many other citizens' groups, into conflict with the government.

The following story, "Strange Things Happen," is historical fiction. The characters, except for those related to UIM, are also fictitious, but the story and the actors are all based securely in events of history. The chief character is a steelworker who lives in the city of Inchun. The author appears in the story as Missionary Oh. The events in the story are now remembered by only a few, but the workers' struggle for justice and the right to participate in their own society contributed to the wider movement which brought democracy to South Korea.

*   *   *

My mother wanted me to marry early. She was up in years and wanted to see her grandson before she died. She had the bride picked out. I kept resisting. I had no objections to the girl. I just did not want to get married. I was only twenty and would go into the army soon. Using that as an excuse, I delayed the inevitable. Military service kept me for three years, but soon as I was discharged, mother was at me again. This time I knew I could not escape, so begrudgingly I gave my consent. Then a strange thing happened. The girl my mother had in mind married someone else. Mother had to start the search all over again. That gave me a reprieve of another year, and much to my surprise and pleasure the second candidate was much prettier than the first and much more to my liking. So we got married. Within three years we had two children and a third joined us on our fifth wedding anniversary. Two of them were boys. Mother was exceedingly happy.

Not long after discharge from the service, I got a job at the steel mill here in the city of Inchun where I live. At first I was registered as a temporary worker, one whose wages are half that of a "permanent" employee. A "temp" can be laid off at any time without reason. After two years as a temp, I was promoted to the permanent bracket. The law said that if a company uses a person for more than a year, it is required to give him permanent status. As a matter of practice, however, some temps are kept on for years and years. The increase in my wages helped me to start paying back my father and brother who had lent me money to rent a house. We have two eight by ten rooms and a kitchen. It isn't much, but we are doing okay and there are times of happiness.

My family going back three generations is Christian. My grandparents were converted to Christ around the turn of the century. I remember my grandfather telling us the story. He lived in a little village near the town of Kongju in the province of Choong Jung Namdo. The village was nestled near the bottom of the Kai Ryung mountain range. A clean, pure stream of water flowed down from the mountains through the village. Some of the water was siphoned off for irrigation of the rice fields; some was used for bathing and household needs; but most of it flowed peacefully through our village on down to the next one. It was the custom of the men of the village to gather in the evenings at a favorite grassy site beside the stream to drink, tell stories and recall the days of old.

One evening as grandfather and the others were in the midst of their story telling, a strange thing happened. Grandfather told it like this:

> A tall blond-haired, angular-faced man with a
> big nose walked into the village. No one had seen
> such a man. Some of us thought he was a ghost or a
> spirit that was known to roam the mountains. With
> great hesitation we welcomed him into our company.
> He sat down, and in what seemed to be our
> language he explained that he was indeed human,
> that he had come from a place called America to tell

us about a new God and His son Jesus Christ. This
was all new to us, but we asked him many questions
about his country, his God and his own personal
looks. He stayed the night. He ate, slept and drank
the same as we did. After that, Mr. Woo (He had a
foreign name, but preferred to be called by his
adopted Korean name, Woo Myung Li.) came to our
village many times.

I listened carefully as he told us about the
strange god of love and sacrifice. Gradually my heart
was persuaded to believe in his God. He then
baptized me, and several others, there in the middle
of the mountain stream that runs through our village.

All of grandfather's family has been Christian ever since.
My wife comes from a Christian family also. We all go to the
Chong Dong Methodist Church not far from our house. As a
matter of fact, I am a deacon in the church and hope next year
to pass the exam to be an elder. My working hours are so long
and unpredictable that I may not be able to attend all the meetings or do the study needed to meet the requirements, but I am
going to give it a shot.

My job at the mill isn't easy. As I take my place at work a
furnace is in front of me. In the furnace are steel bars heated
red hot. The bars are shot towards me. I have a pair of tongs
with which to catch the bars and redirect them towards a cool-
ing-off vat to my right. It is split second work, heavy and very
dangerous. When I first started, I was burned several times on
my legs and arms. Once I slipped while I was turning and fell
right on top of a hot bar. My thick clothing and quick action by
a fellow worker saved me from serious injury. Fortunately I am
strong and well coordinated. Now I seldom miss.

I had been working at that job doing the same thing for
thirteen years when a strange thing happened. A new man was
put on the job. I could tell with one look that he was a green—

horn. Why they would put him to do such dangerous work, I could not understand. He could get hurt bad. It fell to me to show him the ropes. He was young and eager, and much to my surprise before long he was handling the steel right along with the rest of us. Our rhythm was to work for a half hour and rest ten minutes. The work was so draining that to do more than that would increase the number of accidents.

Once when the new man and I were taking a break, he told me he was a Methodist minister working with a church group called Urban Industrial Mission, or UIM. I was a Methodist, but had never heard of the organization. Apparently some clergy were going out to work in factories instead of becoming ministers of churches. This guy, Cho, was one of them. It all sounded odd to me, but before I could ask many questions our break time was over.

Several days later another strange thing happened. The president of our local labor union, Chang Do Chan, came walking through the plant. That was not so extraordinary, he came often, but this time he had with him a foreigner of some kind. Chang seemed to be explaining the work process. They came over to where I was standing taking a break. He introduced the man to me. We shook hands, and much to my surprise he spoke pretty good Korean. He was a Christian missionary from the United States with the same group, Urban Industrial Mission, as my young colleague Cho. Mr. Chang informed us that the missionary would be visiting the union and the work area once a week or so. I did not say much, but at first I thought it odd that a missionary would be spending time inside a factory. Then I remembered the old time missionary who unexpectedly had appeared in my grandfather's village. After that, I saw Mr. Oh frequently when he stopped to talk with me or with some of the other men on the line.

On one occasion when we had a slow down at the job some of us gathered around an old saw dust heater. The stove was made from a 50-gallon drum cut off at one end. The fire, fed constantly by a spray of sawdust, burned red-hot. The metal of the drum was at a meltdown pink. Those of us gathered around the stove were hot in front, but the cold wind that swept through the run-down factory kept our backsides shivering. The roof and part of the walls had been blown away by the war. All that was left was a shell of a building constructed many years previously when the Japanese controlled Korea. The men who worked inside this shell of a building were constantly exposed to the outside elements. The machines were old, often welded together with nothing more than the ingenuity of the workers. Signs of injury and accidents were everywhere. Of the twenty or so men gathered around the fire that day, seven of them were missing thumbs or fingers. The furnaces had exploded on a couple occasions because hand grenades, hidden in piles of scrap metal since the time of the war in 1950, had accidentally been shoveled in along with the scrap metal.

As we sat around the stove, eating our lunches, Pak Yong Hi, our foreman, and the missionary came by and sat down with us. "We have a foreign guest," Pak declared. " He is a missionary from America. He wants to talk with us about the Christian faith. I invited him to come and sit with us."

With that, Pak turned to Oh and gestured for him to talk. "I am honored to be allowed to visit you today. I hope that you will be able to understand my Korean. I am still studying. As Mr. Pak said, I would like to talk with you about faith and its relation to our everyday lives, but I do not want to preach. I want to share and discuss and hear about your faith as well as my own. If you are interested, I will come each Wednesday at lunchtime. We can meet right here around the stove and stay warm. Talk it over. If you want, we will begin next Wednesday."

Questions came fast. "Who are you? Why do you want to talk with us? Are you going to preach and try to convert us? Do American workers live well? Are they organized? Are you part of the CIA?"

He laughed at the last question and assured us that he had nothing to do with the CIA, but I think many of the men were suspicious.

"Why are you here then?" The question came from several places at the same time.

"I belong to a church organization called Urban Industrial Mission. We are trying to do two things. Our Korean society is rapidly becoming industrialized so we are trying to discern where God would have the church serve in this new situation. At the same time if we can be of any pastoral help to you or your families, we would like to do it."

I heard what missionary Oh said, but I did not understand so I threw him a question. "What could Jesus have to do with our life here in the factory? Isn't he the way we get out of this world into heaven?"

His answer was perplexing. "Well, Jesus was a poor man and lived his life among the working class, people like you all. We think that a good way to learn about Jesus is to learn about your physical and spiritual situation. So we are here to learn, and where possible, be of help to you all."

About then the foreman broke off the discussion, "OK guys, it's time to get back to work. I am going to ask Reverend Oh to come back next Wednesday. We'll continue the discussion then."

So each Wednesday for several months about twenty of us ate lunch together around the old saw dust-heater. The discussions roamed with our interests, all the way from Jesus and salvation to Buddhism, Confucianism and Shamanism. Several times we talked about Korea's role in the Viet Nam war, and often someone would bring up the topic of labor unions.

It happened early on the morning of the third Wednesday. As the men in front of the blast furnace were shoveling in scrap metal, they inadvertently threw in one of the old hand grenades left from the war. The blast rocked the whole factory and, left the furnace area in shambles. Two men were killed and nine were injured, two of them badly. The injured were carried to the nearby Christian Hospital. Our foreman, Pak, phoned Missionary Oh and told him what happened. "Will you visit the men in the hospital with me?" he asked.

"Of course I will. What time shall we go?

"Right now—say we meet in front of the hospital in a half an hour."

"I'll be there."

Families of the injured men lined the hospital halls. In the patients' rooms wives and children cried and groaned. Nurses were coming and going as they tried to take care of the men. Foreman Pak introduced each of the wives to Reverend Oh. After finding out the condition of each of the men, he asked if it would be all right for him to pray for the men. Though only one of the injured was a Christian, they all quickly agreed. Reverend Oh knelt and gave a short prayer: "Our father God, have mercy upon these thy servants. Receive the souls of brother Choe and Song into thy Kingdom, and put thy healing hand on all those who were injured by this accident. Give the families strength and peace of mind. We ask your mercies this day. Amen."

That afternoon at lunch all the discussion was about the explosion and the injured men. Reverend Oh told us he had visited the men and gave us a report on how they were doing. Before we left the sawdust stove that day, word came that the general manager of the plant wanted Reverend Oh to come by his office. Later on we learned through the grapevine (namely, via the young woman who works as personal attendant to the manager) that the conversation went approximately like this:

"Thank you for visiting our men this morning."

"I know several of the injured men. They come to the discussion meetings we have on Wednesdays. So I was glad to make a visit and pray with the families."

"I, of course, knew of your visiting the labor union offices and walking around the floor with the union president. That is the prerogative of the union. We have also been aware of Wednesday lunch meetings."

"We have kept strictly to the time so as not to interfere with work. The men seem to enjoy it. If you find it disruptive in any way—"

"No, no. Do not stop. You are welcome at any time."

This one pastoral visit gained Missionary Oh recognition and respect through out the plant. When, after three months we discontinued our lunch discussion groups, men from other sections of the company invited him to start discussions with them.

A few weeks after the incident of the explosion, I saw Reverend Oh in church. He had two other men with him. One was Cho Moon Gul, my fellow worker at the plant, and another fellow I did not know. As soon as I saw the three of them, I sensed that something was up, something related to me. Sure enough, soon as the service was over, the three of them came over to me. After greeting me, and introducing the third man, Rev. Cho Sung Hyuk, Moon Gul asked if I had time to talk with them for a little while. I said yes so the four of us went to a near-by tearoom. Cho Sung Hyuk did most of the talking. Urban Industrial Mission was going to hold a training program just for Christians who worked in Inchun's factories. They had selected twelve people from twelve different companies, ten men and two women, to participate in the program. I was one of those whom they had chosen. They asked me to become one of the twelve. This put me in a real quandary. If I were to join this group, there was no way I would make elder this year. There would just not be enough time or energy to do both. "I will have to talk it over with my wife," I heard myself say. I was a bit surprised to hear those words come out of me since I seldom discussed important matters with my wife. But I did not want to answer right then so I used my wife as an excuse to give me time to think.

Again, something strange happened. I actually did talk it over with my wife. I laid out the pros and cons. Explained to her that the twelve people who would take the course would be commissioned as "factory apostles," and asked to act as modern day apostles in the work place. To do this would put additional demands on my energies and thus on hers too. I would be away from home even more often than usual. With hardly any hesitation at all she said, "Do it. Since you live at the factory more than anywhere else, learning how to relate your faith and work sounds like a good idea. Try it. If it gets too demanding, you can quit can't you?"

We met once a month for six months. After work on Saturday, the twelve of us workers, the two Cho's and Missionary Oh, would gather for a bowl of rice and soup. After supper we began to study. The routine was always the same. We began with a period of Bible lectures on one of three points: *palkyun* (discover), *bongsa* (serve) or *hapsai* (unite). *Palkyun* directed us to discover leadings from God within our fellow workers and within our working situation. *Bongsa* gave us ideas of how we could help our fellow workers in trouble either at home or at the job. *Hapsai* was the hardest for us to grasp. It meant uniting with others to create a more just factory life. That would mean some kind of a union and it might at times bring us into conflict with the company over wages, safety, health care, and supervision. The Bible study was then followed by discussion of events at our factory that were related to the Bible study. Where did we discover a witness to God? What problems were our colleagues undergoing? How can you help develop solidarity among the workers? We were scheduled to have prayers and retire at eleven o'clock, but our discussions often took us far beyond that. Whatever the time, when we finished we would lay down on the floor and go to sleep.

At six-thirty we were up. After a quick breakfast, we had assignment time. With the help of his comrades each person would assign him or herself a task to complete by the next meeting. Each task would fit within one of our three guidelines. At assignment time during the next meeting, each person would report on how the assignment was carried out and what the results were. Before adjournment, we had communion together and departed in time for each of us to get to worship at his or her own church.

To fulfill my assignments I had to change my style of living. I began to interact more and more with the other men in my department. I visited homes, and though I do not drink, I even went to the wine house on a couple special occasions. Frequently I made visits to the hospital to see buddies who had been injured. Sometimes Rev. Cho or Missionary Oh would go with me.

When it came time for our section of the plant to elect a representative to the union governing board, a strange thing happened. The men selected me to be their rep. I had never paid much attention to the union, but now I was one of its leaders. It seemed to fit into the definition of *hapsai* taught in our Apostles' class. What I discovered about the union, however, was not very pleasing. Instead of joining together to work for justice and the rights of the workers, it seemed like everyone was fighting everyone else. After listening to a fiery encounter between two men, both of whom wanted to be union president, I could no longer keep quiet. I stood up and called the two men to account. Remembering some of the words that I had learned at the Apostles' course I called upon them to leave off their personal ambitions and join together to work for the benefit of all the workers. When I finished my little speech, there was resounding applause. The two men were not exactly happy with what I said, but neither of them attacked me.

At our annual meeting in the fall, when the election of officers is held, these same two guys put themselves up as candidates for president. The speeches were loud and angry. A fistfight broke out. Finally a ballot was taken. It was a tie. Neither side could command a majority. Then on the third ballot a strange thing happened, someone wrote in my name. On the next ballot I was elected by a large majority. All of a sudden I was the union president. I was at a loss. I did not know what to do. I knew practically nothing about how a union functioned or what its main tasks were. Fortunately the Urban Industrial Mission was available to help. After work that night I walked over to the offices of the UIM to talk with Rev. Cho.

We talked long into the night. We laid out a plan with two parts. First and foremost, I had to strengthen my relationship with the men throughout the plant. Being president of the union meant I did not have to work on the floor so I had time to develop solidarity with the other workers. (My plans for becoming an elder at church were again postponed.) Second, along with the other officers I had to get ready for a new round of negotiations with the company next spring, only a few months away. In this Rev. Cho was a big help. He introduced me to other union leaders who were experienced in collective bargaining. With their help and with considerable guidance from Rev. Cho we got our act together. An increase in wages would be our primary concern.

The week after my election, I was invited to the offices of the vice-president in charge of labor relations, Mr. Kim Bae Oon. He gave me a warm welcome and asked the office girl to bring us tea. As a gesture of friendship, Kim came out from behind his large desk and sat across from me at a little coffee table.

"I wish to congratulate you on your victory," he said.

"It is more of a heavy responsibility than a victory," I replied.

"We did not know that you were seeking the job as union president, or we would have met before so that you could know what the job requires as far as relations with the company is concerned."

"I was not running for the position, but I believe I understand what is required of me. I appreciate your concern."

"Well, I want you to know that I am here if you need help. The company wishes to cooperate with you in any way possible. If you run into problems of bookkeeping, or finances or anything else, just come in at any time."

"Thank you. We will try to handle the job."

"You know that the yearly negotiations come up in the spring. We should probably meet, the two of us, a couple times before the official business gets started—just to iron out any preliminary problems. The business has suffered some financial difficulties during the last year, but we know that the workers understand and will continue their loyalty to the company."

"Yes, we are getting ready for the spring negotiations, and would be glad to receive any reports about the company's financial situation."

As I was leaving Mr. Kim's office, one of his clerks walked to the union offices with me. The clerk was a union member. "I see you had your first talk with Mr. Kim. He is very friendly with all the union leaders. Be careful. He also is known to start rumors that the union chiefs receive favors from the company. By being seen with you frequently, he sets the background for making the rumors credible." At least part of the clerk's prediction came true. Mr. Kim paid an unusual amount of attention to me and frequently visited the union offices that were located on company ground not far from his office.

By the time springtime came, we were prepared. Our negotiating team consisted of five men. The company's side also had five. Negotiations over safety, work assignments, and overtime dragged out because each item had to be approved by the headquarters in Seoul. Finally we reached agreement on everything except wages. The cost of living for the year had increased about fifteen percent, so the union asked for a twenty percent increase. We could have compromised at about fifteen, but the company would not budge above an offer of ten percent. The stalemate dragged on for a month. Finally the union put a strike vote to the workers. They voted almost unanimously to go on strike if there was not a settlement within two weeks. No one wanted to strike. Life was hard enough as it was. Going without an income even for a day would be hard for the families to take.

Then something strange happened. The president of the company came down from his headquarters in Seoul. He sent a message asking if he and I could have a meeting with Rev. Cho Sung Hyuk. I had no idea as to how he knew Rev. Cho, but I was quick to accept the offer. The three of us met and went over the arguments on both sides. It was clear that there was no easy way of getting a solution, but Cho made the unheard of suggestion that the union and company together invite a certain university professor to act as an arbitrator. It was acceptable to me and to the company president. I had to check with the other union officers. They agreed. The strike date was delayed. The professor did his job and kept good relations with both sides. In a short time, he proposed a compromise that consisted of a pay increase of thirteen percent and a possibility of a year-end bonus if productivity were increased. We put the proposal to a vote of the members. It passed by a large majority. I think that was the first time in our history that a third party was invited to act as arbitrator.

After that, my reputation and the status of the union soared. As I made my rounds among the men on the floor, I was met with warm greetings. A large number of members began to attend union meetings. Being president of the union had become an enjoyable task. For about a year we floated along in that kind of euphoria. Then we got caught up by something much bigger than we were.

As the year 1971 came along, the political situation in the country deteriorated badly. President Pak Chung Hee, a former military general, refused to leave office after his second term, as the constitution required. Instead, he forcefully changed the constitution to allow him to run for a third term. He won, of course, but he was not satisfied. He wanted total control. No independent groups were to be tolerated. Union activities and collective bargaining were suspended.

The significance of the political change did not hit home until one afternoon in October. I was about to leave the office when two men in black jackets pushed open the door. "Won Ji Hun?" The one guy growled.

"Yes."

"You are wanted for a short visit at the university."

"Why? Who wants me?"

"Don't ask questions, Let's go"

"Okay, but let me make a phone call to my wife."

"No, that won't be necessary! You'll only be gone for a short time."

They grabbed my arms and half-carried me out to their waiting jeep.

In Inchun at this time the word "university" was the code word for the Korean Central Intelligence Agency (KCIA). It was not considered polite or healthy to make direct reference to the KCIA, so the euphemism of university was applied. The interrogators at the "university" were at first very solicitous, apologizing for any inconvenience they were causing me. They asked a volley of questions about the union and the members and relations with the company.

Then their attitudes changed. "You know, Mr. Won that our nation is in a dangerous emergency. We have information that the communists have initiated a new offensive to infiltrate the working classes of the South and through them to over throw the government."

No, I had not heard about any such communist initiative, but I made no reply. "Mr. Won, what do you know about an organization called Urban Industrial Mission?"

"I know several people there, and have attended some of their meetings. But they are Christians. No one opposes communism like the church."

"You would like to think so, but the new communist scheme is to infiltrate that organization which is under the least suspicion—the church. Do you know Rev. Cho Sung Hyuk? Do you think he could be deceiving you and others? What do you know about the foreigner who is called Missionary Oh? He could be a contact with North Korean spies through Japan or even the United States. You know Rev. Cho Wha Soon, the woman minister, who works at UIM? She has been arrested just today on charges of giving comfort to the enemy by causing disturbances among the women workers in the textile mills.

I was dumbfounded. "That can not be true. I know them. They are good Christian men and women who are working for our people."

"You think so? Mr. Won, you are being duped. Rev. Cho introduced you to a professor to help in negotiations with the company last spring, didn't he? Do you know that that professor has been a suspected communist for a long time? Of course you don't. We have just been waiting for the right time to take him in. Mr. Won, our nation's entire future is at stake. Please be careful whom you associate with. We will help you all we can."

I was not released that night. I think they wanted to inject as much fear as possible into my family and friends. The next morning just as the night shift men were leaving and the day shift fellows were arriving at the factory, they saw a black jeep drive up to the union office. In sight of everyone two men in black jackets pulled me out of the jeep and deposited me roughly on the ground.

For several weeks nothing happened. Everyone was bewildered and afraid. Stories of other union leaders being arrested and beaten floated through the grapevine. Fear was spreading rapidly. Black-jacketed men showed up unexpectedly just to stand around. They seldom spoke to anyone. Kim Bae Oon, the company vice president in charge of labor relations, discontinued his visits.

One evening as I returned home, my wife came running out to the gate to meet me. "Quick, come into the house and listen to the radio." I followed her into the room where we kept the radio. "Listen!" she whispered with a touch of fear in her voice. At first I could not make out what was going on, but gradually it came together. I was listening to a radio dramatization of a communist attempt to take over the South. Urban Industrial Mission was being portrayed as a traitorous organization being used by the North to undermine the working class's loyalty to the democratic government of Pak Chung Hee. I began to shake. My wife began to cry. We were in real danger. Even innocent association with someone charged with being communist could get me, and my wife, arrested and sent to prison for a long time. What to do? What to do?

It turned out that I didn't have to sweat that one. The answer was forced upon me. The time for collective bargaining was coming around again. The union was moribund. No one had the courage to talk or act. A summons from Kim Bae Oon's office was brought to me. I went. This time there was no tea served—no friendliness. "Mr. Won, the company will find it difficult to negotiate with you. I suggest you resign. We will see that you get your old job back."

I made no reply, but got up and left. There was a meeting of the union leadership scheduled for the next day. Everyone gathered. No one spoke. I opened the meeting, but before I could say what was on my mind one of the men interrupted and said, " I move a no-confidence vote in our president and call for his dismissal immediately." I had to put the vote to the members. It was secret ballot. The room was as quiet as death. Ten of the twelve votes went against me. I was no longer the union president. After three years, I was back at my old job catching hot steel rods. Men in black jackets paid me no attention. I stayed to myself. My fellow workers hesitated to talk or be friendly.

I wanted to go and talk with Rev. Cho and Missionary Oh, but I was sure their offices were being watched. I could not afford to be seen with them right now. I did not believe the KCIA's slander that they were communist. That was absurd, but for the sake of my family I had to be careful. I worked. I slept.

I went to church. I spoke to no one about the events at the union or "the university."

In the following months the heavy hand of the KCIA was felt everywhere. More union men were arrested, students were imprisoned in large numbers, and a state of emergency was declared over the entire nation. Any behavior that could be construed to be anti-government was called pro-communist and punishable by long years in prison or worse. The black jackets seemed to reign supreme. UIM ceased to be an active player in labor affairs. Rev. Cho Sung Hyuk was arrested on a couple occasions; Cho Wha Soon, the woman pastor, returned from her arrest to carry on education programs for the textile women, but she was always under surveillance, and the police threatened the workers who associated with her. After a while she moved on to take a pastorate in a rural area. Churches, which at one time had financially supported the work of UIM, withdrew their money. Missionary Oh was arrested and deported back to the United States. A UIM organization continued in name, but its ministry among the workers was reduced to practically nothing. The twelve of us who had taken the "Factory Apostle" course gradually drifted apart. Several of the other men had also been taken to the "university" and treated the same way I had been. We were pretty much discouraged. As one of us said, we had walked the walk with Jesus as apostles in our work places. Now we were experiencing the cross, but there did not seem to be any resurrection in our future.

Ten years passed and the oppression of the KCIA was not lifted. On a Saturday night in early 1981, I made a visit to a friend in Yongdongpo, an industrial area in Seoul. My friend and his two sons work in near by factories. As we ate the evening meal of rice, soup and kimchee, I began to share with them my experiences as a "Factory Apostle." When I had finished, one of the young men said to me, "Uncle, will you come with us tonight?"

"Where will you go?"

"Just come. I will explain later."

This was highly mysterious, but I knew the young men to be trustworthy as was their father. I told them I would go with them.

A few minutes after the curfew blew at twelve midnight, the three of us left the house. I followed the brothers down several twisting back alleys staying in the shadows of the buildings. The boy in front opened a door of an old shack and the three of us went in. We went up a flight of stairs and into a large room. The room was lighted with a few candles. Forty young men and women were seated cross-legged on the floor, pencil and paper in hand. A man, of perhaps thirty years, stood in front instructing them in labor law and techniques in collective bargaining. He went on for about an hour and a half. Then another young man, addressed as Reverend Song, lead a discussion on how to be a follower of Jesus in these difficult days.

A strange, astounding thing happened. Reverend Song said to the gathered young people, "I want you to remember three words," he said. "Keep these words in your mind. They can be your guide. The three words are *palkyun* (discover), b*ongsa* (serve) and h*apsai* (unite)."

I could have shouted with joy! Here was the resurrection! How could that be? How did this young man come to use the very same words that Rev. Cho had taught to us ten years previously? I never found the answer to that question, but that is all right. It makes it more mysterious like a resurrection should be.

WE WON'T GO BACK

Background

The economic expansion of South Korea is due in large part to the blood, sweat and tears of young women who moved from the farm into the textile factories of the large cities. Women workers have consistently provided thirty to forty percent of the industrial work force. Their labor, repaid with low wages and horrendous working conditions, has been the leverage that Korea has enjoyed in international markets for a long time.

The story below depicts experiences common to these young women during the decade of 1965 to 1975 when military dictatorship and the march to economic development determined the course of the nation.

Names of places, events and people, with the exception of the woman pastor Cho Wha Soon, are fictitious. Reverend Cho is a close friend of the author.

*   *   *

The young women of the village were excited. The announcement had been made a few days before. Tomorrow Mr. Ko would come. He would invite a number of girls to go to Inchun to work in the Tongbong Textile mill. Any girl over fifteen who was in good health and of obedient disposition was eligible. The life of a peasant's daughter was not easy. She worked the hardest jobs and bore the brunt of male meanness. It was a life that offered minimal excitement and maximum boredom. The

95

opportunity to move to the city took on an aura of romance in the imagination of the girls. This was true despite a number of gruesome reports from women who actually had spent some time working in the mills.

The tradition of recruiting country girls for work in the textile mills began long ago under the Japanese. When Korean managers took over after the Japanese left in 1945, they continued the practice. For the last ten years now the same recruiter, Mr. Ko, had come to the village of Danjin. He knew the families and watched the children grow up so he had a good hunch as to which of the girls would best fit into factory life. The parents of the girls certainly regretted seeing their daughters go, but on the other hand their labor usually was not really needed at home and the factory wages would be shared with the family.

This year Mr. Ko came to talk with the father of Moon Sunhe. Ko knew that Sunhe was now sixteen and in good health. He had never heard of her giving trouble to anyone. He also knew that she had two brothers and two sisters. She would hardly be missed. Sunhe's father and Mr. Ko had no trouble reaching agreement.

"You understand, don't you, that you are responsible for her behavior? If she does not work well or causes trouble, we will return her to you."

"Of course I understand that," replied Sunhe's father. "Put your mind at rest. She is a good girl and works hard. You'll have no trouble from her. Our contract is for one year and it can be renewed. Is that correct?"

"Yes. She will live in our dormitory. We will provide food and pay her a fair wage. That is all in the contract. This year I am in need of ten new workers. I would like them to be in Inchun, Wednesday of next week. We will meet them at the bus station. Can you arrange that?"

"Yes, of course."

For two days recruiter Ko repeated similar conversations

with fathers of nine other girls. Sunhe, of course, knew all of them, but most importantly her very best friend Kim Kisook was also going. The two of them at an early age had taken an oath to always be loyal sisters to one another. They were sisters forever. Sunhe was the older by six months. One would certainly have protested if the other one had not been selected to go at the same time.

On Wednesday morning the ten girls with their few belongings gathered at the bus station. Mothers and sisters were there to see them off. As usual, the old dilapidated bus that passed through the village was an hour late. Already it was jammed pack with people and an assortment of plants and animals. The girls pushed their way in and stood squashed up against each other.

The driver tried to make up for his lost time by slamming the gas pedal to the floor. Each stop was an abrupt re-ordering of the passengers' positions, accompanied by moans, groans and protests. But they made it. No accidents. No one hurt. And when the bus pulled into Inchun Station it was only an hour and a half late.

The company bus was waiting. In comparison to the one they had just been on it was new and very comfortable. The girls murmured with pleasure. After only a short ride they arrived at a tall brick wall that extended for a whole block. At the end a large metal gate swung open and the bus drove in.

What Sunhe, Kisook and the other girls did not realize was that they had just become part of a work force of 600,000 women upon whom the economic development of the entire nation depended. It was their high productivity and low wages that made the economic five-year plans a success. The other thing they did not know was that it would be many months before they again saw life outside those gates.

The dormitory housemother, Mrs. Pak, a woman of about forty years of age, greeted the girls in a kindly way. "The company welcomes you. We are one big family here. If you have any problems, come to me as though I was your mother. Treat each other as sisters and share the burdens and we will get along fine. There are, of course, a few regulations that we have to follow. Three hundred girls live here. They work three shifts, so at any given time a third of them are sleeping. Please keep the noise down at all times."

"Second, bathroom facilities are limited. Follow the rules as nailed to the doors. And third, until you are adjusted to our factory's way of doing, you will not leave the compound. After a few months, that will be reconsidered. We are responsible to your parents for your conduct and safety so we will have to act accordingly. There are other rules, but we can take care of those as we go along."

There was a short pause while Mrs. Pak shifted to another subject. "You begin your work tomorrow morning promptly at 8:00 AM. Therefore, you must get up and be at breakfast by seven. You cannot be late. Being tardy will earn you a demerit on your record. After breakfast, a foreman will show you to your job."

Again Mrs. Pak hesitated and looked around at the girls. They all stood in steep silence unable to take it all in, and by habit making no verbal response.

"Very well. Now I will show you to your rooms. You need to get your sleep to be ready for tomorrow." Mrs. Pak then proceeded to give each girl a room number.

"Mrs. Pak, Kisook and I would like to room together," offered Sunhe.

"Sorry, but that is not possible. There are no double vacancies."

"Could you put us close together then?" asked Kisook.

"You will take what you are given. We can not play favorites." Mrs. Pak's voice changed from that of a kindly matron to that of a strict warden.

Sunhe opened the door to her room. Two girls were already lying on the floor asleep. They took no notice of her. One of them snored in a loud rhythmic beat. The room was small like the ones at home. The sleeping girls were stretched out on small floor mats. There was one mat and a small space left for Sunhe. The room was already crowded with clothes and bundles of things that belonged to her roommates. Sunhe laid her small package of belongings on her mat. She would use it as a pillow. As she laid waiting for sleep to come, a sense of isolation and horrible loneliness clutched her heart.

She finally slept, but time and again she awoke, fearful that she might over-sleep. She need not have worried. All of a sudden her two roommates were up noisily getting ready for the day. They grunted hellos to Sunhe, but engaged in no talk. Sunhe followed their lead and got to breakfast on time. At exactly 7:45 AM, the new girls were called together and given their work assignments. Sunhe and Kisook held each other's hands waiting for their names to be called. Kisook's name came first. Sunhe squeezed her hand for good luck and whispered good-bye. A young man claimed her and three other girls and led them off to a far corner of the mill.

Another young man called Sunhe's name and took her to a jungle crowded with endless lines of clamoring machines that were twisting thread out of cotton fibers. The noise was so great that the young foreman made no attempt to verbally tell Sunhe what to do. Rather, by means of gestures he indicated that Sunhe was to stand beside a girl who was already at work and learn from what she did. The machines demanded total attention. The worker gave Sunhe a half a smile, but did not try to speak. She moved up and down the line in front of the machines making sure the threads did not break, or if they did come apart, to quickly repair them. If a thread were to break, and not be repaired immediately, a whole line of machines might be brought to a stop.

It was not a skill difficult to learn. After an hour or so, the foreman motioned for Sunhe to follow him. She was taken to a line of machines that were not running. "These machines will start up in ten minutes," he yelled. "It will be your job to do just as you saw the other girl do. Since you are new, you will have only half as many machines as she. I will be here to help. Just do your best."

Sunhe learned quickly, but after only an hour or so muscle spasms gripped her back and her fingers began to bleed. The air was so thick with lint and cotton dust that the workers all resembled moving snowmen. Breathing was not easy. But it was the noise of the machines that caused the most pain. Sunhe's head ached and pounded like a thumping drum. She motioned to the foreman. He came up close so that he could hear.

"I have a bad headache. I must rest," she yelled.

"No way! There is a ten-minute break in two hours—no resting before then. Be careful now not to stop the line." The answer came back without sympathy.

How she finished the day Sunhe was never able to recall. She could only remember the pain that wracked her body as she lay on the floor of her room and the laughter of the older girls as they mocked her pain. Sleep never came, only fits of troubled dreams. The night passed slowly, agonizingly. She cried. She called for her mother, for Kisook, but there was no one to give her comfort.

When morning finally came, she felt unable to move let alone get out of bed. Promptly at 6:00 AM, however, house-mother Pak came in. Her voice was not harsh, but it came in command. "Get up! Wash! Go to Breakfast!"

Sunhe knew there was no refusal. She got up. Washed. Went to breakfast. She found herself in front of the machines. The ache in her head began where it had ended the day before. She heard a whistle down the line. The foreman was telling her to work. Several times during the day he hit her on the head with a little stick he always carried. He did not hit hard, just enough to keep her awake.

She moved in a trance. Fatigue and pain so controlled her body and head that only sleep seemed real. At meals, she and

Kisook clung to each other. Kisook's legs had swelled up to double their normal size. Her once pretty face was weary with tears and exhaustion. They exchanged looks of desperation when they had to separate.

It took Sunhe and the other new girls several months before they began to come out of the stupor that their new work had inflicted on them. Gradually, however, their young bodies began to reassert themselves. The air, noise and heat in the factory did not improve, but the pain became less. Their fatigue decreased and they began to sleep and eat in something like a normal fashion again. Color began to reappear in their cheeks.

Sunhe was not sure how long it took her to work through her pain. She had been more dead than alive. Now she became aware of her fellow workers. No one was happy or kind. Every one seemed to be angry. Everyone was on her own, pitted against everyone else. It was impossible to even talk with a fellow worker. Yet one person's mistake resulted in loss and pain to others on the line. Every mistake was accompanied by shouts and curses.

The foremen set the pattern. Week after week they would hoist up new banners exhorting the workers to greater heights of production: "Save our Nation! Produce More!" "Join Hands and Work together!" "As One Family, Let Us Go Forward." But regardless of the slogan, the attitude was always the same: a command issued in low, degrading terms. Words of respect or encouragement were seldom heard. Supervisors and foremen were men of higher education and economic class. They saw the country girls as inferior and capable only of obeying orders. They did not hesitate to give out demerits if a girl talked back. Ten demerits could have a person fired and returned to her village.

The girls in their relationships with each other repeated the same pattern. Two or three would make tight friendships but these little cadres always seemed to be in conflict with other groups. Sunhe's two roommates, though close to one another, never permitted her to enter their friendship. On occasions when the three of them were in the room at the same time, the two would huddle together, talk, giggle and whisper so that she could not hear. Kisook was her only friend. There was never time nor inclination to become close to any one else.

The first incident occurred after she had been there for about six months. The foreman, Mr. Lee, a man of about thirty years, instead of hitting her with his stick, placed his hand on her shoulder and in a friendly way said, "Stay awake little sister." It was the kindest word she had heard in months. She responded to him with a smile. The next day as she reported to work, he said, "good morning." Again she smiled. His kindness warmed Sunhe's lonely heart. It became easier to get up and go to work.

Not long after that a thread broke, and one of Sunhe's machines was stopped. The usual practice was for the foreman to blow his whistle and yell at the worker to get it fixed. This time, however, foreman Lee came over. "Let me help with that. These things happen." He reached into the machine and quickly repaired the errant threads. In so doing he brushed himself up against Sunhe's thigh. He looked at her and said, "Sorry about that."

The look in his eye, however, suggested that he was considerably less than sorry. Sunhe had little experience with men, but she instinctively sensed that something more than an accident had taken place. "Thank you," she yelled against the clatter as the machine started up again. After that, his attention became obvious. Several times a day he would pass by, or say something kind or touch her lightly on the shoulder or thigh. Even the other workers became aware of Lee's infatuation. Word started to spread that Sunhe was Lee's woman.

At the far end of Sunhe's work line, there were a few moments when she was out of sight of everyone else. She was concentrating on the threads and the hypnotic up and down motions of the machine. She turned to the left to tend to the last thread, and walked into Lee who had planted himself in front of her. His hands reached for her breasts and his mouth tried to find hers. Instinctively Sunhe hit him hard across the face and pushed him away. The surprised foreman was caught off guard. He stumbled backwards into the churning machine. Immediately the whole line stopped, bells sounded, whistles blew, and workers and supervisors came running.

After a fellow foreman extricated him from the tangle of threads, Lee bellowed for all to hear, "The bitch! She pushed me. I could have been killed!" With that, he swung around and hit Sunhe across the face with the back of his hand. She fell to the floor and began to cry.

By then the department supervisor had arrived. "Get this mess cleaned up and the line moving again." He pointed to another foreman and said, "You're in charge. The rest of you get back to work. Mr. Lee, and you," pointing his finger in Sunhe's face, "get to my office at once."

Still in shock, Sunhe lay motionless on the floor. Miss Suh, the only female foreman in the plant, took her by the arm and led her to the office. Lee and the supervisor were already there. "You have got mixed up with these little bitches before, Lee," yelled the supervisor.

Much subdued, Lee pleaded his innocence. "She was the one who was after me. When I turned her down, she lost her temper and pushed me." Lee lied without much effect.

"Get out of here! I'll take care of you later." With that the supervisor turned toward Sunhe, who was standing just inside the door, bent over crying, her hands covering her face. She was so ashamed she could not lift her head.

"You, you little bitch! We have given you a home here. We've given you a place to stay and paid you fair wages and you repay us like this? That one episode has cost the company more than you are worth. You will be returned to the village at once. Let your parents try to make a lady of you."

The supervisor's words had a strange effect on Sunhe. His

accusations were so unjust and his attitude so insulting, that her crying stopped. She became calm. Much to her own surprise she heard herself reply to the supervisor, "You are being unfair. I am a good worker. Look at my record. Lee was trying to seduce me. He has been all over me now for months. Ask any of the other girls they will tell you what kind of a guy he is. If you send me back to the village, fine, but I will not allow pigs like that to rub over me."

Her words also had a strange effect upon the supervisor. He was taken aback by the young girl's spirit. There was a long pause. Then with anger still in his voice, he responded, "I will not send you back this time, but as of now you have nine demerits. One more and you are out of here for good. Tomorrow you will be transferred to another department. Get out."

As Sunhe walked to the dormitory, she felt everyone's eyes on her. No one spoke. She made it to her room, collapsed on the floor and continued her crying. When she heard her roommates coming, she wanted to hide or run away, but there was no escape. She would have to endure their ugly words. The door opened. "Sunhe, are you all right? We heard what happened. Good for you. You did what a lot of us have wanted to do and never had the courage. Are they going to return you to your village?"

Kind words coming from her roommates? Sunhe looked up and saw that both of the girls were crying. They knelt and embraced her. Again the door opened. Kisook and several other friends came in. Soon the room was full of crying women, but the tears of pain changed into tears of joy as they found themselves bound together by the "heroic" behavior of Sunhe. She had found the courage to stand up for herself in a way that most of the others had only fantasized about doing.

For a few days after the "Lee incident," life in the plant and dormitory lightened up a bit. The foremen were quieter than usual and the women spoke to each other more often. After only a few weeks, however, the rhythm of the machines reasserted itself. Foremen returned to their usual habits. Workers again cursed and insulted one another. The friendship between Sunhe and her two roommates, Okja and Mia, however, did not die.

A year passed. Mrs. Pak, the dormitory mother, made an announcement. "The company has decided to close down most of the dormitories. It costs too much to keep them up. The company will allow a grace period of three months. Then all of you will have to find your own quarters. You must vacate before the end of the three months. After that, the dormitory buildings will be torn down."

The three friends sat in their room talking about the news. "It will be a mess moving things out, but actually I like the idea of living out on our own. Being in the dorm and under the restrictions of the company all the time is a pain in the you know what." started Okja.

"What will they ever do with the dormitory mother if we are not here for her to order around?" smirked Mia. "Maybe they will return her to her village." Everyone chuckled and laughed as they pictured Mrs. Pak being returned.

"But we've got to stay together."

"And Kisook too."

"Okay then, the four of us. What do we do?"

Okja was the oldest and most experienced. She came up with the first idea. "We have two rest days a month. Mine is coming up the day after tomorrow. I will begin the search, and report back to you."

Sunhe's day-off coincided with Okja's so she volunteered to go along.

The two girls walked through the neighborhood. It was an industrial area called *Mansukdong*. Narrow, garbage-strewn, alleys wound around in no noticeable pattern. Small *hakabans* (shacks) made of scrap wood and rusty corrugated sheets stood tentatively, jammed up against their neighbors. Little children ran around pursuing each other or kicking the remnants of a ball.

A railroad, that fed the many factories in the area, ran through *Mansukdong*. Several times a day, trains, raining down dirt and noise, edged their way slowly through the mass of children who used the train tracks as their playground.

Okja and Sunhe slowly acquainted themselves with *Mansukdong*. They talked with the women who squatted along side the alleys doing their chores: cooking, cleaning, and nursing children. Several of them offered to rent space, but few could accommodate four people.

Toward late morning they came upon a shack that was about one and a half floors high. The owner invited them in. He was renting to several other girls and would be glad to take in a few more. On the bottom floor there were two rooms. His family occupied one of them, and three girls from the mill were in the other. The second floor was empty. He would let the four girls use it. It was right under the roof like an attic, and hardly high enough for a person to stand upright. Yet it was not much more crowded than their space at the dorm.

Okja talked to the owner about cost. It was agreed that each of the girls would pay the same amount. After a time of bargaining, they reached an amount that Okja and Sunhe thought they could afford. "We must talk to the other two girls and make sure it is okay with them," said Okja after an agreement had been reached. "I will come back tomorrow after work and settle the deal."

The two women reported to their cohorts that evening. It was decided to accept Okja's advice. The next day Okja returned to finalize the agreement. This time, however, the man was hesitant. "To be honest with you, after you left yesterday, two other girls from another factory came by in need of a room. I couldn't turn them down. But I think it will work out. They sleep, I am sure, on a schedule different from yours. While you work they can sleep and when you sleep, they will be at work. How about it? I will lower each person's rent a little."

After again testing the proposition out with the other girls, Okja agreed to the owner's proposal. So for the next several years the six girls shared the cramped quarters. In the winter the roof kept the wind out, but was not very effective against the cold. In the summer the roof became an ally with the sun and baked the residents inside.

Despite the discomfort of the place the four girls preferred the relative freedom to the dormitory. They arranged to share their days off so that they could wander around the city. Sunhe especially like to explore the city's central market with all its labyrinth of paths and stalls, and to talk with the market women who peddled everything from onions to rice to chickens. It reminded her of market day at home in the village.

Then simultaneously two things occurred to disturb their pattern of life. One was a picnic and one was a love affair.

Sunhe was the first to notice. Something was wrong with Kisook. At times she seemed unusually bright and happy, but at other times she became moody and withdrawn. At work she would lose her concentration. She caused two accidents and received five demerits in only one week.

When walking back home one evening after work, Sunhe discovered the reason behind Kisook's unusual behavior. A young man stepped out of the shadows, said hello and asked Kisook if he could speak with her. She hesitated only briefly and then asked Sunhe to go on. She would catch up. But she didn't catch up. It was late, after supper, before Kisook came in.

"Where have you been? Do you have a boy friend?" Sunhe asked in a cheerful but teasing voice.

Kisook immediately became defensive. "He's my friend. That's all. There's nothing wrong with that. We just ate some noodles together. Can't I have a friend without you thinking I'm bad?"

"Kisook, I don't think you're bad. I was just teasing. Who is he? Where did you meet him?" Suspicion and fear now awoke in Sunhe's mind. "Tell me all about him."

Kisook hung her head and spoke quietly. "I met him on the way home a few weeks ago. He works in the shipping department at the factory. He saw me in the plant and wanted to meet me so he waited outside after work until I came. We talked— that's all. After that, we have met several times."

"What does he want?"

"Sunhe, don't be angry. I like him. I like being with him. He's fun to talk with."

"What does he want?" persisted Sunhe. She smelled a rat in the woodpile.

"I'm an adult now. I can do as I please. Do you think you are Mrs. Pak?" Kisook retorted sharply assuming the attitude of one being falsely accused.

"Kisook, remember I am your older sister. We must be loyal to each other and you must tell me everything. What does he want?"

Kisook's spine stiffened. She sat up straight and looked Sunhe in the eye. "He wants me to move in with him."

"He wants to marry you?"

"Yes—Not now. Later when he gets a better job."

"Kisook, you must not do this. You do not know this fellow. Let us find out more about him. If he wishes to marry, let it be now, not years from now. Don't meet him again until we ask some of the other girls about him. Okay? Promise?"

Kisook meekly nodded her head in submission.

Nevertheless, three days later Kisook did not come home.

Kisook's betrayal ached inside Sunhe, and every minute she worried about what might happen to her friend. Okja and Mia were angry. They were sure that Kisook was being deceived and foolish. At every turn one could hear stories about how lecherous men had seduced textile girls.

Maybe they should just kidnap Kisook and forcefully keep

her at home. Mia suggested that they wait in the alley and beat the devil out of the son of a bitch.

Then out of the blue, Okja said, "Let's go to the picnic on Sunday."

"Okay, good idea," chimed in Mia. "Where is it going to be?"

"What picnic," quizzed Sunhe? "I don't feel much like a picnic. What about Kisook?"

"Kisook will have to wait. Let's go play. We're hiking up Pupyung Mountain. The plan is to meet at the bus station and go together."

Sunhe was a bit mystified. She had not heard of a picnic, and Okja was talking as though she were heading the thing up. "Slow down. Who's having this picnic? Who's going? What does it cost?"

"It is sponsored by the church. Reverend Cho Wha Soon puts things together. You will like her. She is a nice lady."

"I'm not a Christian. Have never been to a church," objected Sunhe.

"Neither have I," said Mia, "but it doesn't make any difference. Only a few of the people who go are Christian. It's fun. We have time to talk, and Reverend Cho usually teaches us some interesting things. I have gone two times."

The other girls' enthusiasm finally persuaded Sunhe. On Saturday evening they prepared some rice, seaweed and a little pickled cabbage. By nine the next morning they were at the bus station in front of the Inchun train station. Thirty girls gathered. Okja seemed to be the leader. When she said the word, everyone got on the bus and in an hour they were at Pupyung. From there they walked to the foot of the mountain. Ten other girls were waiting. As they started up the mountain, one of the girls began to sing, and before long everyone else joined in. Sunhe noticed that one person, whom she guessed was Rev. Cho, walked around talking to everyone. She came Sunhe's way. " I am Cho Wha Soon. I work at the church. I am glad to see you. Are you from Tongbong?

"Yes but my home village is Danjin. Several of us are from the same place." Cho's words and attitude were friendly so Sunhe told her about herself and how she lived together with Okja and the others. Cho repeated her words of welcome and went on to speak to other new girls.

The top of the mountain was shaped like a sway-backed horse. Here they stopped and spread out their food. One of the girls raised her voice to be heard. "Before we eat Rev. Cho is going to talk to us. After we eat, we have a couple games to play, and after that you will be free to do as you wish. We have to get the return bus at four o'clock.

Rev. Cho's message was very brief. "The Bible tells us we should love one another. All religions teach that. The problem is that we often do not know how to love one another. Instead of my preaching, I want you to break up into groups of five and discuss among yourselves the following question: what are the problems that we face in the factory and how do we show love in those situations?"

Those who had been with Rev. Cho before knew exactly what to do. New people followed along. Sunhe found herself in a group along with Mia, but she did not know the other three. One of them took the lead. "First off, everyone has to give her opinion. That's the rule. How can we show love to each other when we face problems? I guess that means how do we help each other? When one of is in trouble, how do the rest of us help out?"

"I have a good example." chirped in one girl. "A girl on our line collapsed the other day. The foreman was all over her trying to get her on her feet and back to work. Two of us told him to leave her alone for a while. We divided her work up, and the two of us by working faster did her job for a few minutes until she recovered."

"Well, one of our friends fell asleep on the job and got her hand caught in the machines. Cut her pretty bad. The nurse bandaged her up, but the supervisor had her returned to the village right away without any compensation at all. They said that since she couldn't work she was of no use to them. How can we help? I don't think we can. Love might be a good thing, but in some cases it's not what is needed."

Mia broke in. "Okja says that the labor union is supposed to help in those cases."

At the mention of the labor union the other girls laughed. "Don't hold your breath. The union is in the hands of the company. Don't expect any good to come from it."

"There is another problem that we have to face," continued Mia. "That is the insulting way that the men treat us. They think they can use as their sexual playmates or worse. Sunhe, you haven't said anything. Tell us about your run-in with foreman Lee."

This was really a new experience for Sunhe. To speak about a personal matter in front of strangers! But under the gaze of the other girls she couldn't refuse. She told her story. When she came to the place where she pushed Lee into the machines, the other girls clapped their hands and gave loud guffaws. "Good! Good! That is a good way of solving that problem and showing love to each other."

For more than an hour the discussion went on. Sunhe had never been so energized. She never dreamed that women could get together and act on their own. She would have been glad to continue, but the person who had spoken earlier again raised her voice declaring that the discussion time was over. Time to eat. Slowly the groups broke up and everyone reassembled around the food.

"Before we eat, let us thank God for the food. Reverend Cho, will you ask a blessing?"

Everyone stopped talking and bowed their heads. This also was a new experience for Sunhe. She listened to what Reverend Cho was saying. "Father in heaven, hallowed be thy name.

Let thy kingdom and its justice be among us. Thank you for the life you have given us. We thank you for each other. Teach us to love one another. Thank you especially for this food. Amen." In a loud voice many of the girls repeated the word amen.

The rest of the day was spent hiking up to the top peak of the mountain, talking, laughing and singing. For Sunhe it was glorious— maybe the happiest day of her life.

As they were coming back down the mountain, Sunhe asked Okja, "What is a labor union?" "Do we have one at Tongbong?"

"A labor union is an organization of workers. It is supposed to represent the interests of the workers and negotiate with the company about wages and working conditions. We have one, but since we workers are women, the men control it and run it for their own and the company's benefit"

"I've been here for almost two years and haven't even heard of it. How do you know so much?"

"I've studied about it with Reverend Cho. She lets us read the law that sets up unions, and she teaches us how it is supposed to work.

The idea is that workers should have the right to organize and bargain about wages and working conditions. Workers form a union. Then the union representatives and the company bargain to resolve their common problems.

"Why is Reverend Cho so interested in unions?

"She worked in a factory for a while and understands our situation. She says that Christianity teaches that there should be justice and equality among all people. To build justice workers have to stop being cliquish and work together. We have a meeting this Saturday. Come along with me if you want."

The subject for the Saturday meeting was startling. "Can we women workers become leaders of the union at Tongbong?" Reverend Cho laid out the questions and let the participants do the discussing. "Question one: why is it desirable for women to run the union? Question two: how is the union organized? Question three: what strategy is needed to enable us to become leaders?

The discussion raged on late into the night. It was not concluded. For many meetings after that the same topic was continued. Finally a consensus was reached. A three-pronged attack was going to be needed. According to the present regulations, once a year the workers in each department elect a union representative. Department representatives then meet and elect union officers. Usually the process was quite perfunctory. A few men gathered together and elected department reps from among their group. The reps in turn elected union officers whom the company suggested.

This was the pattern that the Japanese established when they controlled Korea. After Korean employers took over they just continued on the same way. The women, however, now decided to change things. Their first strategy was to attend each of the departmental elections and cast votes for a woman of their choice not for a man.

Second, the women had to agree on a candidate for union president they would all support. And finally, the newly elected women officers had to have a slate of goals that would rally the workers in support.

The strategy worked perfectly. The company had no inkling of what was going to take place. When the day for election of department representatives came, for the first time ever, women workers attended. In every department a woman won the race for representative. Several days after that, they unanimously elected Okja president of the union.

The plant manager found himself in a dilemma. For the first time in history he was being called upon to recognize a woman as head of the union. He would have to sit down with her and bargain about plant problems. That was embarrassing. He would not—could not— do it. Yet he could not deny that the elections were honest and legal.

Okja took the initiative. Along with Sunhe and two other

department representatives, she walked into the company office and requested to see the manager. She had sent a letter
ahead asking for a meeting to discuss common concerns. The
company president, they were told, was in Seoul and could not
see them.

They returned the next day and the next day and the next.
The manager was never there. On the fifth day Okja declared
that they would wait until he returned. The four women, joined
by the rest of the union officers, began a sit-in. The company
retaliated by calling the police. The women were charged with
trespassing on private property and thus breaking the law.

The police relished the assignment. They gleefully beat the
women over the head with their clubs and dragged them out of
the offices. Okja and Sunhe, as the perceived leaders of the
group, were thrown into a black police van and carried off to
the police station.

For three days they were allowed to languish in the jail en-
during all the sexual barbs that their keepers could heap upon
them. Okja ground her teeth, and fumed in her frustration. Sunhe
spent much of her time crying. She was so ashamed to be called
all those ugly names. If her father ever learned that she had
been arrested, he too would have been ashamed, and would
probably disown her. At the end of the third day two men dressed
in black suits came from the company. As soon as she saw
them, Okja began to wail and cry. Sunhe knew Okja was put-
ting on an act to impress these two guys, and make them think
she was a poor, repentant, country girl. Okja's machinations
made Sunhe stop crying, but she was still too embarrassed to
look at the men.

"Okay you two, time to go home. Be on time for work in
the morning, and no more of this labor union nonsense. Do
you understand?" Okja just cried louder and Sunhe hung her
head even lower to keep from laughing at Okja. They were
driven back to their room in a big black car.

The plant manager had miscalculated the women's determination. The day after she got out of jail, Okja contacted the National Union of Textile Workers in Seoul. At the time there were seventeen nation-wide industrial union organizations, one of which was the textile union.

Okja pleaded with the national chairman to come to Inchun to give them support. This was a bad mistake. She had no way of knowing that just a few days before she made her request the military government, which now ruled in South Korea, had taken over leadership of the national union organizations.

The man who came down from Seoul was a newly appointed agent of the secret police. For two hours in the morning he huddled with management. In the afternoon he called all the union officers together and gave them a lecture. "Our nation is going through very difficult times. The North has become more threatening. Any turmoil on our part will encourage them to attack. Furthermore, as you all know, we are in deep economic competition with other nations around the world. We must keep up production. Any work stoppage hinders our economic development. In this time of crisis it is the role of our labor unions to stay in line with the policies of our government. So I urge you, be patriotic! Work as a patriot for your nation. Follow the leadership of the company."

Okja was furious. She yelled, "You call us unpatriotic? We give our lives every day in this contemptible factory! Our wages are hardly enough to live on. We work in jeopardy of being hurt or even killed. I thought you were a union man! Who do you work for?"

Several other girls also began to yell and scream threats at the man. He departed quickly back into the shelter of the company's office. The women were incensed. They marched to the door where he had gone in and shouted a demand that he come out and explain who he worked for. The crowd of workers began to grow. Those going to and coming from work joined the rally. Before long several hundred women were shouting and chanting.

The company manager responded by calling in a gang of thugs that the company seemed always to have available when needed. They waded into the women knocking them down and ripping off their clothes. The thugs were soon reinforced by the police who once more expressed their pleasure in roughing up country girls.

Sunhe was down on her knees trying to ward off a blow by a policeman when she saw the policeman's truncheon smash into Okja's head. Blood squirted out like a fountain. Okja collapsed. Sunhe let go a piercing yell, "Help! Okja is dead! Okja is dead! Help! Please help." Her high shrill alarm was heard over the bedlam. An ambulance was called. Okja was barely alive when they arrived at the hospital. Sunhe and the other union leaders were again carried off to jail.

Okja lay in a coma for three days. Reverend Cho sat by her side, praying and helping the nurses tend to her needs. On the fourth day Okja regained consciousness. The very next day the company served her with official dismissal papers. She no longer worked at Tongbong Textiles. She was forbidden to ever again step on to Tongbong property.

Several days later when Okja was able to stand, police came to arrest her. Reverend Cho protested loudly. "You must not do this. Don't you see she is too weak to be taken out of the hospital? Can you be responsible if she dies? She is not going to escape. At least leave her here for a few more days."

"We've been ordered to bring her in, and that we shall do. Get out of the way." One policeman shoved Reverend Cho into a corner. The other picked Okja up and carried her to the police wagon. The next day Okja was taken before the judge, and despite all the arguments and pleadings of Cho Wha Soon, she was sentenced to six months in prison.

Sunhe and a dozen other women, who had taken part in the melee, lay in prison for three days. On the fourth day a judge sentenced each one of them to a year in prison, but then exercised clemency and left them out after only a month.

Sunhe would always remember the date of her release from prison. It was the same day she heard about Kisook. She had just returned home when Mia came rushing in.

"Sunhe, quick. It's Kisook. She's in the hospital. She may die."

"What happened? Why?"

"Come on. I will tell you on the way. I heard it from a friend who is a nurse at the hospital."

As they took off towards the hospital, Mia told the story. Kisook had gotten pregnant. When her boyfriend found out, he was angry and beat her. He wanted no baby, and he certainly did not want to marry Kisook. He left. Kisook thought he would come back if there was no child so she went to an old crone in the neighborhood to have an abortion. The old lady had done hundreds of such operations, but she was now old. Her eyes were not clear and her hands were not steady. She messed it up badly. Bleeding and in pain, Kisook had dragged herself to the house where her boy friend was now staying and laid herself down at his doorstep to die. Someone found her and called the police. They took her to the hospital.

Kisook was lying unconscious with a maze of tubes piercing into her. Sunhe was driven to her knees with anguish and guilt. If only she had stayed closer to her friend, her little sister—if only they had stayed home in the village— if only—

When the doctor came in, Reverend Cho came in with him. She immediately embraced Sunhe and tried to assure her that Kisook was going to be all right.

"Kisook has lost a lot of blood. It will take many days before she is out of the woods, but her chances are good. We have already operated and mended the damage that the old lady did. It's just a matter of time," comforted the doctor.

"I am her only friend, her only family in the city," said Sunhe. "I should stay here with her, but I still have to work. I'm due at the factory in a few minutes. What shall I do?"

"I will see to her," offered Cho. "Between the nurses, doctor and me we will take good care of her. She probably won't be able to visit much anyway for several days. Put your mind at rest. Go on to work."

Each day when her shift was over, Sunhe made a pilgrimage to the hospital. With each visit Kisook seemed to be gaining in strength, but her load of guilt was heavy. She condemned herself for committing such a terrible sin. Her self-respect was gone. She had betrayed Sunhe. She would never be able face her parents. Her fellow workers must certainly think of her as a slut or worse. There was no way out. She began to think and then talk about suicide. That seemed like the one honorable escape.

One evening Kisook seemed quieter— more at peace with herself. "Sunhe, Reverend Cho told me a story today. Do you want to hear it?"

"Of course. What is it"?

"It's in the Bible. Some men brought a woman like me to Jesus and asked him if they should stone her to death. You know how he answered them? He looked at them and said, "the one of you who has never sinned, throw the first stone." Since they also had done wrong things, no one dared throw a stone. So Jesus looked at the woman and said, 'Daughter I do not condemn you. Go and sin no more.' He forgave her. I think God is forgiving me too." She looked up at Sunhe. Their eyes met in the warm love of sisters reunited. "When I get all better, I think I would like to go back to work."

That night as she walked back to her house, Sunhe was in a good mood. Kisook's change of heart had been a blessing to her too. "Perhaps we can forgive and be forgiven." She thought. "Tomorrow I will ask the company to allow Kisook to come back to work."

The next morning she went to the company offices and asked to see the manager. The manager refused to talk with her, but he did send out a clerk to hear what she had to say.

In a quiet and sweet voice Sunhe began. "Hello, I am Moon

Sunhe. I work in the winding department. A friend of mine, Kim Kisook, has missed work for several days because she has been terribly sick and in the hospital. Now that she is getting better she would like to return to work. She should be ready to begin in another week or so. Will that be all right?"

The clerk only looked at her. He said nothing, turned and retreated into the inner office. When he reappeared again, he had a folder with Kisook's name on it. "Yes we are well aware of that case. We cannot condone behavior like that of Miss Kim. This will reflect poorly on the company. It has been decided that she will be returned to her father as soon as she is able to travel."

"And what about that scoundrel, Song, who did this to her? Will you return him to his village also?" Sunhe's sweetness was swept away by bitter sarcasm.

The clerk gave Sunhe a cold stare. "You are being insubordinate Miss Moon. What we do with Mr. Song is our business, not yours. Now please leave."

Sunhe now knew what she had to do. She thought about it all night and then contacted the union leaders the next day. "Meet at my place tonight right after supper." They all came, but they brought with them a rumor that increased their fear and anxiety: "Cho Wha Soon has been arrested. They say she is a communist, a spy from the North."

"I don't believe it. She's no communist," was Sunhe's immediate reaction, but still a shiver of fear swept through her. It was twenty years since the war, but all the stories of the terrible things that happened still lay deep in the collective memory. And even now, spies from the North continued to infiltrate into the South to cause trouble. Intuitively Sunhe knew that Reverend Cho was not a communist. The government which now was being run by the military probably made up the accusations. But still, what if . . . Doubts were sewn by the accusations.

Gradually the whole story came out. On the way to her

office at about six in the morning, men in a black jeep had
picked up Reverend Cho. Rumor had it that she was now at the
Korean Central Intelligence Agency (KCIA) headquarters in
Seoul.

She was charged with causing disturbances among the
workers at Tongbong. The company had sent a spy to her classes
about labor unions. The spy reported that Cho had spoken
harshly against the company. She was the one who told the
innocent country girls that they needed a union. To the company and the military such teaching could only have come from
communism. All the girls who attended the classes or the pic-
nics were now under suspicion of being subversives.

What could they do? Would they have to drop their plans
for the union and submit to what seemed to be the inevitable?
The company, the national union, the police and now the KCIA
were against them. No one could say, "Let's give up," but no
one had the spunk to say, "let's go on." Without Okja there was
no one to take the lead.

The rumor about Reverend Cho's arrest stoked the anger in
Sunhe's heart. All the humiliations she had suffered since she
arrived at Tongbong rose up in her. The stupid, demanding
machines, foreman Lee, the low condescending talk, the miserable wages, the disrespect, the beatings by the police, the
crass names, Okja's beating and Kisook's very life. Anger boiled
in her like a pot of hot blood soup.

Sunhe spoke. "We have eaten enough disrespect, been
called too many foul names. I propose we go on with trying to
organize the union. It is one way to honor Okja and it is the
only way that we will get any justice in this company. I will
stand for president."

A cheer of support wavered across the room. At Sunhe's
insistence they quickly set out a plan of action. The next day
would be used to get the word out. The day after that the meeting would be held.

Before they left, Sunhe had another word. "We've got to be

strong. Let us give up being timid, docile country girls. Remember what they did to Okja. Remember Kisook. Remember what they have done to Reverend Cho." The women clung to each other half crying, half cheering.

The next day all went well. Word was passed from person to person. "The union meeting will be held tomorrow at noon. Sunhe is the candidate for president."

After work that evening, Sunhe and Mia contacted each of the union department representatives. They were all in agreement. The conspirators planned late into the night getting every detail correct. The stage was set.

Before the sun had risen the next morning, however, the plans were rendered useless. Just before dawn, while it was still dark, two black-jacketed men burst into the room where Sunhe and Mia lay sleeping. Looking at Sunhe one man snarled, "Get your clothes on. You're going home."

"Who are you? Get out of here," yelled Sunhe.

Mia in a panic screamed over and over again. "We're being murdered. Help save us. We're being murdered!"

One of the men hit her hard. She stopped screaming.

"Put your clothes on or I will put them on for you," commanded the first man.

Sunhe slowly obeyed. The entire neighborhood was now awake, gazing in fear at the two men as they dragged the young woman to a black automobile, and threw her on to the floor of the back seat. The two men then got in the front seat and drove away.

Sunhe lay on the floor of the car. Her shock was quickly overcome. She was no longer an innocent village girl. Her first thought was how to get out of there. Quickly she devised a scheme for escape. She made sounds like she was weeping.

The two men, after the usual barrage of verbal abuse and threats of rape, turned to their own conversation and left her alone. Sunhe slid up onto the seat. She waited. The street they were on had stoplights at every intersection. She knew what she was looking for. The car came to a stop in front of central market. Just as the driver was about to accelerate, Sunhe pushed opened the back door and darted out into the market place. It was a maze of little stands that went forever. Already at this early hour, hundreds of shopkeepers were setting up business. The place was bedlam. Sunhe knew where she wanted to go. Zigzagging from one tiny alley to another, she reached a ramshackled storage bin. She plunged in and hid herself deep under the baskets, pots and rags that were kept there. She waited. Peddlers came and went from the bin, but no one saw her. Even if they had, they would not have told the two thugs.

When Sunhe made her move for freedom, the driver had already been picking up speed. By the time he stopped and could get out of the car, Sunhe was already well into the market. They ran from place to place knocking over vendors and carts, but they never caught sight of her. After a couple of hours, they were forced to return to the company and confess they had let a country girl out-smart them.

Meanwhile, after Mia had come to herself, she hurried to the factory. She stood just inside the gate so that she could meet the other union leaders. What to do now? The meeting was only a few hours away, and though they agreed that the meeting needed to be held, there was no unity about who should now be the candidate for president. They needed time to get together. Several of the women might have filled the position, but there had to be discussion before the meeting.

Around eleven o'clock one of the office girls started another rumor. She said that Sunhe had escaped. She, the office clerk, had seen two black-jacketed men go in the manager's office just a short while ago and heard the manager's loud bellow, "You did what? She got away? You're finished! Get out of here! Who needs someone who can't even take care of one little village girl?" Then according to the clerk, the two black-jackets stumbled out of the office and went away.

The plant manager called security and warned them that

under no circumstance should they permit Moon Sunhe to enter the plant. Noontime was fast approaching. Tongbong was in turmoil. Work was stopped. Rumor after rumor swept through labor and management. A few minutes before twelve a large crowd of women gathered around the plant's main entrance. Security tried to disperse them but had no success.

Sunhe stayed in the refuse bin until she thought the thugs would get discouraged and leave. She also figured they might place other thugs around to look out for her. She had to be careful. She rummaged through the rags in the bin until she found what she needed: one big holey piece of cloth that went around her waist and a smaller one that she could pin over her head. She picked up a couple broken baskets and slowly wound her way out of the market towards the factory. She looked like any other of the hundreds of women who bought and sold in the busy market place. As she emerged from a back alley not far from the factory gate, she saw the crowd huddled around the gate entrance. She walked closer. She spotted Mia and went up to her.

"What is going on, little sister?" she asked. Mia turned to answer. Immediately she saw through the disguise. "We are about to elect a union president," she giggled. Quickly the word spread. Without warning the girls jammed into the entranceway all at once. Security guards were swept away. Sunhe, still in her disguise as a merchant, was swept in along with everyone else. The crowd moved to the union hall. The department representatives pushed their way to the front. When it became quiet enough to be heard, one of them stood up and proclaimed that the meeting was now open. "The only item of business is the election of a president for the Tongbong Textile labor union."

Very quickly another woman stood up and without making a speech said, "I nominate Moon Sunhe."

"Are there any other nominations?" asked the chair. For a second there was silence. No one else spoke. "There being no other nominees, I now ask the department representatives to caste their votes by secret ballot."

The vote was taken. It was unanimous. "Will Moon Sunhe please come forward to accept the election?"

Sunhe had stayed to the rear of the hall. At the chair's bidding she walked up the central aisle still in her disguise. At first the audience returned to silence as they saw the woman in rags walk towards the front. Then they recognized her, and by the time Sunhe got to the front, everyone was standing, cheering, laughing and crying. It was their greatest moment.

"My friends and fellow workers, today we have made history. We as women have won a great victory. We now can represent ourselves. We call upon the company to recognize the will of the vast majority of its workers and enter into negotiations with our union. We can be proud of each other. We will never again go back!"

AFTERWORD

I stop the story at a point of victory and hope to symbolize the determination of women workers to press forward in their struggle to gain respect. Unfortunately the employers at Tongbong (a fictitious name symbolizing textile mills in general) and elsewhere still do not accept women as equals, nor do they recognize collective bargaining as a legitimate method of resolving issues of wages and working conditions. They continue to protect their ancient right of domination, often inflicting serious wounds to the very processes upon which a democratic society can be built.

Nevertheless, thanks mainly to persons like Sunhe and Okja, women workers now have a new respect and status in society. As Sunhe said, "We will not go back."

UNFINISHED CONFLICT

Background

President Pak Chung Hee was assassinated October 26, 1979. For ten years more, military generals ruled the land and did not lift the oppression from the people. To suppress the workers' continuing demands for collective bargaining and a living wage, government and employers resorted to violence and accusations of communism.

Under mounting pressures from all sectors of Korean society, President Chun Doo Whan (Pak Chung Hee's successor) announced that he would not run again in 1988. Instead he threw his support to a fellow general, Roh Tae Woo. Roh, sensitive to the rising opposition to military rule, declared on June 29, 1987 that he supported presidential election by direct vote of the people. If elected, he would guarantee the basic rights of all citizens. Roh's speech was like a match set to dry timber waiting to be kindled. Decades of pent-up humiliations were set loose. Wave after wave of worker demonstrations took place. Within four months, after Roh's declaration, no less than 3,400 labor disputes erupted throughout the nation. Within a year 2799 new local unions were organized and 586,167 new members were added to union roles.

The author visited Korea in 1989, two years after the big uprising. The old adage that " the more things change, the more they stay the same" is applicable to Korean labor-management relations. Despite labor's revolt and new vigor, management seems to have learned little. It continues a fight to the finish. The "chaebul," or conglomerates, that dominate the Korean economy adamantly refuse to accept labor as a partner in the production process.

The following five anecdotes are true stories and reflect, I believe, actual characteristics of the South Korean labor-management scene as of 1989, and probably down to the present.

*   *   *

An American Company

The first experience was almost my last. A few days after we arrived in Seoul, I was walking by the Kwangwha Mun intersection when I noticed a large gathering of people in front of the American embassy some two or three blocks away. I decided to check it out. As I got closer, I saw that it was a demonstration of women employees from the Pico Company. Pico, an American company, had treated its employees shamelessly. They closed the shop and fled to the United States without paying the workers wages that were due.

I walked closer, listening to the chants, wondering if anyone from the embassy would come out. No one did, but a few of the women discovered me standing there. They raised a cry that here was one of the dirty Americans standing right among them. Others turned around. In a moment the entire rally seemed to focus on me. At first I thought to speak to them, but that was not at all feasible. Hastily I beat a retreat. In no way did I want to fall into the hands of several hundred angry women.

Later that week, through the good offices of Rev. Cho Sung Hyuk, I met with the leaders of the Pico employees and visited the plant where they were still maintaining their sit-it. The workers, of course, were full of questions and wanted to know how an American company could act in such an evil way. I responded that as an American, I was embarrassed by Pico's behavior, but American companies, like Korean companies, would take advantage of their workers unless there were strong laws and a strong union to stand up for the workers. I thanked them for demanding justice. Unfortunately, however, they never received justice. The company resisted all attempts at a settlement.

Workers' Church in an Industrial Estate

By 1989 the Urban Industrial Mission (UIM), a Christian ministry to industrial workers, had been almost stamped out by the military governments. Staff was under constant surveillance; workers were warned to stay away; churches were ordered not to provide financial support. UIM, the Korean CIA alleged, was communist.

Yet, at Koryudong, an industrial estate near Seoul, we discovered UIM in the form of a "Workers' Church." In the Koryudong Estate there were about twenty separate small factories producing a wide array of goods. Each factory had a wall around its property with worker dormitories inside their respective compounds. The employees were mostly young women and men. The Workers' Church was one of few places where employees of one compound met workers of another. When a wage dispute ignited in the Daewoo Apparel Company, management followed the usual practice of appealing to the police. The union leaders were first beaten and then arrested.

Much to the surprise of everyone, however, a thousand workers from other plants in the estate stood in solidarity with the Daewoo strikers. In rally after rally they demanded the release of the union leaders. It was one of the few instances where workers took action across company lines. In addition, many religious and social organizations also made public demands in support of the Daewoo strikers.

Much of the coordination for this newfound solidarity took place in the Workers' Church. The pastor of the church was a friend of mine and invited me to attend worship service one Sunday morning. After worship, I sat in on a meeting of men and women from various companies inside the industrial estate as they planned future actions. Here was a new mind and a new strategy that was to play an important role in the developments of the next several years.

Giant Hyundai

In no place were labor relations as traumatic and tragic as in the city of Ulsan. The Hyundai *chaebul* had transformed a small fishing village into a gigantic industrial estate. Twelve Hyundai factories producing everything from automobiles, to engines, to ocean-going ships hired about 80,000 people. Prior to 1987 neither Hyundai nor any of the other large conglomerates would tolerate worker organizations. In the heat of the 1987 uprisings, however, within a few days Hyundai employees organized and demanded the right of collective bargaining. The *chaebul* had been founded by a man name Chong Jo Yong. He declared publicly that there would never be a labor union in any of Hyundai's operations. His anti-union attitude and methods were quite representative of most chaebul.

After making his position clear to all his workers, Chung then proceeded to form a *"kusadae,"* a group of specially hired toughs with skills in martial arts. Whenever workers would try to hold rallies, or sit-ins, the *kusadae* would break it up usually inflicting considerable damage on the workers. A second anti-union strategy was to hire a "consultant." The man hired at Hyundai was an American citizen of Korean descent, named James Lee. His methods were similar to those of the *kusadae*.

He heard that union leaders from all of Hyundai's companies in Ulsan were planning a secrete strategy meeting in a small resort village outside of town. He led a band of thugs and anti-union employees in a surprise commando attack against the workers. Heavy damage was inflicted. The Chair of the meeting had his leg broken and several others were hospitalized.

Instead of dissuading the workers, the "James Lee incident" strengthened their determination. Anger against Hyundai raged across the entire Ulsan complex. For three months work at Hyundai came to a standstill. Still the company would not compromise. Finally on March 30, 1989, a force of 10,000 police, in coordination with the company, attacked by land sea and air. Workers disappeared from company grounds, retreating to their own homes. Gradually they returned to their jobs, but under company dictated terms. The union has not been completely broken. It persists even down to the present, but the company shows little intention of ever accepting it as a legitimate partner.

Death at Daewoo Shipyards

Okpo, on the island of Kojedo, was a famous little town. Four hundred years ago Korea's first iron clad ship had been made in its harbor. Admiral Lee Soon Shin aboard the "turtle boat" had attacked and destroyed the Japanese armada that threatened to invade Korea. In the 1970's two large *chaebul,* Daewoo and Samsung, constructed world-class shipyards at Okpo. In 1987 the Daewoo shipyards, like most every other work place in Korea, felt the impact of worker uprisings. A newly formed union demanded a wage increase and the right to be free from company interference. Predictably, the management pleaded hard times and demanded that the status quo be maintained. The result was turmoil that dragged on for a couple years: work stoppages, sit-ins, and marches through the city streets.

In the midst of the turmoil, two men committed self-immolation, a supreme act of sacrifice. In front of his fellow workers Pak Shin Suk poured gasoline on himself and lit a match. As his human torch burned, Pak is reported to have yelled, "Stop oppressing the workers! Increase wages! Be democratic!" Twelve hours later Lee Song Mo climbed to the top of a four-story building and before the eyes of hundreds of his comrades below he set fire to himself and jumped. He too is reported to have screamed, "Stop oppressing the workers!"

The all-night wake was held outside in front of the hospital where the bodies lay. Throughout a long and heavy night, thousands sang and shouted slogans and heard speeches.

Knowing that I was not far away in Ulsan, an old friend, who was a union organizer at Daewoo, invited me to attend the funeral. My friend asked me, as a guest, to take a seat up near the front of the gathered workers. Others cautioned that with the current mood of the workers it might not be wise to attract attention to a foreigner. I stayed in the back.

It had started to rain the night before and it continued in a hard, steady downpour throughout the day. The funeral procession, accompanied by drums, gongs and the moaning of funeral dirges, wound in and out of each section of the vast shipyards. It came to stop in front of the hospital where several thousand people were gathered. Worker after worker came forward to eulogize Pak and Lee's sacrifice, demanding that the company act in a humane way and bargain with the union. The climax came when the elderly father of Lee Song Mo came to the podium. He urged the workers to persist in their demands and make their solidarity even stronger. "We are workers who have built up this company and our nation," he proclaimed. "They call us communists and treat us like serfs. My son sacrificed himself in protest against this injustice. He sacrificed himself to give others the courage to fight for freedom."

Afterwards, the bodies of the two men were transported to Kwangju. Lee Song Mo and Pak Shin Suk were laid to rest beside the martyrs of the Kwangju massacre. The two deaths did not bring about peace or understanding. When asked what the immolations had taught Daewoo about relations with labor, a company vice—president responded that Pak and Lee had both been communists. They had been indoctrinated at secrete brainwashing sessions, and ordered to commit suicide by the communist party. The old often-used accusation of communism is used as a crutch to avoid reality.

Students, Workers and Kwangju

Korean society was in much turmoil in 1980 when the Kwangju massacre occurred. One of its root causes went back to another tragic event that happened miles away from Kwangju. The president of the YH Trading Company absconded with the company assets in May of 1979 leaving some 500 young women employees with unpaid wages. In an attempt to secure their wages the women occupied company property. Police moved in, randomly beating protesters, killing one and leaving many in critical condition. Two days later, three women employees were arrested and charge with unlawful assembly, a crime that carried a sentence of seven years in prison.

That incident, among others, incited citizens around the country. In the southern cities of Pusan and Masan, college students staged massive demonstrations that turned into anti-government protests. Kim Jae Kyu, the head of the Korean CIA, was sent to assess the situation. His report back to President Pak Chung Hee, however, was not what the president wanted to hear. The two men argued violently. Kim shot the president dead.

For a brief moment it seemed as though the world had

changed. Without Pak Chung Hee democracy might have a chance. The moment, however, passed quickly. General Chun Doo Whan saw to it that military rule would continue. Two months after Pak's assassination, he declared martial law and established himself as "president." His seizure of power was immediately answered by giant protests around the country. The uprising in Kwangju, a city in the southwest, turned out to be the bloodiest and the most significant for future events. The day after General Chun declared martial law, students staged an opposition march demanding that Chun step down. Chun's response to their demand was to send soldiers and paratrooper into the city. Students were beaten and bayoneted. Dozens were left dead. Citizens were appalled. In large numbers they joined in the protests. Police stations were invaded and stockpiles of army supplies and guns were commandeered. On the morning of May 27, 1980 the 20th Division of the ROK Army was ordered to take back the city. This they did. Hundreds were killed. Chun won the battle, but also won the hate and disdain of the people.

When my wife, Dorothy, and I visited Kwangju in 1989, Ms. Na Ah Ra, known as the "Mother of Kwangju," escorted us to where students and citizen groups were still keeping vigil in tents set up along side the city's streets. For almost ten years people had slept there beside the busy streets so that the sacrifice of the students and the cruelty of the government would not be forgotten. In the YWCA building we saw a dramatic musical reenactment of the massacre.

People from all over the country come to pay tribute to the martyrs of Kwangju and, like us, make a pilgrimage to the cemetery where many of the slain students were buried. Kwangju was a shadowing spirit that hung over the entire land. By burying Lee Song Mo and Pak Shin Suk in Kwangju, the union at Daewoo Shipyards was intentionally joining the spirit of the two men with that of other martyrs for democracy.

PRAYER FOR THE INNOCENT

Background

In April of 1974, the Pak regime announced that it had uncovered a communist conspiracy to overthrow the government. A thousand or more democratic dissidents were rounded up and thrown into prison. Eight men were charged with being the ringleaders of the conspiracy. Though the evidence against them was minimal, the eight men were tortured and made to confess to deeds they had not committed. Then a military court sentenced them to death. On April 9, 1975, without ever having been permitted a fair trial, the eight men were secretly executed by hanging.

This story is an account of the author's connection with these condemned men and their families, and the consequences that came from that connection.

*   *   *

It was ten o'clock at night when the phone rang. A woman's voice said in Korean, "Reverend Ogle, you don't know me. I heard about you from a mutual friend. I must see you at once. May I come to your house?"

"Who are you? What do you want?" I replied to her insistence.

"I can not talk over the phone. It is not safe."

Given the political situation in South Korea at the time, I knew she was right. The Korean CIA probably bugged many

phones, including our own. "It is already late. Could you come
tomorrow morning?"

"That will do. I will be at your place by 9:00 o'clock," she
answered and hung up.

The next morning at the stroke of nine, the doorbell rang.
Instead of one woman, however, there were eight. I asked them
in. After we got all seated, the women began to introduce themselves. As they spoke their names, I had glimmers of recall. I
had heard their names before. Then it came to me. These women
were the wives of the eight men accused by the Korean CIA as
being leaders of a communist conspiracy to overthrow the government. After the introductions, Mrs. Woo, who had phoned
the night before, explained that each week they had to take
food and other supplies to their husbands at West Gate prison.
While they were waiting to get in, they had met the families of
some of the Christian prisoners who suggested they come to
talk with me.

Several women began to talk at once. "Reverend Ogle, we
need your help. We are desperate. Please help us! Our husbands are in prison. They have been tortured and forced to
confess to something they know nothing about."

I interrupted. "For me to understand we will need to talk
slowly. I have heard of the alleged conspiracy, but only know
what I have read in the newspaper. Will you each take turns
and tell me your personal stories. That way I think I will understand better."

Mrs. Woo began. "I was only eighteen when I first met
Woo Hong Sun. I worked as a clerk in a bank where he did
business. Love seemed to have come at first sight. We married
young and quickly had three children, two girls and a boy. He
worked as a bookkeeper with a small construction company
here in Seoul. Life has always been hard for us, but we always
made ends meet, and our love seemed to get stronger. Even
after ten years of marriage, we would walk up South Mountain
holding hands like young lovers.

"It happened on April 16, this year. Without warning, police broke into our house and turned it upside down searching for what they called "evidence." They terrorized the children and me. My husband was dragged out of the house and charged with taking part in an anti-government conspiracy about which he knew nothing. He was tortured and forced to confess. A military court summarily sentenced him to death. He was given no chance to defend himself. Lawyers were not permitted to talk to him. All appeals were rejected."

After Mrs. Woo, the other seven all told similar stories. It was afternoon before we finished. I believed the tales these humble ladies told me, but I had not a clue as to what might be done. As a foreigner, I was not permitted to interfere in Korean politics. I had no influence with people of power, but the women would not be put off with such excuses.

"You've got to help us. We have no one to turn to. You as a Christian missionary can call for a retrial by a civilian court. That's all we want."

Finally, just to get them to leave and to give me time to think, I said, " I can promise nothing since I have no influence in political affairs, but I will look into the matter." Those last six hesitant words changed my life forever.

After the women left, I paid a visit to a couple Korean friends who were knowledgeable about political affairs. Both of them told me the same thing. The charges against these eight men were fabrications. The military government of Pak Chung Hee wanted to inject a new wave of anti-communist fear into the people of South Korea so that it could tighten its control over the nation. The government made up the conspiracy out of whole cloth. Over a thousand religious, university and union dissidents had also been charged with being part of the alleged conspiracy. There was no evidence to sustain any of the government's charges. The eight men were innocent lambs going to the slaughter.

I decided on a plan of action. It wasn't much, but it was all

I could think of. Many, if not most, of the thousand dissidents who had been arrested under the fabricated conspiracy charge were Christians. Each Thursday morning their families and friends gathered to hold a prayer meeting, pleading to God for their safety and release from prison. On this particular Thursday, October 9, 1974, it was my turn to give the meditation and lead the prayers. I decided to include in the prayers and meditation, not only the Christian prisoners, but also the eight condemned men, none of whom were Christian.

Police agents were everywhere. I could count a half dozen from where I stood. Sitting in front of me were about one hundred people, most of whom had a loved one in prison. I looked out at the congregation that included the black-jacketed policemen and began to speak.

"Christ is often mediated to us through the most humble and weakest of our brothers and sisters. Among those now in prison there are eight men who have received the harshest of punishments. They have been sentenced to die, even though there is little evidence against them. They are not Christians, but as the poorest among us they become the brothers of Christ. Therefore let us pray for their lives and souls. Probably they have committed no crime worthy of death."

As I spoke, the "black-jackets" assiduously wrote down every word, and as I later found out, their notes were quite accurate.

The next afternoon at five o'clock, two agents of the Korean Central Intelligence Agency came to my house to arrest me. I would be gone for only a couple hours they said. Since my wife was not home at the time, I left word that I had gone to "Namsan" (euphemism for KCIA) and would be gone for "a couple of hours" (euphemism for indefinitely).

The ride to Namsan was an experience in itself. The driver darted in and out of Seoul's rush-hour traffic like he was on a mission of death. As soon as we arrived at the KCIA headquarters, I was taken to room 306. The two interrogators waiting for me dispensed with normal Korean manners of introducing one-self and saying something nice. Interrogation began immediately. I was told that I would have to write down every question and answer in Korean. So for the next seventeen hours I practiced my Korean handwriting, as I had never done before.

"Why do you have prayer meetings every Thursday morning?"

The answer of course they already knew, but I explained how we met to pray for the health and safety of our friends and family members who were imprisoned unjustly.

"What right have you to pray for the release of criminals? The government has judged them guilty of breaking the law. What right do you have to try and get them out of prison through prayer or any other means?"

Mr. Huh, the chief interrogator, was indignant. He was the one who was always hostile. Mr. Yun, the other interrogator, played the role of my friend. Once a question was asked, I would give a reply. Then Mr. Huh would harangue me for being insincere. I would give a different version. Huh would not like it. He would alter the question slightly. I would respond again. Somewhere along the line Yun would act as mediator so that some acceptable answer would be recorded. I was told that the answer that I would finally write down was to be of my own free will, but in fact I could write only after Mr. Huh and his miserable disposition had attacked me.

You gave a sermon yesterday at the prayer meeting. What did you say?

"I spoke from the Bible where it urges Christians to serve those who are the poorest and weakest in society, and I said we should prayer for eight men who have been sentenced to death."

"You said the men of Peoples' Revolutionary Party were innocent. You spoke on behalf of communists, didn't you?"

"I believe I said that the KCIA had presented very little evidence against the eight, and that they probably had committed no crime worthy of death."

Mister Huh was outraged. "Such talk is in violation of the anti-communist law. Did you know these men were communists before you gave your sermon?"

I responded that I knew that the KCIA had declared that these men were communists, but I did not know whether they were or not. This reply only infuriated Huh even more.

"How do you dare question the judgment of the government? The government decides these things, not you. You, a foreigner, come into our country and insult our people and culture!"

"I insult no one. I have nothing but respect for Korea, its people and culture. There are a thousand of your countrymen in prison now because they think there should be democracy in the land."

Over and over again Huh and I repeated our opinions about the right of people to have opinions different from the government. After forty minutes or so he changed the subject. "Yesterday, after you spoke, someone prayed. Who was he and what did he say?

"As I am sure you know, he was Rev. Pak. I do not know his first name. His prayers are his responsibility. Not mine. Ask him. Anything I say could be used against him."

Mr. Yun assured me that at the KCIA they did not do things that way. Everything I said to him or Huh would be kept in strictest confidence. When I remained stubborn and refused to answer, Huh then read of from his notes the exact words of Rev. Pak's prayer. "That's what he said, isn't it?"

"You will have to ask him," I replied. I did not know it at the time, but that is exactly what they were doing. Rev. Pak had been arrested a couple hours after I had been. Later when we compared notes, we found that we had been kept in the same building and they had questioned him closely about what I had said, assuring him that everything said would be held confidential.

Again they changed the subject. This time they demanded

that I write down the names and addresses of all the people I knew in Korea and the nature of our relationship. From hearing the stories of friends who had been through the KCIA interrogation, I had expected this question. If I were to give a name, the KCIA would then visit that friend and tell them that I had accused them of some anti-government action. The friend would then be blackmailed into providing names of more people, and, of course, the trust between all of us would be subverted. I wrote down the names of churches and institutions where I had worked in South Korea, but refused to give names. Huh's harangue was loud and ferocious. Yun calmed him down. We were about to return to the topic of communism, when a messenger came in the room and said something to Huh. Our session was discontinued and I was taken to another room. It was, I believe, the main office of the KCIA's sixth section.

One small man sat behind a large desk. He wore a dark blue or black suit. I was ordered to sit down. "Mr. Ogle, I am Mr. Lee. You have been in Korea along time, but obviously you do not know much about Korea, and you know nothing about communism. You have violated our anti-communist law, but because you are a foreigner, we are going to be generous. I am going to prove to you that these eight men you pray for are indeed communists."

Lee then repeated to me the exact same thing that had come out in the newspaper. His only piece of evidence was a copy of a speech by Kim Il Song, premier of North Korea. Ha Chae Won, one of the eight, allegedly listened to the speech, copied it down and showed it to a few other people.

Then an amazing transformation took place. Lee left off showing me "evidence" and launched into a strange tirade. "These men," he shouted, "are our enemies. We have got to kill them. This is war. In war even a Christian will pull the trigger to kill an enemy. If we do not kill these men, they will kill us. We will kill them. If we do not kill them, I will visit the national

cemetery and confess before all those buried there that we have
sold out our country to the communists. I will go to the United
States and tell the brave men who died in the Korean War that
they have died in vain. They must die!"

What was going on? Lee's emotional soliloquy certainly
could not have sprung from the "evidence" that he showed me.
His eyes were lighted up like a warrior about to go to battle. He
was on an emotional high that was beyond me. Later on, a
friend told me that this Mr. Lee had carried on a personal ven-
detta against some of the condemned men for more than a decade. Now he was in a position to secure revenge. That may
have accounted for his weird behavior.

The interview with Mr. Lee lasted for about an hour. I was
then returned to the cubicle with Huh and Yun. Interrogation
began again. This time it was about Urban Industrial Mission,
the mission work I had been involved in since 1960. They
wanted all the details: When did it was start? Who was in it?
What were its goals? Why did we have clergy working in factories? Why were we cooperating with labor unions? I wrote down
answers to these and other questions, but each was a struggle.
Huh would never accept my first answer. Back and forth we
would go until finally we would arrive at a response acceptable
to both of us.

It was about 1:30 in the morning. Huh was getting tired.
He instructed Yun to make me write down the names of the
wives of the eight men for whom I had prayed. How often had
we met and what did we talk about? Huh then stretched out on
an army cot and went to sleep. Yun and I continued for a couple
more hours.

Finally, sleep began to overtake us. Yun said we would rest
for a few hours and then finish up the interrogation. "In the
morning" he said, "you will need to write an apology, confessing your wrong doings and promising not to repeat them." Yun
and Huh had prepared an apology that I was to sign. First, I
was to say that I did not know the eight men were communists

when I prayed for them. Second, I had to promise that in the future I would obey all government policies, and lastly, I was to promise that I would never again pray for or speak on behalf of the eight condemned men.

It was 3:30 am when I was given this ultimatum. Yun said I could sleep on it for a couple hours and then we would discuss it. I crawled into a cot next to the snoring Mr. Huh, pulled a khaki blanket up over me and did not sleep.

We were up and into the interrogation again by 7:00 AM. I told Huh that there was no way that I would agree to the first item in the apology. "The way you have worded it implies that I now do know them to be communists. I do not know any such a thing."

Much to my surprise neither Huh nor Yun pushed me on it. We went to the next point—obeying government policies.

"You want me to say I will obey all policies of the government or all laws?" I asked.

"Policies! You are a foreigner here. You must be obedient to all the policies of the government."

"But there are too many policies, and some I do not agree with. How can you ask me to obey all policies? Not even you do that."

Huh again jumped on to his high horse. "Who do you think you are coming into our country and insulting our ways of doing? You are a foreigner! Don't think that the American Embassy can help you. You can't break our laws and get away with it."

"I have lived in Korea for more than fifteen years and have never been arrested or charged with breaking any laws. I respect your people and willingly live under the laws of your land."

About that time a little man in an army uniform came in and ordered Huh to hurry things up.

This unexpected interruption helped me avoid signing the second part of the apology. Only the third item was left—I was not to preach nor pray for any of the eight. Huh said he would take out the prohibition against prayer, but I must promise not to speak on their behalf. After much debate as to what "speak on their behalf" meant, I finally signed a statement saying I would not talk about them in my sermons. Other forms of "talking" were not restricted.

At approximately 11:00 AM the little army man returned and ordered me to go with him. He took me to the office of the Deputy Chief of Security of the Korean Central Intelligence Agency. He was introduced to me as Mr. Lee. He had lived in the United States for eight years, he said, and he knew Americans very well. He was sorry to see me in this situation, but my offense, he said, was very serious. "If you ever help the communists again, I will either put you in prison or deport you." Then he ordered a big black car to take me home.

The conclusion to this confrontation with the KCIA was not happy. About two months later on December 14, 1974 I was indeed deported. The authorities, however, did not charge me with helping the communists or working in UIM. To deceive the public they concocted a different charge.

In the spring of 1971 I had returned to the United States on furlough. While there I finished up my Ph.D. degree in international labor relations at the University of Wisconsin. Through the good offices of a friend, I was invited to be a visiting professor of industrial relations at the School of Commerce, Seoul National University. I returned to Korea in the spring of 1973 to begin work at the university. I was made welcome by the faculty, assigned office space and told that I would have two classes during my first semester.

One morning, several weeks after I had been detained by the KCIA, I went as usual to the university to prepare my lectures for the day. My office was in an old two-story concrete building. There was no heat. It was cold as an icebox. I decided to try the library. Maybe it would be warmer.

As I stepped outside, noise like a great flooding river hit

my ears. It was a flood all right, a flood of university students chanting and marching towards the university's administration building. The campus vibrated with the din of shouted slogans: "Down with Pak Chung Hee!" "No Dictatorship!" "Secrete agents must leave campus!" "Freedom." "Democracy."

A line of plain-clothes-police and black-jacketed thugs blocked the students' way. Several faculty members scurried back and forth between students and police seeking to avoid violence. Their efforts were futile. The students came on.

No signal was seen nor heard, but of a sudden the police attacked. Some had clubs, but most used their skill at taekwondo. In a brief moment the students were scattered, many with broken noses and bloodied faces. Some lay unconscious on the ground. These were thrown unceremoniously into a police van.

"There's a faculty meeting in the dean's office," a colleague whispered in my ear. I stood for another minute getting over the shock of such a quick, physical explosion. As I headed towards the dean's office, a man, whose very bearing told me he was an agent of the Korean CIA, stepped in front of me.

"Are you Dr. Ogle?"

"I am."

"Could we have a talk?" He did not introduce himself.

"If you wish, we can go to my office. It is cold, but it will be quiet.

Once we entered the office and sat down, he on a long bench and I on the one available chair, he started right off. "You are the person who was detained for speaking in support of the eight communists?"

"I was arrested and interrogated at the KCIA headquarters for praying for eight men who were tortured into making false confessions."

"Did you understand that you were breaking the law and giving comfort to our enemy, the communists?"

"I have lived in Korea for fifteen years and have never been accused of breaking the law. I hold Korea and its traditions in highest respect, but as a Christian minister I always have the right to pray for people who are in prison."

He obviously did not want to pursue that matter. Abruptly, he changed the subject. "Dr. Ogle, we are aware of your background with the subversive organization called Urban Industrial Mission, but how did you get an appointment to Seoul National University? You know you do not have the right visa for such work. We are not insisting that you be removed from the university right now, but—

Before he could finish his sentence, the office door burst open, and a very excited student rushed in. Dried blood was smeared on forehead and a wound on his left cheek still bled. He stared at the man on the bench with a look of recognition, said not a word, but quickly retreated back out the door.

"Do you know him?"

"Of course. He is one of my students."

The agent stood up, ending our conversation. "Thank you for your time. We may meet again." He walked out the door.

Several days later at seven in the morning a black jeep pulled up in front of our house. Men wearing black jackets took me out of the house and escorted me to the Office of Immigration.

"Mr. Ogle, there has been an error in regards to your visa and residence permit. You were given a visa as a missionary. That does not qualify you as a university professor. You have violated our law. Therefore we must ask you to leave Korea."

"How can that be? Seoul National University's Department of Commerce hired me. They knew all about me before I came. Besides there are hundreds of missionaries teaching in schools all over Korea, all the way from kindergarten to graduate schools. Why do you select me for this punishment?"

"We are not talking about other people. Only about you! You are in violation!"

So it came about that I was deported from Korea after having lived there for fifteen years. The government never officially charged me with any wrongdoing. Instead they resorted to chicanery, alleging that my visa had been falsely secured. This allegation was, of course, a sham. Behind the sham was the military mind-set that could not tolerate prayer for innocent people or justice for its industrial workers.

Unfortunately the story does not end here. On the night of April 8, 1975, the wives of the eight men received phone calls from the West Gate Prison. They were told that if they would come to the prison the next morning at nine o'clock, they could see their husbands. When they arrived at the prison each one was ushered into the prison and presented with the bodily remains of her husband. The eight men had been hanged three hours earlier.

MY BODY

This is the story of one man, accused of being a leader of the Peoples' Revolutionary Party, as he goes through the horrors of interrogation, torture and execution. It is a fictitious representation of what the condemned man might have reported, if he had been able to speak to us from the next world.

Though the events and names are fictitious, the story is accurately based upon the witness of the wives of eight men executed by the Pak Chung Hee government on April 9, 1975, and on the stories of others who underwent torture at the hands of the Korean CIA.

* * *

That's me in that box over there, or rather it's my body—what is left of my body. I was hanged yesterday along with seven other guys. After they killed us like that, they played a little trick on our wives. They sent word telling them that they could visit their husbands if they would come to West Gate Prison by nine in the morning. The women came, but by then, we were already long dead. The name of each man's wife was called out. One at a time they were ushered through the prison gate. Inside, each was handed her husband's remains in a crude, wood casket.

In my case, however, they made a mistake. It had not been intended that my body be given up. It had been tortured and battered so badly that it was almost beyond identification. The authorities wanted to keep that little bit of information to themselves. Some one goofed. My body was handed over like the rest of them, but in a few minutes the prison authorities caught their mistake and demanded that it be given back. By then the casket was in a van ready to go the Catholic Church for mass and then burial. The police stopped the van from moving. My wife and a couple foreign priests put up a good fight, but in the end the police prevailed. I am now headed for the crematorium. I wonder what it will be like to see my body go up in smoke.

My body served me well for over forty-seven years. It stayed healthy and was always quite sturdy. I earned my living as a beekeeper. Learned the trade from my father. Beekeeping may seem to be an easy type of job, but it is really quite demanding and requires a good bit of physical strength. My wife and I were ordinary people. We had three children. She sold fruit in the market and earned a little money so that we could make ends meet. The only real conflict in our home was my wife's complaint about my habit of going out Saturday nights to drink with my friends. Often I would come home drunk and make an ass of myself. Have to admit that I did hit her once or twice. I'm sorry for that now, but otherwise we did okay.

One spring morning in 1974, our ordinary life came to an extraordinary end. Before daybreak loud pounding awakened us on our gate. I opened it. Without a word, two policemen pushed me aside and entered. Bit by bit they took our little three-roomed house apart. Everything was turned upside down. My books and my radio were put in bags and taken away. They told me to get dressed. I needed to go with them for a short while. Then they warned my family to say nothing to anybody or else it would go hard on me.

"Why? What is going on? How did they get me mixed up in this—whatever it was?" When I attempted to ask the policeman who sat beside me in the black police car, he smacked me in the face and said, "Shut up you scum." I was blindfolded so I could not keep track of where I was being taken, but after a while we stopped in front of some metal gate. I could hear the sounds of it opening and closing and the driver talking with the gatekeeper. Inside, we rode for a few minutes. When the car stopped, I was dragged out and pushed in through a doorway. Then my blindfold was taken off. Two men were in the stark-empty room with me.

"What is your name?"

"Where do you live?" "What work do you do?"

"Who are your friends and neighbors?"

"What do you listen to on the radio?"

"Why does a beekeeper read so many books?"

The questions came fast. I tried to answer as best I could, but I was still bewildered and disoriented by the whole affair. Even nightmares weren't like this.

"Who do you drink with on Saturday nights?"

I named a few names, but when I mentioned Mo Hee Bong, the two inquisitors gave each other a satisfied grin. This all had something to do with Mo Hee Bong!! But I hardly knew the man. He was a friend of a friend who sometimes came to our Saturday night group. When I insisted to the two men that I knew nothing about the man, they hit me and knocked me to the floor.

"Stand up and let's try that again."

One guy gave me a hand to help pick me up, but as he did so he threaded a ballpoint pen through my fingers and began to squeeze. The pain grew so intense I begged him to stop.

He did, and in a calm tone of voice he said, "Maybe you just need to think things over a bit."

With that he delivered such a blow to my left ear that I heard the roar of an explosion and then complete silence. I never heard from that ear again. I collapsed to the floor.

"You lay there a while and think. We'll be back in a little while to talk some more."

I lay there trying to puzzle out what Mo Hee Bong had done and why I should be associated with him in the minds of the police. Nothing came. I did not know Mo well enough to even know where he lived or what work he did. My ear throbbed like a machine gun.

I lay there alone for thirty minutes or so. The same two men came in, but a third person was now with them.

"Now let us start from the beginning. How long have you known Mo Hee Bong and Choe Young Sam?"

"I have known Mo for a few months, but only at the wine house, and then only casually. Choe Young Sam? I have never heard of him."

"And when did you join the Peoples' Revolutionary Party?"

"The what? I never heard of such a thing. I do not get involved in any politics."

The third man suddenly kicked my legs out from under me, and I went tumbling backward. It hurt something awful. As I tried to get up, he kicked me in the balls and then sent my head spinning backward with a rapid kick of his knee. I lay there feeling more dead than alive. He then came over to where I lay and he pissed on me. Right on my face! I was so outraged that I jumped to my feet, and swung a roundhouse right to his nose. I heard the bone break. He went down. I knew I could take him, but the other two guys were not about to allow a fair fight. They held me while the third guy got up from the floor and proceeded to beat the shit out of me. Somewhere along the line I lost consciousness. When I woke up in a dark, wet cell, my body begged for mercy. From the pain and shame and fear I cried loud deep moans. As hard as I tried, I could not make out what it was that I was supposed to be guilty of. All I knew was that it had something to do with Mo Hee Bong and some kind of a political party. If I had even a clue as to what they wanted from me, maybe I could accept it just to get out of here.

The door opened. I was dragged out of my cell and deposited in the same room where I had been before. This time, however, two chairs and a desk had been added. A new man was sitting behind the desk.

"Mr. Lee, Please have a seat. I wish to apologize for the behavior of that rowdy last night. It was a misunderstanding. You see we have a serious spy case on our hands, and we know that your friend Mo Hee Bong is one of the ringleaders. So all we want is the truth, and then we can let you go home."

"What beautiful words!" I thought. "Finally some sanity!"

" I will certainly tell you everything I know, and help in any way possible," I said.

"Good, now tell me something about Mo Hee Bong."

So I began to describe him the best I could from what little I knew of him, and I guess I added few things that I figured the interrogator wanted to hear. After I spoke for a couple minutes, the man said, "Very good! Just the stuff we needed to know. Now would you please write that all down for me."

I wrote it all down and perhaps provided a few more items just to make a good impression.

All right very good. Now please write what you know about the Peoples' Revolutionary Party."

"But I do not know anything about it. I never heard of it until yesterday!"

"Mr. Lee, you promised to help me find the truth. That attitude is not good for either of us. You think it over and we will have another talk soon."

I was led back to the cell. It was cold and dark and my wounds still trumpeted their despair. What could I do? Some how I had to say something about this Peoples' Revolutionary Party that they would like. This imperative was accentuated by the opening of the cell door. Number three man of yesterday came in.

"Understand you complained to my boss, you miserable traitor. You think you're tough? Come on! We'll take care of that right now."

He beat me until unconsciousness again protected me from feeling more pain.

How long I lay there, I have no idea. When I came to, I was

once again in the room with the two chairs. The man behind the desk was saying in very soft, kindly words, "You attacked the guard when he came into ask you a question? I am sorry he had to beat you like this, but surely you understand we cannot tolerate such action from you. Now let's get down to facts so that we can get you out of here. Tell me about the Peoples' Revolutionary Party, known as the PRP."

My brain worked furiously. What could I say about something I knew nothing about? "It is a group of people led by Mo Hee Bong and . . . and what was that other man's name? Oh yes, Choe Young Sam. They met secretly and tried to get others to join the PRP."

"Go on. How many were there? How did they make contact with North Korea? Did they get money from Japan?"

" I don't know. Maybe there was a hundred or so. I don't know about the rest."

"Okay Mr. Lee, I see you need more time to think, but I must warn you that I am your only hope and I do not have much more time left. If you can not tell me the entire truth within a few days, I will be withdrawn from your case and you will be turned over to the three men you met the first day."

I was taken back to my cell. This time I became aware of the moaning and crying sounds that came from adjoining cells. My own body shivered at the sounds. I had to think. I had to satisfy that man behind the desk—but how? What could I say? What do I know about this PRP business? In response, I said to myself, "You know that it has connection with North Korea and with North Koreans in Japan. And you know that Mo Hee Bong and others were the leaders probably in some kind of political demonstration. That should satisfy him."

Time went by, and some more time and more time. What if the man behind the desk were already replaced? What if I had to face those three guys again? O lord! Help! Don't let it be too late!

The cell was opened. I had not been beaten for several

days and so I walked out, passed the other cells, each with two haggard eyes looking silently toward me. I opened the door into the room, my heart jumped with hope. There was the man behind the desk.

"Good morning Mr. Lee. You are looking much better. Would you like a cup of coffee?"

"Please." I took the coffee and sipped. It was so good! After a couple more sips, I remembered to thank him.

" Since we do not have much time, let's get down to business. Are you ready to write down everything you know about the PRP? Take as much time as you wish. You can write right here at the desk. I need to step out for a little."

I wrote. I thought I was being clever. I just affirmed everything they had insinuated in their questions. And as before, at places I let my imagination fill in some of the holes.

The man came back in. Sat down behind the desk and read what I wrote. "Very good, Mr. Lee. This is just what we needed. Now would you please sign it right there at the bottom, and put your fingerprint right below. I signed. He got up and left. It was the last time I saw him.

For a few days all was quiet. I was left in my cell and once or twice even taken out for a brief walk. Without explanation one morning I was given some new clothes, traditional Korean white, taken out of the cell and loaded on to a bus crowded with many others. We were taken to the courthouse. "Now," I thought, "this ordeal is over. We are having a trial and the man behind the desk will give witness to my innocence. I will go home."

The names of several persons were called out and the charges against them were read. Then I heard my name. I stood. I heard from somewhere a voice: "Lee Sang Sin, charged with conspiracy to overthrow the government of the Republic of Korea." He then read all the things I had written claiming that they were my confession. "The government demands that Mr. Lee be given the sentence of death."

"No, No!!!" I shouted. "I know nothing about this. I was tricked. I was tortured into writing that. NO! I didn't—" I never finished that sentence. The guards dragged me away.

I am not sure how long I lived after that. Time had no meaning. Number three man would not let me alone. He beat me in every way conceivable. My once strong, sturdy body was reduced to a mash. At the end they had to carry me out to hang me. My legs had long since been "neutralized" as they say.

I still am not sure why I was hanged. How did they ever connect me with their damnable conspiracy? Was it only because I had the misfortune of having had a couple drinks with someone named Mo Hee Bong?

I curse them all. I was happy in my ordinary life as a beekeeper. May the man behind the desk sit at that desk forever, and each time he stands up to go let the door slam shut in his face. May the three have swarms of honeybees attack their gonads. They inflicted pain just for sport. At four o'clock in the afternoon, they would enjoy an hour or so of torturing me, along with a few others. They loved to hear the loud screeches I made when they prodded my testicles with their electric rods. At five o'clock, they checked out, went home, ate supper, played with their kids and slept with their wives. While I writhed in pain in their wet, loathsome prison, they carried on the ordinary life that I once loved so much.

TEAROOM

For a decade after being deported by the Korean government, I was not permitted to return. In 1984, however, the government relented and allowed me to visit for seven days to take part in the centennial celebration of the founding of the Korean Methodist Church. While there I managed to have a brief meeting with Mrs. Woo, whose husband was one of eight men executed by the government April 9, 1975. Below is an account of our meeting.

*　　*　　*

I arrived at the tearoom before Mrs. Woo. I found a booth towards the front so that I could keep my eye on the door. She was late. For thirty minutes I waited and fretted. Had she not received the message? Was I in the wrong tearoom? Was she still being followed?

I looked down at the gold ring on the little finger of my right hand and thought back to the afternoon of December 10, 1974, the day I was deported. When I was being taken out of my house to go to Kimpo airport, a squad of police blocked the entrance to our yard. Beyond the police was a ring of friends who had come to give support. As I walked toward the black jeep, someone pressed a small, gold ring into my hand and said, "This is from Mrs. Woo." I took it and put it on my little finger. Mrs. Woo thought I would be put off the plane in Japan where I would have neither friends nor money. So she had given me her gold ring to exchange for Japanese yen. In fact, I was

155

not allowed off the plane in Japan. The Korean CIA forced me to stay on the plane until we reached Los Angeles.

Soon after I arrived in the United States I had written to Mrs. Woo, saying that I would wear the ring until her husband was released. That day never came. Four months later, April 9, 1975, Woo Hong Sun and the other seven men were hanged until dead. I still wear the ring.

Suddenly the door opened. Mrs. Woo rushed in. She looked harried and tired. Quickly I stood up and walked towards her. Neither of us spoke. We embraced and wept freely as memories of the past washed through our minds. I was aware that the eyes of the entire tearoom were focused on us. They were youngsters and could have no way of knowing the story which Mrs. Woo and I shared. Already ten years had passed since the cruel execution of her husband; ten years in which a government controlled by the military suppressed all references to the terrible events of 1974-1975; ten years, long enough for most to forget and long enough for a new generation, without memory of such events, to come of age.

I took her arm and led her to the booth. I ordered tea and we started on the awkward road to becoming reacquainted. We asked about each other's children. She wanted to know about Dorothy, my wife. I asked how she and her children had been able to live over the last ten years. I learned that Father Basil Price, a Jesuit priest from Sokang University, had helped her get work. I carried the conversation further by inquiring about the wives and families of the other seven men. I heard stories about their suffering. Many of the kids had been taunted and teased because their fathers were "communists." The older children had difficulty getting jobs or finding a spouse because of the stigma of being related to the executed men. There was no one to step in and defend them. Neither Mrs. Woo nor I wanted to talk about death, and neither was eager to ask, "What could we have done differently?" The ghost was there, but speaking about it could not have exorcised it. Then it was time for Mrs.

Woo to go off to her second job. She needed two jobs now that her children were in college. We embraced and parted, happy but sad in our awkward reunion. I was not to see her again for many years.

After she left, I stayed in the tearoom, remembering. I had brought with me a copy of a poem that Mrs. Woo had written the day after her husband's murder. I had intended to show her the English version, but I could not bring myself to make her relive those days. I took it out and read it to myself:

> Where should I go?
> Where should I go
> From now on to meet you again?
>
> Turning your head again and again,
> You'd leave our home in the morning,
> And always come back in the evening.
> Always in one piece, you came back to me.
>
> Even that short separation was too long for me.
> I counted the hours until you came back to me.
>
> Where should I go?
> Where should I go
> From now on to meet you again?
>
> Last spring, all of a sudden
> You were taken away, without any reason.
>
> After the spring, summer came, autumn passed
> Without any sign of your return.
>
> All through the long winter I waited for spring to come,
> For if spring came, surely I would see you again.
> I kept dreaming of that joyous day.

Even that dream I am deprived of now.
I am refused to even feel the pain
That I had gone through by waiting for you.

You were all that I lived for,
The spring from which came
My strength to live.

Beloved One!
I would rather lie next to you
Holding your pale tortured hands,
Holding them tightly, tightly and with a smile.

I would rather lie next to you
Peacefully, peacefully and quietly.

I left the tearoom and walked long into the night, thinking, remembering—trying not to do either.

That night I dreamed a dream. I was swimming in a river. In front of me stood a giant of a man with one leg planted on the right bank of the river and the other on the left. He obviously intended evil. There was no way around. I dove deep into the river between his legs thinking to escape, but I saw and then felt the knife cut through my arm and chest.

The scene changed. I observed four men carrying a body draped with a white sheet. They carried the body into a small, gray room. Eight other bodies lay there in a semicircle. The men placed their burden beside the others. On the little finger of the right hand I saw a small gold ring.

ESCAPE INTO BONDAGE

Background

In 1995 and 1996 Amnesty International was gathering information to document the plight of North Korean refugees living in Russia who, because they had no legal status, suffered at the hands of Russian police. They could not return home to North Korea, and there were great obstacles to becoming refugees in South Korea. Some of the men had come into Russia after working as laborers in Siberian lumber camps. Others had secretly abandoned North Korea and had come to Russia through China.

I made two visits to Moscow on behalf of Amnesty International acting as interpreter for Mr. Diedrick Lohman as he interviewed the North Korean refugees. These interviews inspired me to write the following story. The two main characters in the story represent those who had experienced the lumber camps and those who escaped from North Korea through China. Though all the characters and North Korean village names in the story are fictitious, the people and events are quite credible within the historical context. The Christian churches referred to in the story are also fictitious but it is a fact that Korean churches do exist in all the places suggested in the story, and they have played a central role in helping North Korean refugees all the way from Vladivostok to Moscow.

By the time this story takes place, North Korea is struggling to compete with the South. Its communist allies are experiencing radical changes themselves and are no longer able to give support. Kim Il Song, the man who was President of the Peoples' Republic of Korea for nearly a half century, died in 1994. The next year there was unprecedented flooding, followed by more flooding and draught. Years of famine have killed millions of people and caused a severe economic setback.

In 1987 Koreans in the South broke the stranglehold of the military dictatorship that had dominated the country for two decades. Though a three-way race in the Presidential election of 1987 allowed another military general to win, the military was forced to introduce democratic reforms. Citizens again were permitted to discuss issues of peace and reunification of the country without fear of imprisonment. Then in 1998, former dissident Kim Dae Jung, was elected President. Instead of confrontation and containment, he proclaimed a "Sunshine Policy" that engages North Korea with reconciliation and peaceful coexistence.

Reunification and peace, however, are not easily achieved. The forces that have separated the two halves of the peninsula are deep and many. The story below looks at the two Koreas through the lives of two North Korean men. Just as the previous stories in this collection witness to how ordinary people make history, so the lives of these two North Korean men suggest the central significance of ordinary people in creating the future.

Chapter 1

YUN SONG NAM

UNWANTED ESCAPE

I knew I was doomed, but I could not help myself. I picked up the tree limb. I swung it at his head. He went down. He wasn't dead, but I soon would be.

I lived in Sochun, a small village in North Korea. Our commune consisted of fifteen families. We maintained our livestock and machinery in common. The land we tilled, of course, belonged to the community. We were organized to work together. Each of us had his or her regular job assignments, and when some special need came up our commune's Party leader would appoint workers to take care of it. On a day in early spring three of us had been assigned the job of cleaning out the irrigation ditches that fed our village's rice fields. It was not hard work, but it demanded careful construction. Otherwise the water would cut through the side banks and damage the rice fields in the terraces below. Kwan Ho Kyung, the other worker, and I had been assigned this duty many times. The third man, our foreman in charge, Pak Ju Won, was a Party hack who knew very little about any kind of manual labor. Yet he was in charge. His contributions consisted of giving orders to Kwan and me and then cursing at us for not doing it the way he demanded.

My mother and father were both members of the Communist Party. Both had fought in the wars against Japanese and American imperialism. From my infancy they had taught me stories of the heroism of our people under the direction of The

Great Leader, Kim Il Song, as we sought to create a society of justice where all were valued equally. In South Korea and Japan it was not so. There, the rich oppressed the people, living in luxury while the masses subsisted in poverty. There was no such oppression among us. The Party made sure that all were treated equally. Everyone had his duties and his rights. We were probably the only really democratic society left in the whole world. I had joined The League of Socialist Working Youth at the age of fourteen, and later when I became of age, I joined the Party. I loved the Party even though I knew we had not yet reached the perfect socialist society. At times even in our classless society a worthless scoundrel like Pak would rise to positions of authority.

"Kwan, open that gate. Let the water run." Pak ordered.

"No!" I cried. " Not yet! The lower gate is not ready to handle more water. It will tear the bank away."

Pak ignored my warning. He again ordered Kwan to open the gate. The water backed up and then broke through the bank. It poured down the hill into the fields cutting deep ruts into the soil.

"Now look what you have done. You stupid ass!" Pak barked at Kwan. "Did you not hear comrade Yun tell you not to open the gate?"

"But, you told me to . . ."

"Shut up, you son of a dog, The Village Committee will certainly reprimand you for this. I shall recommend the stiffest penalty."

"That's not fair. If anyone is to be punished it should be you." I hurried to Kwan's defense. "The Party teaches us to work together and take mutual responsibility. Let us all three confess that we have made a mistake."

"Yun, stay out of this. You and your idealism! The Party teaches us to be obedient to our superiors. You are being insubordinate! Now get back to work!"

Kwan and I set about repairing the damage. Getting the

upper gate closed was not difficult, but bringing in new rocks and soil to repair the dikes added hours to the job. We worked without a lunch break while Pak went back and forth to his office in the village. Near sundown we decided to knock off for the day. On the road back to the village we met Pak.

"What are you doing? Why are you not working?" he bellowed.

"It's about dark," I interrupted. "We've worked all day without rest. Besides there is nothing more we can do today. We'll get at it early tomorrow."

"In our commune we work until the Party officer says stop. We all have to pull our load as the Party teaches. You work until I tell you to stop, you sons of bitches. You think you are better than your Party officer?" Pak was losing control. His eyes spit fire. His curses could not satisfy his fury. He swung his fist and hit me square on the nose. As I staggered backwards, I saw the tree limb on the ground. I picked it up and let him have it. That one-second of pleasurable outrage ruined me forever. I have gone over that instant a thousand times. If only I could have controlled myself. I am not a violent person. I had a good reputation as a hard worker in the commune. Pak had done wrong, but I knew better than to attack him. If only I had fallen down and then registered a complaint with the chair of the local party. If only— but what was done was done. Pak lay stunned on the road in front of me. I knew immediately I was in for big trouble. Attacking a Party officer was a serious crime.

Quickly I ran to my house. I had seen similar situations before so I knew exactly what to tell my wife. She was in the kitchen preparing the evening meal. As usual we were having rice with barley, pickled cabbage and a mountain grass called *toraji*. Our two children aged two and three, were playing a game in the yard.

I ran into the kitchen and, quickly told her what had happened. "You must immediately go to the *banjang* (the neighborhood leader) and denounce me. Tell him I am an anti-Party influence, an enemy of the people and that you are sorry you ever married me and wish to be divorced immediately. Write that down and sign it. Take it to the *banjang*. Go now. Don't wait till after supper."

My wife had once been a pretty woman, but she had worked so long in the fields and volunteered so many hours to the Party in addition to caring for our two children and me that she had become haggard and skinny. Her tired eyes could not fathom what I was telling her. Her mouth quivered in fear. "Why did you hit him? What will you do? Where will you go?"

"I do not know, but I must leave, hide somewhere. But please do not talk. If you do not act quickly, you and the children might be exiled to Ham Gyung Pukdo, in the north, and left there to exist as best you can. If the *banjang* accepts your public denunciation, you and the children might be allowed to stay on in the village."

My fate was sealed. Either I fled or I would spend years at hard labor in prison. Hitting a party official was not a small offense.

I took a last look at my children; smiled a smile of regret at my wife; took a couple handfuls of rice, a piece of dried fish, a turnip and fled out the door. I would never again see my children or wife. Yet there was no time for sentiment. Fortunately, I lived at the edge of the village so not many people saw me come or go. I headed for the mountains up beyond where we had worked on the irrigation ditch. The higher levels of the mountain were covered with pine trees and scrub oaks, and a series of deep rock formations provided endless hiding places.

I reached a high bluff, got my breath and looked down. I expected there would be a party in hot pursuit, but there was no one. Should I hole up for the night or go on? I decided to move. I knew the mountains, but so did everyone else. I would surely be found out. My only option was to head northwest toward the Yalu River and try to get across into China. I stayed at the highest levels and followed the mountain range as it ran

its course northward. The first day I ate the rice. From then on I nibbled on the fish and turnip, and drank a lot of fresh mountain water.

After a week of night travel, the mountains were behind me. Rolling hills and plains were in front. The city of Sinuiju lay not too many miles away. There I would have to cross the Yalu. That would not be easy. There was a curfew in effect. Strangers could be arrested at any time, and after mid-night, anyone found on the city streets could be shot on sight. I approached the town carefully. I needed food and a way across the river. And I needed both before the sun began to rise. Luck was with me. I spied a small house nestled at the foot of some hills. It was not difficult to find the kitchen. The door was not locked. I pushed it open and went in. It was a typical kitchen. The floor was made of mud. Behind the door fixed into the fireplace were two large pots for cooking rice. On the other side was a table where dishes and leftover food were stored. Several dried fish hung from the ceiling. I wrapped up two handfuls of rice in a piece of paper; took one of the dried fish and put an apple in my pocket. As I closed the door behind me, I offered up a wish that no one was robbing my house like this. In a period of a few days I had knocked a man unconscious; I had become a fugitive, and now I was a thief. My conscience hurt, but what else could I have done?

The main street running down the center of town would no doubt lead to the ferry where one would cross over to China, but I could not just walk down that street; nor could I board the ferry. Guards would be everywhere. I moved alongside a road that swayed northward. Then I pushed cross-country in the general direction of the river, away from the city. I was counting on some enterprising farmer running an illegal night ferry. I got to the river, and found a good hiding place from which I could see up stream and down. My guess was correct. On the very first night I saw a small boat with three people aboard

push out into the water. It did not take long. The ferryman returned within an hour—alone.

I took him by surprise as he stepped back on to his dock.
"Take me across too. I will pay you."

"Who are you? What do you mean? I was just fishing.
Night time is good fishing time."

"Don't lie. I saw you take those two men across. But don't
be afraid. I will not turn you in. I must get across. Please take
me. I will pay. Look, this is all I have, but surely ten won is
enough for one quick crossing."

Begging like that proved to be the wrong tactic. The
boatman's face quickly changed from one of fear to one of
disdain. He had taken advantage of desperate men like me before. "Ten *won*? You must be crazy! I risk my life for ten *won*?
No way! Throw in your coat, and I'll do it."

"My coat? It is all I have. It is still cold around here. Surely
my coat is not worth anything to you. You have one."

"Never mind what it is worth to me. Ten *won* and your
coat. Take it or leave it."

I took off my coat, gave it and the money to the farmer and
got into the boat. Within a few minutes, I was safe in China.

FIRST REFUGE

On the China side of the river there was nothing. For this I
was grateful. After finding a rock formation under which I could
hide, I lay down and quickly went to sleep. At the first light of
dawn I awoke. The area seemed abandoned, but not far below
me there was a well-worn path following the flow of the river. I
stayed in my hiding place and watched. People from the north
began to stream south, on their way to Dandong, the Chinese
city across the river from Chinuiju. I was patient.

Toward mid-morning the traffic on the path dwindled to
almost nothing, only a few stragglers. I waited. If I were to go

into the city without drawing attention to myself, I would need a coat and a pair of pants. My own pants had been torn apart by the mountain rocks. Finally the right guy came along. He was a rather old man, well dressed and alone. I grabbed him from behind, wrestled him to the ground and bound him hand and foot. "Sorry uncle," I apologized as I half-dragged, half carried him up to my hideout space. I took not only his money, but his clothes too, and hat. I tied him up good, and gagged him. It would take him a while to get free. That would give me time to scout out the city and see what alternatives there might be.

It took about three hours to reach the town. I walked along slowly, avoiding police and border guards. The city, Dandong, was a hubbub of buying and selling. It looked like one big open market. I made myself walk casually from one stall to another pretending I was tracking prices or looking for a particular buy. Despite my disguise in the old man's clothes, people looked at me in odd ways, and as a bunch of students went charging past, several of them yelled insults that I could not understand. I changed my strategy and looked for an inconspicuous place from which I could better spy out the landscape. I found such a place on a little balcony that jutted out over the market entryway. It was occupied with various wares, but no one paid any attention as I dug out a little space between three large bags, sat down and began my vigil.

It was near sunset when I caught sight of him. I knew there would be Koreans around here. I followed him through the market. He entered into a small hovel that had a Korean sign above its entrance: *sul jip*—wine house. I entered. It was dark inside, but to my grateful ears everyone was talking Korean. I ordered a glass of beer, and took a seat in a far corner so as not to draw attention. After only a short while, however, a man came over and sat down beside me.

"What are you doing dressed up like that?" Koreans don't wear Chinese clothes, and they don't walk like them nor do they smell like them. You probably robbed some unsuspecting farmer. Coming in here like this endangers us all. Get out. Circle around back of this building, and you will find a cellar door. Go down there and wait. Someone will come and take you to the church, but stay put till he comes."

"Take me where? To the church? What's that?"

"Never mind, just go and do as you're told."

I'm not sure how long I waited in the black cellar, but early in the morning while it was still dark, someone came down the steps. A woman's voice: "Sir, follow me. Please do not speak.

We wound through the streets and alleys of the dirty, sleeping city. The woman in front of me moved silently staying close in the shadow of the buildings. After about an hour, I began to hear noises like some one having an argument. As we drew closer, it sounded more like a crowd of people in a street brawl. We entered into the room from which the noise came. There, lying prone on the floor, were a dozen men and women crying and shouting and praying to some one called *Hannanim*. It was a terrible and mysterious racket. My guide told me to kneel down and pray like everyone else. I knelt and lay silent, trying to decipher something of the uproar around me. After the noise subsided, a young man gave an exhortation about praising *Hannanim* through love and service to our neighbor. The whole group then sang together and the meeting was over. I stayed sitting until the young man who gave the exhortation came over to me.

"Welcome to our prayer meeting. We will talk later. Now, please follow me."

The markets were now beginning to open. The prayer-meeting people walked together talking and singing happily. I followed, wondering what was going to happen next. After a mile or so, we entered into an old warehouse-like building. Inside the courtyard were many small apartments, where evidently many of these church people lived.

The young man directed me toward his quarters. Inside were two rooms with Korean-style hot floors. There was no furniture. He handed me a cushion and motioned for me to sit down on the floor. He sat opposite me and for a few seconds bowed his head in prayer. Then looking me straight in the eyes he began to lay out my future.

"Friend, I do not want to know your name, and I will not tell you mine. That way is safer for both of us. You must quickly decide what you want to do. You have, I think, three alternatives. You may leave right now and be on your own. You may stay here and try to work your way little by little into our society. Or you may travel north out of China, into Russia. Police informants are everywhere. The chances of your not being detected around here are very small. If caught, you will, of course, be sent back to North Korea. We will help you travel to Russia if you decide to go there. But before you answer, let us have breakfast. After you've eaten and had little rest, you will be able to think better."

A woman came into the room bearing a tray of rice, kimchee and steaming hot turnip soup. I almost fainted it smelled so delicious. Only then did the memories of my wife and children flood over me, and I began to cry. For several minutes they left me to myself. Then a prayer was offered to *Hannanim*, thanking him for the food and asking him to protect my family and reunite us soon. I ate like a tiger, paying no attention to the proprieties for which we Koreans are famous. Even before I was finished, however, I felt the fatigue take over. I was shown a mat on the floor in the adjoining room. I collapsed on to it and was immediately engulfed in darkness and then in myriad of dreams and nightmares.

As I woke many hours later, I heard the men talking in the next room.

"His best bet is to go north to Russia, but he may not want to. It is like permanent exile from his home country."

"Yes, but we are in real trouble. Last week the police picked up two escapees who informed on us. The man in charge was sympathetic to our work, but he warned us if we were caught one more time, some of us would go to prison."

"I know, and for him to hang around here right now will mean almost certain capture. Yet we can't force him. One way or the other he will have to decide."

I waited several minutes before I arose from my mat. I lay there once more reviewing my shattered life. Perhaps I should just give myself up, go back and face the music. Running away from the Party, the border guards, and the security police— It might never end. But going back was not a solution either. Not only would I be punished, my wife and kids would also be exposed to a battery of hardships they did not deserve. My only alternative was to move on, go north. I could not stay here and endanger these people who had been so good to me. But I hated the thought. Once in Russia, I'd have almost no chance of ever returning home.

I cleared my throat to let those in the next room know that I was awake. As I entered their room, I bowed to the men sitting crossed legged on the floor. They asked if I had slept well and said they hoped I was in good health.

After the formalities, I told them that I had decided to move north. The other three men seemed to expect my reply. One of them immediately gave me instructions as to what to do: "To-morrow a truck load of foodstuffs and agricultural chemicals is set to leave in the morning. We will hide you away in one of the large straw bags. Chinese officials will inspect the cargo before departure, so you will need to be in your hiding place before dawn."

The inspection was perfunctory. A gift of tobacco was given to the two inspectors. They lit up a cigarette and stamped the truck's invoice approved. After we got out on the road, the driver opened the sack to give me air and water. I was on my way to the Russian city of Khabarovsk.

REVEREND LEE SONG MIN

Getting to Khabarovsk proved highly uncomfortable but quite uneventful. For most of the seven hundred miles I was able to sit in the cab of the truck with the driver. At other times I would have to momentarily return to my potato sack. The police did not patrol very tightly, and my driver always had something to share with a guard or policeman who might stop him—a cigarette, a bag of rice, a few potatoes, a couple dried fish. We made good time. It only took us two weeks to make the trip.

Before I had fled from my village I had known no world other than my own commune and nearby villages. Now in the space of a few weeks, I had traveled across northern China and was about to enter Russia. We had to stop at the border patrol before we crossed the Amur River that separates China from Russia. The Chinese guards were friendly and after a couple smokes waved us on. The Russians, however, were different. Apparently they were looking for something. Later I learned that this was one of the major roads for the smuggling of drugs into the Siberian territory. I thought surely they would discover me with their poking around, but they gave up the search just in time. My potato sack was passed by. Finally the truck driver came through with a bag of rice for the two guards and we were allowed to proceed.

I had been to a large city only once in my life. While a soldier, I had been allowed a trip to our capital, Pyongyang. It has a population of about two million people, but the streets are wide and clean; people live in large white high-rise apartments. There are parks and rivers everywhere. It is indeed a beautiful place. By contrast Khabarovsk, with about the same size population as Pyongyang, is sprawled out with no apparent plan. Multi-story buildings, built when the city was first founded in the mid-nineteenth century, command the downtown government area; factories spew forth white and black smoke so thick it can be tasted; and the Trans-Siberian railroad yards discharge streams of ash and noise. High-rise apartments, like those in Pyongyang, dominate the spaces between the factories and the down town buildings. Though trees still line the main streets, they are covered with dust and look as uncared for as the buildings. Everything seemed to be deteriorating, but the city was busy with trucks, trains, automobiles, bicycles and hordes of people.

We crossed the bridge over the Amur River, made a right turn and headed toward the wharf. Khabarovsk is located near the confluence of the Amur and Ussuri Rivers, and is, therefore, a commerce and transportation hub connecting waterways and railroads throughout the Far East. It is the center from which Russia controls Siberia. The truck driver found the dock he was looking for. We unloaded our cargo. Most of it would be trans-shipped up stream. When that was finished, the driver and I took a bath. We jumped into the river, and though it was dirty too, with the use of a little sand and mud we were able to scrape ourselves reasonably clean.

The strangest thing was yet to come. We got back into the truck and began to wind our way into the middle of one of the worst of the city's ghettos. The alley dead-ended in a circle. In the middle of the circle stood a modest, clean concrete building. On the outer side of the circle a series of small, clean wooden huts were huddled. A few of them even had flower boxes outside the door. A sign, in the Korean language, in front of the circle proclaimed: *"Hannanim Jip,"* (The House of God). The driver stopped the truck. He got out and motioned for me to do the same. He led me up to the front of the concrete building. "They are expecting you," he said. "I must go now. I pray the Lord will be gracious to you." He got into the truck and drove away.

As I stood there befuddled, wondering what to do next, the door of the central building opened. An elderly Korean woman came out. "In the name of God I give you welcome. The pastor has been expecting you. Please come in. Have you had supper?"

I followed her into the building. Inside was a large meeting hall and to the back of the hall a door opened into a private apartment. The woman led me to that door. The apartment was furnished Korean style: one small room with a wooden floor, and two others with floors that could be heated in the winter. At the far end of the wooden floor sat a Korean man. He was reading what looked like a newspaper. He arose and came toward me. "You are welcome. Please take off your shoes and enter." There was nothing special about his appearance. He looked to be about fifty years old. His hair was thin and gray. He had no beard. His voice soft but firm. He stood perhaps five feet seven or eight inches, and weighed probably no more than one hundred and forty pounds. But there was a clarity about his presence, an assurance about his carriage. Both he and his wife moved and spoke in traditional Korean style.

" I am called Reverend Lee Song Min. We are happy that you made it safely, though we are sorry you had to have such a difficult journey."

" My name is Yun Song Nam. I apologize for causing you so much trouble, but I am grateful for your help."

"Let us speak straight out to one another. I am sure you are curious as to who we are, and we certainly want to know who you are and how you came to leave your homeland. Would you please speak first?"

"I am from the village of Sochun in Pyong An Pukdo Province. My grandfather was Yun Tang Jin. My father was Yun Ma Hyung." I went on to tell them the whole story of my life and the incident that caused me to flee. They both listened with close attention asking a few questions as I went.

As I finished my story, Mrs. Lee said, "It is now time to eat. I will bring in the tray. Would you like to wash?"

Pastor Lee showed me a table on which sat a bowl of clean water. I visited the water closet and washed myself. He handed

me a dry towel. Then we sat down to eat—rice, pickled cabbage and seaweed soup. Delicious! We did not talk much during supper. After we finished, Mrs. Lee brought us tea. Reverend Lee began to tell his story. To me it was indeed a strange
tale.

I, too, am from North Korea. I was born in a little
village close to Kaisong. I am sure you know where
that is. When the war began, I was but a youngster of
ten. The very first battle took place in my village. Communist forces under a General Oh Kap Soo burned the
village and killed every person there except me. My
mother saved me by burying me under the roots of a
tree. I stayed there for three days before I dared come
out. I knew I must not be seen so I traveled at night and
hid during the days. I am not sure how long I walked, or
how many days it took, but one day I became aware
that there were others like myself groping along looking for food and shelter.

I attached myself to a woman and three children.
She did not seem to mind so I became an unofficial
member of the family. We walked forever until we came
to Taejun. Unfortunately we got there just as the battle
for the city began. My new mother and her children
were all killed. I lay face down in a riverbed waiting to
die when a strong arm reached down and picked me out
of the mud. The man smelled strange, but I was too near
unconsciousness to look at him. I was carried a short
while and thrown into a truck. The man got in and the
truck took off. When I came to, I was in an American
Army hospital. An American soldier had picked me up.
He saw that I was cared for and fed. When the army
retreated south, he took me with him. I became a kind
of adopted son.

When the war finally ended with the 1953 truce,

this same soldier took me home with him to America. I
was grateful to *Hannanim* for saving me and I knew I
had to pay back the gift of life that I had been given. So
I became a pastor to serve other Koreans who live in
the United States.

"Then just three years ago I met a most remarkable
man. He too was Korean, but he lived in Russia, in a
town I had never heard of, Khabarovsk. He told of the
great work he and others were doing among the poor
Koreans of this city. Though my wife and I have become elderly, we were very touched by this friend's
message. We decided to join him and spend the rest of
our lives serving our Korean people in this area. When
we arrived in Khabarovsk, however, we discovered that
he had gone on to heaven to be with God. Three years
ago now we took over his work, and plan to be here
until we too pass on to heaven.

By the time he had finished speaking, Pastor Lee was exhausted. Mrs. Lee quickly moved to his side. "Now we must
sleep. Mr. Yun, your mat is on the floor in the other room. Can
I get you something before you sleep? Reverend Lee and I will
lie right here."

Many questions about the war, the Americans, his faith,
Hannanim were crowded up in my mind, but I moved quickly
into the adjoining room and lay down on the mat. I slept for the
next twelve hours without moving.

By the time I awoke, Reverend Lee was already gone. Mrs.
Lee brought in my breakfast. "Pastor Lee has gone to the farm.
He will return at evening time. Would you like to see around
the city?"

I discovered that the church called *Hannanim Jip* (God's
House), owned the huts circling the Lee's house. The residents
were all members of the church. They huddled together for
mutual protection and support. The men worked at various

places over the city. The women sold produce and food in the market and took care of the children. Each Sunday they held worship services both in the morning and in late afternoon. The church was also used as a school for Korean children. Pastor Lee was the principal and two church members did the teaching. Mrs. Lee, for her part, was indispensable. She knew the market; she had knowledge of medicine; she acted as midwife; visited the sick and taught Bible to the women each Wednesday evening. That afternoon she took me to visit every house on the circle and introduced me to the open market where all kinds of things were bought and sold. Nothing like this existed in my country. The noise and confusion were befuddling. We walked through the downtown area where the old government buildings had been built a hundred years ago, and at the conclusion of the tour she took me to visit the "Great Patriotic War Memorial" situated on a bluff overlooking the Amur River.

That evening after supper we had the discussion that was to decide my future for the next several years.

"Mr. Yun, I do not mean to push you, but the sooner you make a decision about your future the easier it will be. Now as I see it, you have four alternatives. You can move from here deeper into Russia. The further you go from here the safer you will be. Even though this is a big city, informers are everywhere. Second, you can go south to Vladivostok. There are large numbers of Koreans there. You might be able to lose yourself in the crowd. But there, too, is the problem of the informers. Third, you can stay around here and again try to lose yourself in the crowd."

He hesitated before he went on to the fourth option. None of the first three was very appealing. Getting back home some day was still paramount in my mind. I missed my wife and children. I waited for Lee to speak again.

"I have given this a good bit of thought. I think it will work. You could stay here and work with us. You are a farmer. You know how to raise rice, corn and sweet potatoes. You have had experience with irrigation. The church owns a farm a few miles across the river. We gain enough from it to support our church's social welfare program. We could use another experienced farmer."

"But why would I not be exposed there as well as anywhere else?"

"You would, but I think I can cover for you. You see, at certain levels of society government has broken down. Those who really control the world of everyday commerce and agriculture are not the same as those who control the official apparatus. For centuries the czars dumped their political and criminal prisoners into Siberia. The communists did the same. Over time an underground of mafia-like organizations have evolved. Now with the demise of the Soviet Union's authority, the power vacuum has been filled by these mafia groups."

"I do not see the point. Is the mafia not more difficult to deal with? Wouldn't they be more willing to hand me over for a price?"

"Yes, except for two things. Around here the mafia leaders tend to be very superstitious. They see all religions as though they were magic of some kind. Usually, they do not interfere."

"And besides that," Mrs. Lee interrupted, " I have delivered three of the top man's children. His family name is Nabokov. His wife helps us out in some of our services to the poor. I think we could explain your presence so that Mr. Nobakov would give you protection."

So that is what happened. I became a worker on the church's farm just east of the Ussuri River. The land was fertile. The harvest was plentiful. I was even able to add a bit to the farm's income. I had kept bees at home, and here in the Amur region some of the best honey in the whole of Russia is made. After a couple years, we had a thriving business in honey sending our product as far as Moscow.

Each Saturday evening I would hike up to see Reverend and Mrs. Lee, stay the next day for worship and then hike back to the farm on Sunday night. This became my routine. It was a happy routine. Even my homesickness began to fade. One Saturday as we were eating the evening meal together, I asked a question that had been on my mind for some time. "Reverend Lee, when I was growing up, we learned that the story of *Hannanim* was a superstition. It was made up to keep people's mind on heaven and forget about the evils of the wealthy classes. You worship *Hannanim* like he was a living, super-person. Is it superstition or reality? I can't figure it out."

"Communism's basic flaw is that it does not recognize that there is a God and that we humans have his spirit in us. As part of God, we are to do justice and love one another. If man denies God, then he has no measure of what is good or bad, and so the strong take over and the weak are oppressed. That is as true of communism as it is of capitalism. Have you not seen injustice and oppression in your home country?"

"Yes, but that is not the intention of the system or its values. Communists are taught to serve each other and to build a just society. Just because some do wrong doesn't mean the whole system is bad."

"True, and even godless people or godless societies, can love and work for justice, but unless responsibility to a higher being is recognized, greed and corruption is likely to take over. I would like to go further in this discussion, but I really must prepare for tomorrow's service. Let's pick it up again when you come next Saturday."

Fate determined otherwise. I was never to speak to Reverend Lee again.

CATASTROPHE

The next weekend, my usual Saturday visit to the Lee's was delayed. The bees were beginning to swarm and I had to stay to make sure all went well. By late night, however, the bees had quieted down and were again in the hives. Even though it would be near midnight by the time I arrived at the Lee's, I decided to go on. I looked forward to resuming our discussion about *Hannanim.* Our relationship had become quite close. I felt about them much as I would about my own father and mother. They returned the affection and always welcomed me regardless of what time I showed up.

As I approached the circle, I immediately sensed that something was wrong. Then I saw that the church's sign had been knocked down and the church doors hung open off their hinges. The inner door to the Lee's apartment was also wide open. There was not a sound. Fear grabbed my spine. I took off my shoes and moved quietly through the door. There on the wooden floor immediately in front of me lay Reverend Lee. His head lay in a pool of blood. He was dead. He had been beaten viciously. I stepped over him, my whole body trembling with fear and anger. In the next room, Mrs. Lee's slight body was crumpled up in a corner as though cringing away from an assault. She too was dead.

I fell to the floor in shock. Who could have done such a thing? Why would any one want to kill such kind people? I sat there numbed by the horror of what I saw. How long I sat there, I do not know. When I came to, my first reaction was to raise the neighbors to find out what had happened, and who had done this, but immediately my self-preservation instinct took over. Surely I would be suspected. I would be arrested, interrogated and probably tortured. Russian methods of treating Chinese and Koreans suspected of crimes were well known. My desire to know what had happened was overcome by my desire to avoid the Russians.

Without touching a thing, I moved quietly out of the church. There was no one on the streets but nevertheless I stayed in the shadows and made my way to the railroad yards. I knew freight trains moved out from there every hour. By the time the Lees' bodies were discovered, I could be miles away. I climbed into a boxcar that was loaded and ready to be closed up. I pushed my way into the back corner, pulled sacks over the top of me and waited. The fate that controlled my life was malevolent indeed.

Chapter 2

OH KI SOP

THE LEGACY OF OH KAP SOO

"Into the caves! Hurry, Hurry! Run! Get into the caves. The planes are coming."

The siren had not gone off. The American bombers were overhead before they could take shelter. My grandfather tried mightily to warn the people, to save them, but it was too late. The bombs fell like rain in a violent storm. When it was over, my grandfather and thousands of others lay dead.

Grandfather had been a Freedom Fighter alongside our Great Leader, Kim Il Song. When the Japanese took over our country, the Freedom Fighters fled to the mountains and for thirty years carried on guerrilla warfare against the invaders. The mountains gave them protection, and the people gave them food.

In 1945 when the Japanese imperialists were finally thrown out, the Americans tried to take their place, but once again The Great Leader came to our rescue. Though the Americans were strong enough to take over the southern part of the country, Kim Il Song thwarted their efforts to gobble up the whole peninsula. Until he was killed that night in 1950, Grandfather stood as one of the most trusted lieutenants and companions of The Great Leader.

Because of his close ties with the Great Leader and his heroic death, Grandfather was declared a Martyr for Freedom. His son, my father, was appointed Chairman of the Labor Party for the Wonsan District, a post that he held honorably for thirty years.

I was born many years after Grandfather's death, but stories of his heroism and The Great Leader's wisdom were told to me each night before I went to bed. Seldom, however, did I see either my father or mother. Father was always engrossed in Party affairs in Wonsan or in the capital of Pyongyang. I saw him, but only briefly at great national celebrations like the birthdays of The Great Leader. At those times it was required that the heads of the Party appear in public ceremony with their entire families. Mother, by the fact that she was Father's wife, was constantly called upon to lead women's groups in everything from new farming methods to political education. Our family, the Oh Kap Soo family, named after Grandfather, was given respect everywhere. Ours was a classless society, but certain heroes and martyrs were granted awards for their contributions to the state. We, the Oh Kap Soo family, received bigger rations of food and lived in a larger apartment than other citizens.

From the very beginning I was spoiled by those who looked after me. In day care and later in school the teachers paid me deference and seldom complained about my sullen, insolent attitude. I got whatever I demanded, but never got the reprimand or honest evaluation that I deserved. Father and Mother, off in their own worlds, had no reason to suspect that their own son was becoming an "unhealthy element in society."

When I went for my military duty as a young man of eighteen, my reputation preceded me. I was assigned to the Motor Vehicle Repair Unit, not because I knew anything about mechanics, but because it was thought that I would be in the least harm and also cause the least trouble. Much to everyone's surprise, and especially my own, I took to mechanics like the proverbial duck to water. When I was discharged eight years later, I was not a better man, but I was a licensed mechanic and I knew how to drive a variety of trucks and automobiles.

After my discharge from the military, I was expected to report to the Job Placement Office for work assignment. In our country, unemployment was not permitted. I thought, however, that I could get around the system by appealing to my father. Surely he would find me a place in the Party apparatus, or I was even willing to act as his chauffeur. I should have known better. Father was a strict communist and was not about to bend the rules for anyone, and especially not for his own son.

"Just because you are the grandson of Oh Kap Soo does not give you special privilege," he reminded me. "Go through channels and take the exams. Your first step is the Job Placement Office, like everyone else." I felt sorry for Father. I could tell by his voice that he was disgusted with me and disappointed that his son was trying to undermine the Party's discipline. But he was the one who looked guilty. His eyes steadily avoided mine. Having left me to my own devices for most of my life I was now a stranger to him.

Having no other options, I went to the local Job Placement Office, reported that I had recently finished my military service and that I was now ready for job assignment. The office manager had a much better attitude toward me than did my father. In his mind, my being Oh Kap Soo's grandson meant big backing from important people. He offered me several positions within the bureaucracy, none of which I was qualified to do, but I immediately accepted the one I thought was the most prestigious.

I started the next day. I was a section vice-chief in the office of procurement for the city government. When I appeared at my post, my chief and all the other staff were already aware of who I was. I was welcomed with diffidence and given a desk and chair. Each morning I was served tea and each afternoon I had coffee. On ceremonial occasions I was dragged out and introduced to the visiting VIPs. There was not a lick of work involved. Yet I received my weekly ration of rice with a little extra for meritorious service.

At first I thought I had pulled something over on the system and my father. I played my position to the hilt. I took advantage of everyone I could and acted as though I were indeed a big shot. But then after a couple years, I began to tire of the whole thing. My mind returned more and more to my years in military service. Though I had enjoyed privileges there too, at the same time I had been occupied with learning and doing something worthwhile. Or perhaps it was the reassertion of genes from Oh Kap Soo and my dedicated father that made me restless. Whether it was conscience or boredom, I'm not sure, but I finally came to the conclusion that I had to find a new job, something with a challenge. I was a man of twenty-eight. I wanted a change from the charade that I had been living.

Back I went to the Job Placement Office. The office chief was surprised to see me. He had received glowing reports about my performance at the procurement office.

Much out of character for me, I confessed that I wanted a job that would challenge me, help me grow and develop, a job where people would not know that I was from the lineage of Oh Kap Soo. Needless to say the chief was flabbergasted.

"But I do not understand. I gave you one of the best appointments. Now you are dissatisfied? You are asking too much, comrade."

"No, please understand me. I am grateful for your kind appointment, but I am a young man. I want to do something hard. Something with meaning for my country and family."

At first the chief stared at me in disbelief. Then he smiled in a way that made me wonder if somewhere in his past he may have had a change in attitude something like my own. Only later, when it was too late, did I realize that his grin was one of duplicity. He had me and I did not know it.

"The Great Leader is asking for volunteers to go to Siberia to work in Russian lumber camps. Our patriots go there to work and, in exchange, Russia pays our government in international currencies. Do you think you are up to such a strenuous assignment? It comes with the highest commendation from The Great Leader."

I did not hesitate. It sounded just like what I wanted. "How do I get there? How do I live while I am there? Do I work under Russians? I cannot speak Russian."

"While you are there, you will live in a camp with other Korean comrades, much like at an army base. Your pay is quite generous. The average worker makes about 80 won per month. I see from your records that you are a mechanic and driver. You could make up to 200 won."

I was staggered. 80 to 200 won in one month! That was two or three times more than one could make here at home. "How long must I stay? How about clothing?"

"Not to worry, your physical needs will be taken care of. If you are accepted, you will travel by train across the border into Russia, around Lake Khanka and on up to a place called Chegdomyn. It is about five hundred miles north. There you will be assigned to one of twelve camps. Your term of duty is three years."

For the first time in my life I was excited. There would be adventure in a new land, earning money for the motherland, and making a high wage all at the same time. The chief saw my excitement and acted swiftly. "The Overseas Manpower Sending Committee" has its offices here in this building. I will give you a memo to take to the Chair, Comrade Kim Do Sun. Give it to him. He will show you what must be done."

Comrade Kim received me gladly. He glanced at my record. "Are you sure you want to do this?" He sounded skeptical.

"Yes sir," I replied.

"All right then. Everything is in order. Prepare to depart within ten days."

The suddenness of it all was puzzling, and should have given me reason to hesitate, but when I told Father of my intentions, he smiled broadly and kissed me on each cheek. He was proud that I had undertaken such a patriotic task for the sake of

The Great Leader. Ten days later, along with two hundred other men, I was on the train heading north to Siberia.

LUMBER CAMPS

At the border, before we passed over into Russia, we were taken from the train and assembled in a big hall. Pictures of The Great Leader and his son, The Dear Leader, hung on the walls. We were instructed to line up in military style. After a visual inspection, each man was given a paper and told to sign it. The paper said:

> While staying on the territory of Russian Siberia, the undersigned must not speak disparagingly of his homeland, The Great Leader, Kim Il Song or The Dear Leader Kim Jong Il.
>
> The undersigned will abide by Russian laws and rules and will avoid contact with Russian Koreans.
>
> If the undersigned hears any of his comrades speak ill of the homeland or its leaders, he will immediately report it to his superiors.

We all signed. Our passports were taken from us, and we were given ID cards instead. I became "Camp 3, # 7747-Q478." My name did not appear on the card.

We were put back on the train and taken across the bridge over the Tumen River. We were now in Russia. Again the train stopped and we were ordered out. The train returned across the border. An awful sense of isolation and foreboding filled my heart as I saw that train disappear. For the first time in my life I was on my own. My ancestry would be of no help. I knew no one, and the attitudes of those in charge made me suspect that we had not been told everything about the job to which we were going.

"As of this moment you are under the protection of the Korean Workers in Foreign Lands Department. You will do exactly as you are told and there will be no problem. Make trouble, and you will bear the consequences. We are now going to march up the tracks where we will meet the trains going to Chegdomyn. Follow directions and do not talk."

The man who gave these orders then gestured to a group of armed security guards who gave us orders to take ranks and march. Those who did not react fast enough were pushed or hit with the rifles. We were herded into a boxcar. No windows. No air. No water. No toilet. Several times a day we would stop for water and toilet needs. It took a week before we got to Chegdomyn.

As we were being hauled off the train, I heard my name called.

"I am Oh Ki Sop, comrade." I was so weak I could barely walk. A push from the back sent me stumbling in the direction of the voice.

I was led to a nearby shed. The commandant of the camp sat behind a desk. He arose, and came over to where I stood. He was a tall, thin man, a long nose and a face coated with arrogance.

" I do not know why you are here. There must be a mistake, or some one is trying to spy on us. Why would Oh Kap Soo's grandson be sent to a lumber camp? You will be watched every minute. A violation of any of the rules will bring quick discipline. You will not deceive me."

"Comrade commandant, you have it all wrong. I volunteered to come here as a sign of my patriotism and love for The Great Leader. While I am here, I will obey your every order." With these words I took from my pocket a Japanese watch given me by my father as a going away present. I handed him the watch, bowed and said I was honored to serve under him.

Without apparent confusion or embarrassment he took the watch and returned to his seat. "Very good! In a few days after I have looked over your records, I will call for you again."

The next few days were brutal. Fourteen hours a day we worked. With little or no training, we were commanded to cut pine, larch and birch trees that grew two hundred feet or more. Some of the birch were as hard as iron. Few of us had ever seen trees like this, and even fewer had ever handled an ax or a saw. I was assigned to crew number six. My work identification number was 143. Two of the stronger men in our crew were given the job of cutting the trees down. They, however, were not experienced lumbermen. Often the trees fell in directions they least expected. The very first tree they cut came crashing down on our heads. By some miracle no one was hit directly by the trunk, but several of us were knocked down and scarred by branches. One man was knocked unconscious and had to be carried back to the truck for return to the camp. The rest of us were given handsaws and told to cut off the branches of the fallen tree.

It was in the second week or maybe the fifth, or tenth, I don't really know. By then I had become so disoriented that time had no meaning to me. With my brain numb and every muscle protesting I set about doing my job—sawing limbs and more limbs, a never ending supply of thick, resisting tree limbs. All of a sudden a loud voice yelled out: "Number 143 (that was me) report immediately to crew number eight."

I grabbed my saw and headed that way. Before I reached my designation another voice shouted out: "Timber!" That time my reactions were wrong. The birch tree covered me like the night and one of its lesser branches struck me from behind and buried me beneath itself. How long I stayed there I do not know, nor did I care. I was sprawled out under the tree and was determined to stay there as long as possible. I did not yell or protest. I went to sleep. When I unfortunately was dug out, I found that my legs were paralyzed from the hips down. I could feel nothing. My comrades carried me over to the truck where the dead and wounded were waiting for shipment back to camp. There were no medical personnel in the forest, only at the camp headquarters. After some hours, a truck was made available. Four dead men were laid on the truck bed. A second deck was laid atop them. The seriously injured, me among them, were stretched out at that level, and on a third tier were a few comrades who had suffered only minor harm.

I lay in the hospital among a crowd of other injured men. On the fourth day I began to sense the feeling coming back to my legs. I almost regretted it. I tried to hide it as long as possible, but eventually the nurse and doctor both realized that the trauma had passed and that I was able to walk again. I was ordered to rejoin crew six. Escape and suicide both suggested themselves to me. Escape I knew was impossible and suicide's appeal was only temporary. That evening I joined my comrades in the dining hall. The menu was rice with barley, beans and cabbage soup. For a bed, a narrow shelf had been built around the whole room so as we finished eating, we pulled ourselves on to the shelf and went fast asleep, our bodies tangled together like one long noodle.

In the morning as I prepared to march to the forest with the other men, a guard pulled me out of line. "Come with me," is all he said. I was taken to the commandant's office. If I had joined my comrades that day, I'm sure the appeal of suicide would have increased greatly. Every ounce of energy had been wrung out of me. Comrade commandant was, as before, sitting behind his desk when I entered. He looked up at me and smiled. The guard was dismissed. We were left alone. "Comrade Oh, you do not look so well. I hope you have not been mistreated. An important person like yourself has to be taken care of. That is my duty." Sarcasm dripped from his self-satisfied grin. He knew he had me. And I knew it too. I stood at attention, said nothing in response.

" I have a proposition to offer you. Perhaps we can work

together. Sit down,"

I sat, and was grateful. "Comrade Commandant, I am more than happy to work with you. What can I do to be of service?"

"Your record says you are a mechanic and a truck driver. Is that correct?"

"It is. I learned in the army. I am a licensed mechanic and driver."

"Very good. Running a labor camp is at times a boring job. So I work a little "hobby" on the side. I have developed a small business, and could use a partner. There is a shortage of most everything around here—food, tobacco, boots, coats, vodka, drugs. I have access to a steady supply of these items. With you as driver and deliveryman, we can sell these things around the whole area, to prisoners, guards and even to some Russians. You get your salary as a driver and twenty percent of the profit."

"What is my salary as a driver?"

"180 rubles a month, but half of that goes to the government, and half of the remainder pays for your food and lodging. You get what's left over—.45 rubles. You will need more than that to exist for three years."

"What do I have to do, and when do I start?"

"First you must learn where all the twelve camps are. I will show you a map and you can do a practice run even today. Chegdomyn is the headquarters from which the other camps are supplied. You will be in constant motion going from one to another. I will tell you who to do business with at each camp. I'll make the contacts. All you have to do is deliver what I give you to the people I tell you to. And remember. No tricks! Or else back to the lumber camp you go. Your predecessor in this job was returned to the camps just a few days ago. He tried to cheat me."

I spent the rest of the day looking over the maps, checking on which cargo went where and inspecting the trucks. They were old, 1950 Zhiguli models, but they were still in working condition. I had driven worse in the army.

I was given sleeping space in another part of the camp. The men slaving in the lumber camps knew I was collaborating somehow with the commandant. They probably would have killed me were I to have stayed in the same building with them. I felt sorry for the poor bastards, but there was nothing I could do to help them. With a shock it came to me that we communists had fallen into the capitalist way of thinking: dog eat dog! So be it. I would do anything to keep from going back to the camp.

The next day I had my first assignment, a load of rice to camp #4. It was a long trip. The roads were unpaved and cut up by bumps and holes. At each checkpoint along the way I had to get out and undergo inspection. That first night I arrived at camp #4 after dark. After the cargo had been stored in the warehouse, I was told that the camp commander wanted to see me. I knew what he wanted. I had secreted a box under my seat. I put the box in my duffel bag and went to see the commander.

He was an abrupt kind of guy. Without preliminaries, he asked what I had in the bag. I opened the bag and handed him the contents. He took it, put it under his desk and grumbled, "That is all. Go"

"Yes sir. Where shall I eat?

"You eat with everyone else. When the men get back into camp, you can eat with them." I watched as an army of ghost-like men dragged themselves out of the forests and slowly lowered themselves onto benches in front of long tables. A bowl of rice soup and beans was set in front of them. They ate in complete silence. I took my bowl and went out side. I felt ashamed to see my fellow countrymen treated this way. My way of avoiding a life like theirs was not honorable, but certainly there was no honor in being a slave. Within one short year my life had been twisted out of recognition. From a spoiled grandson to an idealistic patriot, to a slave, and now I had become a flunky to a corrupt politician. I was stuck and could not get out.

My life in Chegdomyn was not uninteresting. It demanded that I meet and relate to variety of different people, and it required a good bit of ingenuity to keep everyone supplied and happy. Each day I was on the road carrying cargo from one camp to the other. After a few months, I became friends with the camp guards and the police who manned the checkpoints on all the roads. They all expected, and received, some "gift" each time I went by. With several of them I developed little businesses on the side that the commandant was not aware of.

A guard at Camp #6, for example, approached me one evening after supper. We were sitting outside enjoying a cigarette. He took a puff and rather nonchalantly said, "I have a proposition for you. We can earn a little bit and do a good deed at the same time."

"I'm busy as it is. I don't need any more business. I already have more rubles than I know what to do with. I'm trying to figure out how I am going to transfer what I got into Korean won so that I can take it home, when I go."

The guard laughed. "You may be one of the lucky ones who will make it back home, but there is no way they will allow you to take a big bundle of money. You'll need to have much more than you have now to pay off the big guys between you and home."

He was right, but I'd do anything to get back home. If I needed more bribe money, I'd make more. "What do you have in mind?

"Last night a buddy and I had a prostitute. Not far from here there is a house with a couple dozen women. Here's the proposition. The loggers have been here for months and years without a woman. They will pay most anything they have, or can get, to spend a few minutes with a woman. We cannot take the men into the city, but we can bring the women to the men. That's where you come in. You drive the ladies out here. Park the truck in the repair shop. No one will be around at night. We can put maybe ten women in the bed of the truck. We allow ten men at a time to get in with them for fifteen-twenty minutes. In just a couple hours, two or three nights a week, we could clean up."

"How could you pay the girls? The men have no money."

"They will sell their lives and indenture themselves forever for just twenty minutes. I know."

That was one kind of business that I was never very proud of, but it was amazing how the most wretched of men will debauch themselves even further for just fifteen minutes of sex. It worked just as the guard said it would. Where they got the money I never figured out, but they came; they handed us their coins; spent a few minutes in the truck and then were gone. Within a month they were back, coin in hand. Slowly I became wealthy.

So my life went. In three years I piled up a lot of money. With the commandant's help I even opened up an account in a Russian bank, and then without his knowledge I made a small deal with one of the bank clerks and opened up a second account where I kept most of my money.

I had never been much aware of my conscience. I took things as they came without trying to figure the good or bad of it all. Since I usually had the advantage in any dispute and lived well it did not occur to me that I might have a conscience. Here in the lumber camps, for the first time my soul was made heavy by all the evil that I had become a part of. I actually grieved for the pain I had inflicted on my fellow Koreans—but in a lot of ways I had helped them too. In any case, it would not be long now before I would make my move to get back home.

CATASTROPHE

It was on a Saturday night, or rather early on a Sunday morning. I had just gotten back from a hard day's journey. As I pulled into the camp gate, I was unexpectedly met by Chun Ho Bin, the orderly for the commandant. He and I had done some business and had become good friends. He jumped up on to the running board and put his head through the open window.

"Whatever you do, do not go into the commandant's office. They are after you. They are going to arrest you for treason."

"Who is after me? What do you mean treason? If I am arrested for the "business" we are in, the commandant will be involved too. Why would he arrest me?"

"No! No! It has nothing to do with the business. The enemies of your grandfather, Oh Kap Soo, have come up with evidence that he had a cousin who was a general in the South Korean Army, and did not report it to the authorities. Your father has already been arrested. Your mother and sister are to be exiled to Hamkyung Pukdo Province in the far north. If you are caught, you too will be tried for treason."

I could not breathe. "My father? My grandfather? Preposterous! Who told you such lies?"

"I saw the communiqué myself. The Great Leader is dead. The Party is in turmoil. Those who were out of power are seeking revenge against those who were closest to The Great Leader. Your family is among those who are being purged. But I cannot stand here and argue with you. If I get caught, my neck can be broken too. Take the truck. Drive to Camp #5. A railroad spur from there connects with the Trans-Siberian Railroad. Once you get there you can go any direction you wish. Go! Get out of here!" He jumped down from the truck and disappeared into the night.

A few hours later I approached Camp #5. I had been there many times. First I hid the truck in a thicket where it would be hard to find. Then I found the railroad tracks. Flat cars stacked high with logs were standing on a sidetrack waiting to go west. I squirreled myself in under some of the large tree trunks and waited. After a short while, an engine backed into the sidetrack and coupled with the flat cars. The train moved with starts and bumps as it slowly picked up steam. Within a few hours we arrived at the juncture with the Trans-Siberian Railroad.

I lay still and waited. Except for the usual sounds coming from a railroad transfer center all was quiet. I squeezed myself out from under the logs and crawled to a nearby signal shack. I hid in its shadow till I could locate the lines that were handling freight. Four tracks over from where I stood a work crew was busily loading freight in to box cars. I watched, then crept closer. The job was just about complete. Most of the work crew moved off down the track to their next job. "Close her up, boys!" came the order from the foreman. In the instant before the order was completed I hurled myself from out of the shack's shadow through the door into the blackness of the car. The door banged shut, locked from the outside. I was on my way . . . somewhere.

Chapter 3

BROTHERS

ROSTOV

From his refuge behind two crates of machinery in the corner
of the boxcar, Yun Song Nam watched the workers load and
unload their cargo. He heard their grunts and groans as they
lifted the heavy loads. Then the order went out: "Close them
up! We're moving out!" The workers jumped out of the car. A
minute, perhaps two, elapsed before the doors were closed, but
in that instant he saw a man throw himself through the door,
into the boxcar. Apparently no one saw him. The door was
closed. The outside lock was sealed shut.

Yun Song Nam could not see the other man's face, but heard
his long sigh of relief as he collapsed to the floor. Just at that
time, however, Yun's leg cramped and he had to move it. The
man heard him, stiffened and dove into a hiding place.

Both men knew the other was there, but neither dared to
speak. Both looked around for a weapon, but found none. The
boxcar was in darkness except for slivers of light that came
through the car's rotted sideboards. Each man dug deeper in
his hole to keep from throwing a shadow that the other could
locate. After several hours, the fear began to subside and curi-
osity began to take its place.

In the best Russian he could muster, Oh Ki Sop finally
said, "I do no want to fight. Let us help each other."

The response came back: "I no speak Russian. You not
Russian I think. You have accent. Who are you?"

"I am Korean."

Yun Song Nam practically jumped out of his hole. He was so glad to hear that the other person was a fellow countryman, he abandoned all caution and moved toward the voice. In Korean he cried out, "I too am Korean. We are comrades."

These words brought Oh Ki Sop out of hiding. The two men met in the middle of the boxcar. Awkwardly at first they peered at each other in the shadows. Then they sat down and began to talk. Over the next several hours each unfolded his story to the other.

All of a sudden the train began to slow down. The men were jolted back to the reality of their situation. Where were they? Which direction were they heading? South meant China and probable prison. North meant Siberian slave camps. East would take them to Vladivostok and police. They had to go west. Their car was transferred to a sideline and let sit. There was nothing they could do. For two days the train sat still. Yun and Oh were beginning to get desperate for food and water. Then on the third night they heard something that gave them hope. Two men were outside their car speaking Korean. They were checking the seals and destinations of the trains. Yun and Oh waited until the two men came close then Yun whispered through an opening: "Honorable sir, please save us!"

The Korean workers came closer. "Who are you? What are you doing in there?"

"We are two men who are fleeing from the Russian police. We are innocent of any crime, but they are trying to arrest us. We have not eaten in three days. Please save us."

"We will let you out, but come out one at a time with your hands in the air. We have weapons. No tricks."

The door was slid open. Yun and Oh slowly climbed out with their hands in the air.

"Is there water? Food? Anything. I have some money. I will pay." Pleaded Oh as soon as his feet touched the ground.

One of the railroad men handed them a jug of water. " Who

are you? Where are you going? Speak quickly. We do not have much time."

Yun and Oh drank deep of the water retching part of it back up.

"We have escaped from the forced labor camps in eastern Siberia," Oh explained using his own experience to cover both men. If we are caught, we will be sent back or killed. Please, you must help us."

"What do you want us to do? Speak quickly. If we get caught with you, we could lose our jobs or worse. What do you want?"

"We need to go west, as far away as possible from Siberia. Help us get on a boxcar headed west. And food . . . Can you give us some food?"

The two railroad men looked at each other. One nodded his head and the other one disappeared behind the train.

"You are in luck. The train on the third track over is on its way to Rostov on the Don, near the Black Sea. It will take at least fifteen days. The car will be sealed. So you will not be able to get out until you arrive at Rostov. By friend is bringing you some food and water. Hurry now."

We got into the boxcar without incident. Soon after, the second railroad man reappeared. He carried a bag of food and two jars of water. As he reached them up to us, he advised, "Eat and drink sparingly. This will have to last you the whole way."

Before the door closed on their new entombment, Yun bowed to the two workers and thanked them for their kindness. "Excuse me for asking, but are you by chance Christians?"

"Yes, why do you ask? "

"In the last several years I have received much help from that group. Do you know whether there are Christians in Rostov?"

"I do not know for sure, but there are Koreans most everywhere, and where there are Koreans there is likely to be a church. Do this. When you arrive at Rostov, keep your ears open. You are likely to hear some one speaking Korean. Many Koreans work on the railroad, most in maintenance crews like us. Now go. May the Lord God give you peace and health."

The last fifteen days of the journey were luxurious compared to the first ten. They took care to ration out their water and food; they slept a lot and spent hour upon hour comparing their experiences at home and in Siberia. Oh Ki Sop made no mention of his famous grandfather and left off most of the stories about "businesses" he had run on the side with the security guards, and said nothing about the use of the prostitutes. Yun Song Nam's life had been typical of most village people. It was only that one moment of anger that changed his fate. Even so, he was still a communist and would gladly return home, if given a chance. He told Oh about Reverend Lee and his pilgrimage from Korea, to United States, to Khabarovsk, and how he had been so cruelly murdered.

As they confided in each other they began to take on traditional Korean, family patterns of speech. Yun, being the older, became "older brother" and Oh was now referred to by Yun as "little brother."

The prediction of the two Korean railroad workers was on target. On the sixteenth morning the train came to a halt. Glimpses of the outside told them they were in the railroad yards of a large city. The weather was warm and bright. They lay in the yards for two days before the seal on the car was finally broken and the doors pushed open. The workers who were to unload the car, however, still were busy in the car behind them. This gave Yun and Oh time to climb down from the car without being detected. Slowly they walked across the tracks. No one seemed to mind or pay any attention to them. They kept walking till they entered the main terminal, a large building that looked like a castle. Inside it was neat and clean. Sculptures of Russian heroes graced the staircases. Painted murals decorated the walls. To the two refugees it indeed looked more like a castle than a train station.

Thousands of people crowded the station rushing hurriedly

to their destinations. Yun and Oh were at first carried along with the busy swarm of people, but after a while, Oh began to recognize some of the Russian signs: restaurant, water closet, baggage. "Baggage" is what they wanted. After a couple of misses, they finally found themselves in a wide open area where bags were coming and going on conveyer belts and bags by the hundred were piled up against the wall.

They settled down to watch. At first it seemed quite haphazard. Who was carrying whose bags? There was no way of knowing. People from all the nations of the world were there. All colors, shapes and sizes. The languages were all garbled. How would they ever pick out a Korean carrying other peoples' cargo?

As it grew late, the crowd began to thin out. After midnight only a few remained. A group of very shabby looking men gathered at one end of the building. It looked like they were going to settle down and even sleep there for the night. A few policemen pranced back and forth seemingly to keep watch over this colony of rags. Now and then they also cast a look of suspicion towards Yun and Oh.

Then all of a sudden a noise of many people talking rang throughout the grand hall. It was the sound that Yun and Oh had been waiting for. The loud clamor of many voices was that of a new work crew coming on duty. They were speaking Korean. The women among them began the job of scrubbing and waxing the floors. The men began to move the bags into an interior room apparently for safekeeping.

Now was their chance. Yun sidled up to a fellow carrying a bag. "Brother, I need help. I have come a long distance. I have money. Can you help me?

The porter recognized immediately that Yun was a foreigner. His Korean sounded too different. "What help do you need? He asked quietly not slowing down his pace.

"My friend and I need a place to stay for a few days. Like you, we are Korean. We are refugees from Siberia."

"Go back to your place. Wait. When you see us leave, follow. Outside we will stand in a group to say good night to each other. Join us. I will meet you there."

Yun and Oh watched the working people do their job. After a few hours, both men fell a sleep. Yun was awakened by the absence of noise. The workers had finished and were half way out of the terminal. The two men dashed to the exit just in time to see them go through the formalities of bowing and saying good night. Without a word they picked out the man that Yun had talked to and joined him and five friends as they walked down the broad avenue.

A few turns off the avenue brought them to a small alley from which a loud clamorous noise arose. Oh was apprehensive. "What is going on? Are we walking into some kind of fight? Where are these guys taking us?"

"You won't believe it, but we are on our way to a prayer meeting," Yun predicted. "Christians seem to do it every where, every morning at sun up. The shouts are prayers to *Hannanim*. It's harmless. Come along."

Inside the small building with a cross on it, a dozen or so people lay prostrate on the floor wrestling noisily with their God. Yun and Oh lay quietly trying to understand the petitions that were flying upward. After prayers, a woman gave a short talk about service to others. They sang a song from the songbooks that everyone carried.

The woman who had given the sermon came over to the two strangers. "You came along with the railroad friends? You are welcome. If you will come with me, we will eat breakfast and talk."

Rostov turned out to be the haven that Oh and Yun both needed. It was big and multi-racial. The police ignored them. Through the good offices of the churchwoman, they both were employed, though illegally, in a small factory run by a Korean-Russian. The factory made industrial ball bearings. One section made a "specialty bearing" out of "iron birch" from Siberia. Ironically they were now earning their livelihood from trees felled by the same slave labor in which, until recently, Oh Ki Sop had been involved. It was hard work, ten hours a day, six days a week. Wages were barely enough to live on, but within a year both the men had become skilled workers in the plant and outside of work they became accepted members of the Korean community.

But then it happened. Oh Ki Sop fell in love. She was a Russian girl, named Tatyana, who worked at the shop canteen. Her eyes were a lucid green, almond shaped suggesting oriental ancestry. Her smile was broad and generous. Oh first met her when he went to get coffee for his boss. After that, he made sure his daily path took him past the canteen. Each time he smiled and waved at her. She always returned the greetings.

One Saturday evening he, along with friends from the plant, went to a disco. The music was loud. The noise even louder. Thick tobacco smoke substituted for air. Bodies, swaying with the music, were jammed against one another. Oh Ki Sop was absorbed into the flow. A woman's hand caught hold of his. He turned. It was Tatyana. Her eyes took him captive. They embraced. Oh had never danced before, but that night he danced until daybreak. When it was over, he took Tatyana's hand and walked her home to the apartment where she and her mother lived. At first they were quiet enjoying the touch of each other's hand.

She broke the silence. "Where did you come from? I have worked at the company canteen for two years, but have not seen you until recently. Where is your home?"

At first Oh Ki Sop tried to reveal only bits and pieces of his background, but gradually the whole story came out. They sat on the outside steps of her apartment as he finished his talking. The sun had already come up, but they had no thought of parting. "Now tell me about you. Are you from Rostov? Have you and your mother always lived together?"

"My father was a Tartar. That accounts for the shape and

color of my eyes. My mother is Russian. My grandfather and his family lived on Tartar ancestral ground not far from here in the Crimea. But Stalin accused us of helping the Germans in the war and deported all the Tartars to Kazakstan. Recently the courts have reversed Stalin's actions, but now it is too late. The Ukrainians control the land of our ancestors and they refuse to return it to us.

"I was born in Kazakstan, but several years ago my father moved us back here hoping that some time in the future we might be able to regain our land. Unfortunately, he died just a few months after we arrived here. My Mother and I have lived together in this apartment ever since."

When she spoke of her father's death, Tatyana wept silently. Ki Sop kissed her gently on the forehead.

After that, every Saturday night they met at the disco. Just before dawn, they would leave off dancing and stroll along the path looking over the great Don River. One Sunday morning they walked up *Budyonnosky Prospkt* and entered Gorky Park. There under a large weeping willow tree they made love for the first time. The tree itself seemed to shake as they surrendered to each other. "Now we are husband and wife. Tatyana, marry me?" Tatyana's immediate response was, "Yes. Yes. I will love to be your wife." Happily they joined hands and started towards her apartment.

As they walked out of the park, towards *Pushkinsky Bulvar,* they passed beneath a streetlight. Two drunks were slouched over a bench. As Oh and Tatyana passed by, one of them looked up and saw the Russian woman and the oriental man. "Dirty whore!" He hissed at Tatyana. Oh acted with quick instinct. He grabbed the man by the throat and rammed his fist into his face. They fell heavily back over the bench.

The other fellow ran away screaming, "Murder! Murder!"

Tatyana pulled on Oh's shirt yelling, "Run! Run quickly. The police! Go! Go!"

But Oh did not hear her. In his fury he jumped on the fallen drunk and began to beat him. The police dragged him off. Oh Ki Sop was taken to the local jail and two days later went to trial.

"Mr. Oh, you are in our country illegally. You have no passport, no visa, and no identification. Therefore you shall be deported to the country of origin, namely the Democratic Peoples' Republic of Korea. Until then you . . ."

Tatyana's scream interrupted the judge's sentence. " No! No! You mustn't. You can't. He is my husband. Your honor, please have mercy. He is my husband."

Tatyana's plea was heard. "If you stand by him as his wife and get his papers regularized, then I will withhold the deportation judgment for a period. In the mean time he will spend six months in jail for assault and battery.

During the second month of his incarceration Oh was taken to a room where, he was told, a visitor was awaiting him. He expected Tatyana or younger brother Yun, but it was neither. A well-dressed middle-aged Korean man stood as he came in.

"You are Oh Ki Sop?

"And who are you?

"I am Song Moo Hyun. I come from the consulate of the Peoples' Republic of Korea. We have heard of your case, and feel it unjust for a North Korean citizen to be treated as you have. Your defense of your sweetheart is laudable. You should not have been arrested for beating that skinhead. We are negotiating with the court to have you released in a few days."

"But why are you doing this for me?" Suspicion ran up and down Oh's spine. 'They obviously know who I am. They know I escaped from the lumber camp. What are they up to? I must be careful.'

"An insult to any of our countrymen is an insult to the motherland and to The Dear Leader. We cannot just stand by. Tomorrow or the next day they will ask you to sign a paper that says you regret the incident, and you have great respect for Russia and its people. Can you do that?"

"I am grateful for your assistance. Yes, I can sign a statement like that."

"Good. Then I will return in a few days and get you out of here."

Two days later, true to his promise, the consulate representative reappeared. "All has gone well. We will now go to the warden's office where he will ask you to sign a statement like the one I told you about."

Oh Ki Sop received clearance from the warden and the two men walked out of the prison together. "Be careful," Oh told himself. "There is a trick somewhere." But then his attention was captured by Tatyana. She was standing at the gate with Yun. She ran to him. They embraced. Tatyana cried, "My husband, my husband!" Oh was holding back the tears so hard he could make no sound at all. They held hands and walked down the path away from the prison. A car was waiting beside the street, but they were oblivious to anything beyond themselves. The man from the consulate walked in front and opened the car door. Yun held back to allow Oh and Tatyana to be alone. Then he saw the big man come from behind the vehicle.

"Young brother, quick run. Treachery!'

But it was too late. Oh Ki Sop was so caught up with his love that he never saw the blow that knocked him unconscious. The big man heaved Oh into the back seat, knocked Tatyana to the ground, and casually got in the back seat along with Oh Ki Sop. The car sped away.

CHAPTER 4

MOSCOW

For two weeks I hid in the back streets and slums of Rostov. I dared not go back to my room or to the church. I begged food and slept in garbage dumps. I could not forgive myself, for being so dumb. How could I have ever allowed Ki Sop to trust those guys? Why hadn't I been closer to help fend off the attacker? My conscience would not relent in its condemnation.

Finally, on a Monday morning at sunrise I found myself walking down the alley toward the church. Already I could hear the loud shouts of wrestling with *Hannanim.* I entered. As I prostrated myself, my body began to shake horribly and I cried like a small child. "Forgive me! Forgive me! Oh God, Save my brother Oh Ki Sop. Let him live." The prayer sprung from me spontaneously and would not stop.

After a while, I felt a hand upon my shoulder. "The service is over. Come with me."

I looked up. It was the woman, Kim Sun Wha, who led the morning services. I meekly followed her, saying nothing. We went to her home. Five or six others were gathered. After breakfast, one of the men began the discussion. "Brother Yun, we think that it will be safer for you to leave Rostov. You have been a good person to have among us and we would like you to stay, but . . . ."

Another man broke in. "North Korean agents have been everywhere since the kidnapping of your friend Oh. They want you since you are the only witness to the event. The woman, Tatyana, they disregard, but your rooms have been under constant surveillance. You have not gone back there have you?"

"No. But all I have is there. I've been able to save a little money. It's there. Where can I go? What can I do? Must I always run from one unknown land to another? Would that I had not fled my homeland!"

"Brother, in days past many of us here have suffered in the way you now suffer. We know how deep your anguish is, but you must not give up. Your life must go on. You do not yet know what future *Hannanim* has for you. We have gathered some money for you to travel to Moscow. It is not a nice place for foreigners, but you will have less chance of being detected by North Korean agents. When you get to Moscow seek out Rev. Whang Jin Ho. Here is his address. He will help you." As he said these words, he handed me an envelope filled with Russian money.

I took it and thanked them for their kindness. The next morning before I left for the train station, one of the men showed me how to divide the money up for safety sakes. "Keep a little change and small bills in your pocket and wallet. Put some larger bills under the insole of your shoes, tape some around your stomach and some around the inside of your thigh," and with a laugh he added, "Stick a few bills right inside your underwear."

They handed me a ticket and I was on my way via third class coach to Moscow.

The trip of three days was uneventful, but as soon as I disembarked I was in trouble. The station consisted of two unpretentious brick buildings. Two or three warehouses stood close by. It was bedlam. Thousands of people were pushing and shoving in no observable pattern. I wanted to find the trolley that I was told ran on the south side of the station, but my directions were mixed up. It was not where I expected. The crowds swept me one way and then another. Finally I broke out to the periphery and began a new search. Several times I walked around that station house before I finally found what I was looking for. But unfortunately my meandering had caught the attention of a gang of young thugs. Four of them surrounded me and forced me to walk behind one of the warehouses. They called me a "Chink" and took all the money I had in my wallet and pockets. To increase their degree of pleasure a bit more they beat and kicked me till I was a bloody mess.

After my head cleared, I stood up and stumbled toward the trolley line. I got on number 25, and after a dozen stops, got off. The landscape was the same in all directions: dozens and dozens of high-rise apartments. I did not count, but each one must have been fifteen or twenty floors or more. This time my directions were true. I cut behind a building that had shattered windows on the first floor, and there nearly hidden among the high-risers was a one-story building, with a little park around it. It was a church. My heart leaped up when I saw the sign written in Korean.

Reverend Whang Jin Ho was a young man probably no more than thirty or thirty-five. He had come to Moscow as a missionary five years previously. Not only did he pastor a church mainly for Koreans living in Moscow, he also ran several welfare and education programs for poor Russians. He was of medium height, with strong muscular arms and shoulders. I found out later that he was a Taek Won Do black belt. He wore dark horned-rimmed glasses on a round expressionless face. We bowed to each other in old time Korean fashion and then shook hands.

"I see you have already met some of our local boys," he said as he looked over my bruised face and torn clothes. "*Ajumoni* (auntie)," he called as he opened the door to an adjacent room, "We need your help. Clean this brother's face and see if you can get him a new jacket."

The *ajumoni*, a woman of fifty or so, came with a first aid kit. She washed my cuts and put salve on my several bruises. After that, she brought me a coat.

"Now," she announced, "it is time to eat. For the noon meal we all eat together and you are welcome to share with us." Twenty-five or so people were gathered in the dining room.

Most of them, I learned later, performed some volunteer function either in the church or in the neighborhood.

After we finished eating, once more I had to sit down with a stranger and plot my future. Before we could get to the future, however, we had to clear the past. Reverend Whang asked me to tell him my story. I told him everything in detail, left nothing out.

After I finished, the reverend took the lead. I had been this way so often I could almost predict what he was going to say. "Moscow is not a friendly place for Asians to live, as you have already found out. You are apt to be assaulted by gangsters, police, local bureaucrats and even ordinary citizens. Since you do not have identification papers and no legal status in the country, you will not be able to find a job or rent a room. The Russians do not want us here."

"But how will I live if there is no job and no room? I should have stayed back in Rostov."

"Don't be too depressed. There are some things that can be done. First, there is a compatriot of yours from North Korea who occupies an apartment not far from here. It is not legal but many extra-legal things happen these days. He would be glad to have a roommate. Second, we can get you a job with some one who hires illegal laborers. The pay will be miserable and the work hard, but it is doable. Third, you can join us for the mid-day meal until you get settled in. And, of course, you will be welcome to come to all the meetings we have here at the church. Several refugees from North Korea do come. And fourth, I will try to get you registered with the United Nation's High Commission on Refugees. Registration may give you a little protection from police, and might even give you a chance to resettle to United States, Canada or South Korea."

All of this was too much for me to take in. I did not know what to say. My heart was so heavy I thought I would never lift up my head up again. I felt a great urge to cry, to wail: "This is me, Yun Song Nam. Am I a dog that everyone should kick? I hate Russia. I hate life. I loathe myself! Why? Why?" I choked down my emotions and sat in silence.

Pastor Whang waited for me. He had seen others go through the same kind of torment.

"How do I find the apartment? How do I locate a job?" I spoke, and felt, like a dead man. I had no options. I was a slave.

"Your apartment mate is Lee Ho Chong. He will be here this evening. He will also help you find work. We have a room here where you can lay down and rest a bit. Why don't you do that? When Mr. Lee comes, I will come to wake you up."

I did as I was told. Mr. Lee came. I went home with him. He found me work with a cleaning crew at one of the high-rise apartment complexes. Maintenance work on these buildings had been neglected for years. Some of the walls were beginning to crumble. Halls and stairwells were cluttered; elevators didn't work and electric lights mal-functioned. It looked like Moscow was disintegrating before our eyes. The work was not too strenuous. I was used to hard labor, and cleaning up the clutter took no particular skill. Only the foreman made the job miserable. He constantly taunted me, called me "chink" and gave me the dirtiest jobs. Why was I working at all? Just to maintain a senseless, dead-end life. It was hardly worth the effort.

A year, or more, went by. I worked. I slept. I learned to bribe the police so that they would allow me to walk the streets. When I got really hungry, I'd take a day off and go to the church for lunch.

One day a summons came from Reverend Whang. He handed me a card with the words United Nations High Commission on Refugees stamped at the top. In Russian and English it said I was a bona fide refugee under the protection of the UN.

"This may give you a little protection on the street, and it is the first step in emigrating to another country. You remember, I told you about that when you first came?"

"Yes, I remember, but I have heard rumors that the United States and Canada no longer take refugees. Is that correct?"

"Yes, they have withdrawn from the program."

"Then South Korea is the only place that will accept me?"

"Yes. It will be hard, but perhaps easier than here, and you will be close to your home—land if unification ever comes about."

"But how could I ever go over to the enemy of my motherland? Already I hate myself for the things I have done over the last ten years. How could I live if in addition to all that I became a traitor?"

"I cannot answer for your soul, but the sins you have committed were not from evil intent. They can be forgiven. You have heard me and others preach. You know if you confess your sins before *Hannanim*, he will forgive you. But as far as going to South Korea is concerned, that is something you will have to wrestle through. I will be here if you need me."

I put the UN document in my wallet and started back towards my apartment. I was in deep thought measuring the idea of immigrating to South Korea. My insides revolted from the idea, but my reason told me it could be no worse than here. I would be closer to my family; I would know the language; but still, going there would be like denying my family and the ideals I was brought up with. Back and forth my brain argued with itself.

I was returned to consciousness by a rough hand on my shoulder. "You! What are you doing here and where are you going? Show me your identification." It was a policeman. I had wandered out of the district where I usually walked and was facing a cop I had never seen before. I handed him my newly acquired UN identification card. He glanced at it, tore it in two and threw it on the ground. "The UN is not boss around here. I am. What else do you have in that wallet? He emptied the content on the ground, stole the few rubles I had in there and then beat me around the legs and hips with his nightstick. "Next time you had better have more than this!" I lay on the ground wondering what it would be like to be dead. How could I make myself dead? Once again my brain was in paralysis. Then it became quite clear to me that I did not want to be dead. I wanted to be alive, and somehow get back home.

Though the policeman had humiliated me, stolen my money, and beat me, he had also done me a service. It was now clear that I must leave Russia. My only option was South Korea. I picked up the pieces of my UN card, put them in my pocket and returned to Reverend Whang.

" I am very sorry that things like this happen," sympathized Reverend Whang, "but these days there is no authority, no credible government on the streets. It is everyone against everyone. I think your decision to go to South Korea is wise. We can visit the embassy tomorrow and begin the process. It will take a year or more. South Korea will not be easy for you to adjust to, but you can start a new, permanent life. Who knows what God may still have in store for you?"

That really got under my skin. With irritation in my voice, I replied,

"From Siberia to Rostov to Moscow you followers of *Hannanim* have been telling me that. Yet each stage of my life gets worse and worse. I feel like He is scheming against me, not for me. And what about poor Reverend Lee and his wife back in Khabarovsk? When the chips were down *Hannanim* gave them no protection."

The pastor listened to my disbelief. " It is true. It is true. Often we think we have been deserted. Yet we believe that at the heart of life is a God who wants us to love and be love for each other. Evil spoils many lives, but Jesus has taught us that the only meaning to life is to praise God and be kind and just to one another. Even though we live in the midst of evil, yet there is the conviction that the best life is one of love and faith that good will prevail. I do not know why much suffering has come to you, but you must admit that at each step since you left home, you have also received unexpected help from people you never knew before. Often they were followers of Jesus who were just going about their day by day life doing good for others as best they could."

The Reverend spoke with kindness and sympathy. His words made me realize what I already knew . . . the life of love is the best one. That was the way I was brought up. As a child, I had learned how to take care of others and work for the benefit of everyone. As a father, as a communist, I tried to teach those same values to my children. I said no more right then, but one point had been clarified: the ideals held by the Christians and by the communists had a good bit in common. Despite all the tragedies of my life, I could still hold on to hope rather than be dead in despair.

The process did indeed take more than a year. Belligerent South Korean agents made me justify my actions at every step since leaving North Korea. I filled in legal papers, and wrote statements about political belief. For thirteen months after the process started I heard nothing. Then the South Korean embassy notified Reverend Whang, as my sponsor, that I had been accepted as an immigrant. The day before I left Whang sent word through my roommate that I should come to the church.

To my consternation he greeted me with these words: "Your life has been a most unusual one. You may not realize it, but your story is often told among other Koreans here in Moscow. Ironic, but your suffering has served as an encouragement to others. Thanks for being with us."

That was beyond my understanding so I said nothing in reply, but it did give me an opportunity to say something that had been on my mind for a while. "Pastor, I am grateful to you and to the other Jesus people who have helped me. I would like to join you. Could I be baptized?"

This took him by surprise. Now it was his turn to be speechless. "I would be honored to baptize you, but let me make a suggestion. I am going to give you a letter of introduction to my brother who is also a pastor. He lives in Seoul. Go to him. Receive instruction in what being a Christian means and then if you like, let him baptize you there. It will be a good entrance into your new life. Who knows what God has in store for you?"

CHAPTER 5

IMMIGRANT IN SOUTH KOREA

We four "escapees," as we were called, arrived in Seoul on March 22, 1995. We did not know there were four of us until we arrived and were led to a waiting room reserved just for us. They had seated us separately on the plane. A male flight attendant had seen to our needs and had guided us to the right waiting room. I knew none of the other three and they did not seem to know each other. Probably we were selected from different parts of the Russian empire. We exchanged no words of greetings, but our eyes measured one another wondering why the other guy was here.

We were taken from the waiting room, put into to a small bus-like vehicle and driven away. There was no conversation. It was evening. The sun was beginning to set. Large high-rise apartments and skyscrapers outlined the horizon. The noise of the city grew into a clamor. Not even Moscow could compare with the noise of Seoul. A foul smell and taste began to invade my nose and taste buds. I learned later on that the smell and taste came from air pollution of the city.

The streets were so crowded with vehicles we drove slowly, often bumper to bumper. After an hour or so, we entered through a large gate into a secluded compound part way up a mountain.

Inside one of the buildings we received our first instructions. Each of us was assigned to a separate room. Supper would be served in an hour or two. That evening we were to rest. In the morning we would begin our orientation to the world of "free Korea."

For the next six months we lived on that compound. In the

morning we underwent intense interrogation. They called it a "debriefing." They already knew my entire story. I had withheld nothing, but yet they insisted that I go over it again and again. They kept asking questions about motives. Why had I acted in such and such a way? What was behind my behavior? But every response I made seemed to be unacceptable. To say that I had lost my temper and hit Pak with a tree limb was followed by a further question-accusation: "What made you lose your temper?" To explain that I attacked the old Chinese fellow in order to get his money and clothes was inadequate. "What led you to such barbaric action?" I would go back and try to explain what had happened. They would not accept my words. After several weeks of this kind of befuddlement, it began to dawn on me what they were after. They wanted me to plead that it was the communist system that caused me to hit Pak, leave my home, abandon my family and flee from one place to another. Confessing that communism was the evil behind my troubles would, they thought, set me free psychologically to enter into the new world of south Korean democracy.

That was ridiculous. North Korean communism had always been good to my family and me. I loved its idealism and its intent to build a just society. I did not hit Pak because of revolt against the system, but purely revolt against him. Sure I had to flee, but that was because a few guys like Pak were abusing the system. To say such things out loud or to defend my homeland would only put me in conflict with those who now held sway over me so gradually I began to say what they wanted and toward the end of our stay at that compound, I wrote a statement saying that I was grateful to now be "a free man in a free society." A few days later my statement was broadcast by the government's radio station as an example of how superior the south was to the north.

In the afternoons during the period of our orientation we had group meetings. The four of us, with the help of two "facilitators," went about the task of criticizing each other. That was a sorry mess. Each of us carried heavy loads of guilt for coming over to the "enemy," and we were suspicious of the others' motives, condemning others for the very act that we ourselves had taken. We spent many an hour listening to each other's stories, trying to catch each other up in inconsistencies, while the facilitators manipulated the process toward accusations against North Korea and its government. The only thing really achieved was to intensify the suspicion that the four of us held for each other.

In the evenings we were given lectures and shown movies about the differences between North and South. These actually were helpful in giving us some understanding of the society into which we were about to enter.

Towards the end of the orientation we were told that from here on it was our responsibility to integrate ourselves into South Korean society. The government would help us in several ways. We would be given a stipend to live on for three or four months. During that time a counselor would help us to find a room to stay in and a job to work at. After that we were on our own.

It was not easy. I was assigned a job with a construction crew. The first day on the job I was introduced to my fellow workers as a "commie." That was a stigma that I could never completely overcome. Even when I became friends with some of the men, there were others who persisted in calling me "red." Differences in my language and theirs produced derisive laughter. The hardest, most menial jobs, of course, were given to me. The pay, however, was good. My wants were few. I saved most of what I was paid.

Then one day after work, I got a break. A man who did not work at our construction site came up to me. " I'm Kang Hee Churl, business manager for our local union. You are going to join the union aren't you?"

"Union? What union are you speaking of?"

Kang looked bewildered. He must have thought I was trying to be a wise guy, but that was not the case. I honestly did not know exactly what he was referring to.

"The labor union, of course. What other union is there? Construction workers are joined together in the "Construction Workers' Labor Union. We want you to join too."

I was more than a bit confused. We had labor unions at home, in the North, but everyone was automatically a member. We did not choose to join or not join. "What does a union do? It's okay if I don't join? I don't exactly know what you are talking about."

"Tell you what," Kang rejoined. "Let's go have a drink and I'll explain things to you."

This was the first offer of kindness. We walked across the road and entered a little run-down shack. Inside it was dark, unbelievably loud and emitted a stench of old, old booze. We did not have such places in the village where I lived. Men would drink, but usually by themselves or in small groups around the fringe of the commune. We sat down. Kang ordered us two glasses of Korean beer, milky white, sweet liquor with low alcohol content.

"In the South we do things differently from the way you do up north," Kang began. "Down here workers have a right to organize together and then negotiate with the employer about wages and working conditions. You understand that?"

No, I did not understand that. Never heard of it. "You will have to go slow. Doesn't the Labor Party take care of things like that? Are you from the Labor Party?"

"Labor Party? I am not sure what you mean."

"In our country there is one political party that runs the government. It is called the Labor Party. Under the Party's direction there is an organization of workers. The Party takes care of setting wages and work conditions. It is the union's job to increase production. You do have a Labor Party, don't you?"

Kang laughed. "Let's have another drink. I see where this will take a long time." This time he ordered *soju*. The first sip made my head spin. I was not used to drinking hard stuff. Kang kept pouring and talking, but after the second small glass, I heard only noise. I must have passed out. Not sure how I got home.

The next morning the attitude of my fellow workers seemed to have changed. Several of them smiled and said good morning. Others ribbed me, but in a good-natured way. "Yun, how do you like soju?" "Let's go out drinking tonight, comrade." "Hey Yun, are you going to join the union?"

I joined the union. And on payday did go to the wine house with the other workers, but I was careful to restrict my intake to beer and only one small soju. Though I became friends with several fellows, including Kang Hee Churl, I knew I always had to be in control. Frank criticism of the South, or praise for the North, I sensed, would not be received very well. My brief experience of living in Seoul had led me to see capitalism as inefficient and unnecessarily complicated. The surplus of things in the market made everyone dissatisfied with everything. Consumers wandered from place to place looking for what they called "the best buy." And I had seen the vast extremes between the rich and the poor. We had nothing like it in the North. But these observations, I felt, were best kept to my self.

After I had been in Korea for about a year, I had another unexpected visitor. It was Reverend Whang Jin Mo, the brother of Rev. Whang in Moscow. He looked like a twin. The same broad, muscular body and round pleasant face that held up thick, brown-rimmed spectacles.

"I have been looking for you for some time," he said. "My brother sent me a letter from Moscow telling me about you. The authorities, however, would give me no information. Only yesterday did they consent to give me your address. How long have you been here? What are you doing?"

"I have been here for almost a year. After our re-education period, I was given a job with a construction crew. That's what I do each day. Not much else."

"Do you like it? Have you made any friends?"

I hesitated to respond to that. I did not want to come across as a complainer, but finally I told him the truth. "The work pays well, but it is very hard. My body aches through and through. Friends? Yes, I have a few friends, but many still see me as a "commie.""

My words were not what the pastor had hoped for. "I am sorry. I apologize for my countrymen. They should not act that way."

"No need to apologize. That's the way it is and recently it has lightened up."

We sat silent for a while. Then he spoke again. "We would like you to come to our church on Sunday morning. Will you come?"

"I will come. Your brother and other Christians have shown me much kindness. I will come, but please do not make a spectacle of me. Don't show me off as a prize of war. In truth, I long to be back home with my family."

"It will not be that way. I assure you. Come at ten o'clock. Here, I will draw you a map of how to find the church."

On Sunday morning, I put on the new shirt that I had bought the day before and went off to church. Reverend Whang was waiting in his office. Another man, an older fellow, was with him. We bowed to each other and exchanged names.

"Please sit down," said the pastor. "Mr. Yun, This is Elder Han. He has agreed to act as your older brother until you get better oriented to our society and to our church. That is, if you would like him to do so." Elder Han was about sixty-five or seventy, taller than most Koreans. His thin, long face and sad eyes suggested prolonged suffering. His words and attitude, however, were calm and even cheerful.

"I am much too old to be your brother, but perhaps I can help you with some things as you adjust to life in South Korea. Also we would like you to become a part of our church community, and I will be glad to help you along that path."

"I must prepare for the morning worship," interrupted Whang. "The two of you stay here and talk it over. Just let me know what you decide and I will help in any way I can. Mr. Yun, I have written my brother and told him that we were finally able to locate you." With these words the pastor arose and left the room.

There were only a few minutes before worship so Elder Han suggested that afterwards we have lunch together. We found a small shop that served cold noodles and went in. As we slowly ate the noodles, Elder Han told me his story.

> I also am from North Korea. My father was a small landowner near the village of Sucho. Perhaps you know where it is. He had two acres of land, one acre was wetland and one was hills and dry land. The farm supported my father and mother, two sisters, my wife, me and our small daughter. We were much afraid when the Russians came in 1945, but when Kim Il Song took over, he assured us that land would be taken only from the large Japanese and Korean landlords. But that policy was soon canceled. All land, it was ordered, would be re-organized into collective farms. Landowners of all kinds were labeled as "enemies of the people."
>
> One day in 1948, word came to us that soldiers were on their way to our place to take over the farm, arrest my father and induct me into the Red Army. Before they arrived, Father hid me in the hollow of an old tree. He, himself, hid in a small, deep cave in the hills behind our property. On the night of the third day, Father came for me. We crept down to the house. There were no soldiers, but neither were there any women or children. We never saw them again. For several more days we hid and waited. When our women did not come back, we turned southward and began to walk. The war had not yet begun, but the borders were already closely

guarded. We traveled only at night. It took us many days, but we finally got across the border.

Before we could get settled the war broke out. Father and I along with millions of refugees walked three hundred miles down to Pusan. We found space on the side of a hill where a myriad of shacks sprang up. One morning I left Father to scrounge for food. I ran into a squad of soldiers who were looking for young men like me. I was detained, taken to army barracks and inducted into the South Korean army. It was six months before they would give me leave to visit my father. He was gone. I never found out what had happened to him.

I got out of the army four years later. Fortunately I found a job with a small company that supplied food to the army. I won't go into details, but I was very successful, and gradually built up my own company. I am now well off. I have never remarried, always hoping that one day I would again be united with my wife.

Elder Han's voice became almost inaudible as he brought his story to an end. His sad eyes reflected the suffering of his tragic story.

We had long since finished our noodles. The afternoon was nearing its end. Nevertheless, the Elder did not wish to part. "Let us go over to the 'New Moon Tea Room' for a cup of coffee. Now that I have told you my story, I want to hear yours. Do you mind?"

He spoke in a tone that made me think I would be doing him a favor if I were to share my background with him. We walked to the tearoom. It was crowded, but we found a table in a deep corner. A young hostess came. Han ordered coffee. I ordered ginger tea.

My story is much different from yours, Elder Han.
I hope you will not be offended by what I have to say.

Under the Japanese my grandfather and father were tenant farmers, actually more slaves than farmers. In their minds, landlords were all oppressors. They did not make distinctions between small and large.

When the Russians swept away that system, people like my grandfather and father were overjoyed. The Russians and the Great Leader, Kim Il Song, promised them land. That was the fulfillment of their dreams. Readily they supported Kim Il Song and the communist government.

As you said, the first land reform program was to have given land to individual farmers, but that later was changed to a system of collective farming. Father and Grandfather accepted this change in things. It was still their land and it was a system that would bring justice to the poor. In addition, by then they had an implicit faith that the Great Leader knew what was best.

I can recall Father telling stories about the landlords who were brought to trial. Most were found guilty of crimes against the people. Some were executed. You may not like to hear this, Elder Han, but grandfather told these stories with great pride. "Finally," he would proclaim, "the landlords got what they deserved. Justice was done."

I was born ten years after the war. Stories of heroism in the struggle against the Japanese, the valiant struggle against the American imperialists and the glorious return of the people to the land made up the tradition in which I was raised. As a youth I joined the Party and worked all my life as part of a collective farm. Father and Grandfather worked hard, long hours in the fields, but they were better off than they had ever been. I followed them as a member of our collective farm. I was proud of our work and the Party that guided us. I did not at all mind the hard work. We were proud of our nation's struggles for liberation and justice.

Then, I made the blunder that has ruined my life. I lost my temper and hit a Party leader with the limb of a tree. But I think you have heard that part of my life story so there is no need to repeat it."

Since I have been here in the South, I see that your standard of living and economy is much richer than ours, but it also looks like it is based more on capitalist greed and contains more injustice than ours in the North.

Elder Han listened with close attention. He felt the emotion with which I spoke. For a while we sat in silence looking into our empty teacups. "Your life and mine reflect the lives of our people, our entire nation. The differences between us are exactly the ones that separate our people north and south. The same history—but experienced so differently."

I nodded my head in agreement, but had nothing new to say. We stood up, paid for our tea and coffee and walked outside. It was dark. We shook hands and thanked each other for the honest conversation. "Next Friday evening there is a gathering of church people at my house," Mr. Han informed me. "Would you like to come? We meet every Friday for an hour or so." I told him that I would be honored to attend.

So, in this fashion, my life unexpectedly became brighter. Gradually I got used to the hard labor of my job; my fellow workers became friendlier; and on Friday evenings I met with the church people at Han's place. The meetings were an extension of the church. Elder Han, or one of the other people, would lead a short meditation on a verse from the Bible. Someone, or everyone, would pray and then there would be free and general conversation with refreshments. At first, several of the members were suspicious of me and expressed their hate of North Korean communism. They had lost loved ones in the war or had had their family land taken over by the government. They took great glee in the economic superiority of the South. On such occasions Elder Han would invariably intervene to remind us that the war was over almost fifty years now, and as followers of Hannanim and Jesus we were expected to practice forgiveness. I kept my peace, spoke of my own life only when directly asked. Gradually the heat that my presence engendered wore down and when I would miss a meeting, some one from the group was sure to appear to check on my welfare.

Fellowship with my countrymen from the North improved somewhat when I joined the "*Tongilhoe*," or Unification Organization. It consisted of a group of refugees who, with the aid of the South Korean government, studied and discussed reunification between North and South. We were allowed to express whatever idea we wanted to, but most of the time we spoke guardedly. The atmosphere was always heavy with suspicion, criticisms and guilt. The Friday night church group became the highlight of my week.

One Friday Elder Han told us the story of a small village in Kangwon Do Province. Heavy rains had washed out most of the rice land of the village. The fields had been terraced up the side of the mountains, but the flooded mountain waters had broken through the gates and destroyed much of the dike system. A church in the area had appealed to the church in Seoul for assistance. After hearing Elder Han's story, it was proposed that we, as the Friday night group, send financial help to the village. For the first time, I spoke without being asked to. "Perhaps some of us could go to the village and work with the people there to rebuild the terraces." Visions of my own village flashed in my head. Many a time I had worked on the terraced rice paddies. On that fateful day that set me off on my long journey, I was doing just that. A new excitement entered me. Perhaps I could return once more to a village like my home!

The practicality of my suggestion was debated at length. Though no one was against it, our group members were city folk or, like Elder Han, advanced in age. It did not seem feasible for them to volunteer work they could not perform. Only two of us were young enough to do hard labor and I was the only one who had experience at such work. Finally it was decided that the group would support the two of us to go to the village and work alongside the people there.

I arranged to take a week off from my work, and Elder Han secured permission from the authorities to allow me to spend a week in the village called Sanku. From morning till night I labored beside the farmers of the village. They too, at first were suspicious of me, but when they saw that I was willing to follow their lead and work as hard as they did, gradually they accepted me. At night after the sun had set, we would gather beside the stream that ran through the village. The women would bring food and drink. We would talk, exchange stories. At times they even asked me to tell stories about my own village and family. There were no communes here in the South. Each farmer owned his own little plot, but when it came to emergency time like flooded terraces or harvest season, the village farmers all pitched in and helped one another. It was the same system that had come down to us from our ancestors. Never had I felt so happy. I would have gladly stayed in the village, but that was not permitted.

The week passed all too swiftly. Villagers and church people came to the bus station to see me off. Over the next few years I returned to the village many times. I was greeted as family. Each time, I worked with the men in the fields, sat with them in the evenings swapping stories. My life in Seoul was made endurable knowing that not too far in the future I would spend a weekend or an entire week at home in the village.

CHAPTER 6

VLADIVOSTOK

When Oh Ki Sop finally opened his eyes, he was looking into the face of someone he dimly recognized. It took several minutes and some cold water before his confused brain recognized Chun Ho Bin, the orderly to the commandant at Chegdomyn in Siberia. "Where am I? What's going on? Where is Tatyana?"

"You are back in Chegdomyn, you fool. How could you be so dumb as to get caught by those bastards in Rostov?"

Oh Ki Sop lay still. He had no answer to the question, no answers at all. A wind tunnel was swooshing through his brain. He remembered Yun's frantic cry and an explosion of lights in his head. After that, nothing. How had they transported him clear back to Siberia? He must have been drugged for days.

"Listen close now, Oh Ki Sop! I give you one more chance for life. Don't screw up again. You are on a train. You and other prisoners are on your way back to the homeland. Before your train leaves this evening a guard will come to check foot and arm chains. He will pretend to check yours, but instead he will loosen them. Tomorrow morning at sunrise your train will stop to pick up freight. That is the time to make your break. Work slowly. Take the chains off; put them quietly on the floor. Go to the door. Without noise push it open and step out. Close it again. Walk away from the train at a normal rate. You will be met. Do as you are told. Do you understand?"

Oh nodded his head to let Chun know that he understood. His head was becoming clearer. He was indeed on a train, and he lay close to a door. Guards were dragging other prisoners in.

"By the way Oh, you might be interested to know that the commandant is no longer with us. His many businesses were finally exposed. But I remain as orderly to the new man. Remember that." With that unexpected threat, Chun left.

Events unfurled as Chun predicted. Soon after Oh left the train, he spotted a truck along the roadside. Someone inside motioned to him. He got in. Beside the driver there was one other passenger. They explained that he was on his way to Vladivostok. It would take several days and several transfers of vehicles to make the journey.

Early in the morning of the sixth day Oh Ki Sop awoke to find that they had arrived in Vladivostok. They drove around the city, built like a grand amphitheater looking out on the Bay of the Golden Horn. The road wound through a hundred enclaves where the land interrupted the water of the bay. At the end of one enclave stood a small building with a big sign: "C.T. McCaffery Ltd. Shipping and Transfer." Inside, three clerks were busy at work. When the driver and Oh Ki Sop walked in, one of them immediately stood up and went out a side door. The other two ushered them to seats and offered tea.

After a short while the front door opened. The man who entered was small of stature with a thick crop of uncombed black hair. Small reading glasses were perched on the end of his nose. His features were oriental, but his carriage was Western. To further mix up the picture, the man spoke in fluent Korean.

"Mr. Oh, I have heard much of you from our mutual friend, Chun Ho Bin. You are welcome to our humble place of business."

Oh Ki Sop was speechless. Who was this guy? How could he speak Korean? What was his business? Where did Chun come into it? What was he, Oh Ki Sop, getting into? He said nothing so the foreigner again picked up the conversation.

"Do not be surprised that I know your language. Besides Korean, I speak Chinese, Japanese, Russian and English. You see, my grandfather was an Englishman who helped open up trade between England and the Far East back in the late nineteenth century. He married a Chinese woman and settled down here in Vladivostok. When the Russians completed the Trans-Siberian Railroad in 1905 his business flourished. Our family has been here ever since. My father followed my grandfather both in business and in selecting a Chinese woman to be the mother of his children. I am now the third generation. As the sign says outside, my name is McCaffery. I differ from my father only in that I am married to a Korean woman, not Chinese.

"But that is enough about me. Let us get down to business. Mr. Oh, McCaffery and Company still carries on trade with England and other countries around the world. Even during the dark days of communism, we were allowed to stay in business, but under strict controls. Now we are beginning to expand our business not only with the West, but also within Russia and into China. We even hope that one day we will be able to serve North Korea."

"I do not understand. What do I have to do with all this? Why did Chun send me here? Please help my feeble brain to understand what is taking place."

"I am getting to that. Let me put in simple terms. I need labor. Our friend Chun supplies me, and other businesses, with cheap labor. You are now an employee of the McCaffery Company. We have work for you to do."

Oh Ki Sup was now not only bewildered, he was frightened. "I have been sold into slavery? What if I do not want to work at your company?"

McCaffery took offense at the remark. In a quiet, but angry voice, he replied, "Quite the contrary Mr. Oh. We are giving you the chance for freedom. If Mr. Chun had not rescued you, you might well be dead by now. You must now repay Mr. Chun for his kindness. I need your labor and skills. I will pay Chun a reasonable amount for his efforts. To you I give safety from the Russian and North Korean police. Remember Oh Kap Soo's grandson is still an enemy of the state. All you are asked to do is contribute one year of labor. You will be given room and board and a small stipend to meet needs, but no salary. If you

prove to be faithful and a good worker, and our business pros-
pers, the next year you become an employee on full salary.

"You said you were a slave. No! Never! You may walk out
that door right now. I do not enslave you. But once you leave,
you are on your own. There is no further protection from me or
Chun."

McCaffery's words baffled Oh even further. Chun had sold
him to McCaffery. After one year, he would be free. Or he could
go now and fend for himself, but McCaffery's voice had a bit
of a threat to it. If Oh left now, he might need protection from
Chun as well as from the police.

"Let me help you, Mr. Oh. You have a wife, Tatyana. She is
in Rostov. Right? After your year is over, I will bring her to
Vladivostok, if you wish."

The mention of Tatyana snapped Oh to attention. "A whole
year? Can she not come sooner?"

"No. Absolutely not. The first year you must pay off your
debt. Then she can come. If you decide to stay, I will get word
to Tatyana that you are alive. She probably thinks you are dead.
You may write her a letter and I will see that it is delivered. I am
not a slave master, Mr. Oh, but I do need cheap labor to make
my business go. Hopefully we will grow out of this stage before too long, but right now we must depend upon workers like
you. So what do you say? Yes or no? Make your decision now."

Oh hesitated to speak, but with the promise of being restored to Tatyana, he knew what his decision would be. "Okay,
I stay and I work one year. Then my wife comes, and we decide
then as to future relations. Is that your proposition?

"That is the bargain I propose," replied a now cheerful
McCaffery.

"How do I know you will keep your word?"

"You don't, but I extend to you my hand. That is the way
my English countrymen seal a promise. When I give a promise, I do not violate it." With that he put out his hand to Oh. Oh

took it and the two shook hands while looking deep into each other's eyes. They both liked what they saw.

That night Oh Ki Sop wrote a letter.

> My Dearest Tatyana,
> I pray that you are in good health. I think of you always and send you my love. I am alive and safe. I cannot tell you much more.
>
> Please wait for me. After one year we will be together again. A year sounds like forever, but it will go fast and then we can be husband and wife.
>
> Forgive me for being stupid enough to let myself be deceived by the North Korean agents. I hope you were not hurt.
>
> You will not hear from me for one year. I cannot receive letters from you. Please be patient and think of me.
>
> Your loving husband,
> Oh Ki Sop

The next morning he gave the letter to McCaffery. "You promise that she will receive this?"

"She will have it in her hands within two weeks," was the reply. "Now it is time for you and me to go to work." McCaffery pulled out a large map of Siberia and northern China. "As I told you last night, McCaffery Ltd. has been in the shipping and international trade for three generations. Under the communists we were limited to importing only items the government permitted. Now the Soviet Union is no more. We are free to expand. Our contacts in Europe, the United States and Japan are eager to do business. The challenge to us is to develop trading partners in Siberia, China, South Korea and maybe later on, North Korea."

The Englishman spoke with such zeal that Oh found himself getting interested. "Sounds like great plans. Where do I fit in? I don't know anything about international trade."

"Be patient, be patient. I am about to come to you. First comes the over-all plan. Then comes your part in it. Your job is important.

"We are ready to begin truck service to Khabarovsk. Already we have orders for industrial and agricultural machinery, chemicals, liquor and cigarettes. To fulfill these contracts, we must be able to guarantee that cargo will be delivered promptly. This is where you come in. You are a driver and a licensed mechanic, and of even more value, you already know the roads and the system of "handling" the guards at the many check points.

"Now look at the map. All the roads connecting big cities such as Khabarovsk, Harbin and Shenyang are shown. These are the remnants of the old post roads built for sledges and carts. They meander all over the place, but already the system is being improved. As time goes on, it will get better. Your first task is to make time and cost schedules for delivery from here to each of those three points using these maps as your guide for distances. Consider the condition of the roads and the interference at road checks. Start with Khabarovsk. Can you do it?"

Oh Ki Sop had been listening with increased enthusiasm. "Yes, I can do it. Give me the price of petrol and oil. Show me the type of vehicle and I can give you an estimate in a few days. Then a trial run should work out the details. I hope your trucks are in good shape. The roads are mean and securing parts is almost impossible, but, I think, we should be able to do it. On the trial run, at least, it might be good to have a partner with me."

McCaffery was more than pleased with Oh's response.

"Okay then. Get to work. Give me a tentative time schedule and cost estimate in three days."

Within two weeks of arriving in Vladivostok, Oh was once more on the road driving truck. This time, however, he felt better about it. He was confident that McCaffery would live up to his bargain. After one year he would not only have a good job, he would have Tatyana. With those happy thoughts in his mind he began to even enjoy the beauty of the Siberian forests and the richness of the Amur-Ussuri plains.

On his first visit to Khabarovsk Oh Ki Sop visited the Church of *Hannanim* that older brother Yun had told him about. The building was there just as Yun had described it. He entered and was welcomed by a middle aged Korean lady. Oh explained that he had a friend who knew the old pastor from the United States. "I heard of his murder. Have they ever found out who did it?"

"They have imprisoned a mentally insane man who used to visit the pastor. They found some of the pastor's belongings in his room, and an instrument that might have been used as the weapon."

Oh thanked the woman and left, thinking of Yun, hoping that some day they would meet again.

After he left the church, he walked over to the bank where he had set up an account so many years before. Much to his surprise he learned that his account was still valid and had been receiving interest. The amount would allow him and Tatyana to find a place to live. His dreams had changed. He was no longer in a hurry to return to his home in North Korea. Now he saw his future in terms of Tatyana—probably in Vladivostok or maybe Rostov.

Oh Ki Sop's skills fit with the needs of the McCaffery Company. His estimates of time and costs proved to be accurate and just as importantly he developed the ways of a smooth salesman, making friends for the company at each port of contact. Pleased with the quality and promptness of delivery, businesses in Khabarovsk, Harbin and Shenyang began more and more to use McCaffery as their means of hauling and transfer. Consequently, several other men were put on as drivers. Oh Ki Sop became the foreman for the group. It was his responsibility to train new men on driving skills and to dispatch them over the several routes. He, himself, spent fewer days on the road, but his work hours expanded. He slept the minimum and worked the maximum. Time was forgotten in the race to do his work.

One afternoon while Oh was in the middle of repairing one of the trucks, he received a message to report to Mr. McCaffery.

"Mr. Oh, you are doing an excellent job. I want now to turn your responsibilities over to another man, and I want you to begin a new venture. We plan to make a bid on importing some heavy machinery for a steel factory in Shenyang. To do that we need to be able to handle the big containers that are now used in international shipping. That means new trucks, huge ones, much bigger than any we now have. Trucks called trailer trucks. Five of them are coming in this spring as soon as the ice in the harbor is melted. I want you to lead a group of five men who will learn to drive and maintain these giants.

"Before that job will be complete, however, your year of service will be up. I'm sure you are aware of that. So I need to know whether you want to extend your time with us. If not, I will have to put another man in charge."

Oh Ki Sop had in fact lost track of time in the excitement of his new work, but he gave no hint of that to McCaffery. "Will you keep your word and bring Tatyana?"

"Yes."

"Will I be on the payroll as a regular employee?"

"Yes. You have my word."

"Very well, I will stay and learn how to drive the big trucks."

"Splendid! Splendid! Now there is one more thing to do before the trucks get here. We have been asked by a charitable organization to deliver a truckload of food and medical supplies to a refugee camp in China. The camp is for people who are fleeing the droughts in North Korea. It is located near a town in China called Dandong on the Korean border. It will be new territory for us, maybe with some unexpected problems. We won't make any money, but it will give us an opening further into China. I would like you to handle that assignment. Is that okay with you?

"I would like to do that. I will need, of course, an assistant driver. But when I get back, you and I begin to talk about Tatyana."

CHAPTER 7

CHINA

When I came back from the country one Sunday night, a letter was waiting for me. It was from Elder Han asking me to come to his house the next evening. As soon as I read the note, I knew that something strange was up. My bones had been through so many cataclysms they now sensed that once more something unexpected was about to happen. I entered the Elder's courtyard at seven o'clock. I cleared my throat to let them know I had arrived, took off my shoes and pushed open the sliding doors into the living room. "Welcome. How was your trip to the country? When did you get back?" were the friendly greetings that met me. Five people besides the elder were sitting cross-legged on the floor. They seemed to have been in deep conversation before my entry.

Tea and rice cakes were served. Light chatter commanded the room for several minutes. Then Elder Han cleared his voice. Everyone fell silent. "Brother Yun, we have been meeting for an hour before you got here. For several weeks now we have been discussing a matter that directly affects you, but we have not been prepared to bring it to you until now. It is a bit complicated so be patient and hear us out to the end. Mr. Kim will speak first. He is the chair of our Church's Overseas Mission Committee."

With that introduction he motioned to Kim Seung Ho. I had met him many times at the Friday night meetings. He was a businessman whose original home was also in the North. "Mr. Yun, I am sure you have heard about the terrible droughts and floods that have hit the North during the last few years. The situation does not seem to be getting any better. As a matter of fact, it is getting worse. There are hundreds of thousands, maybe millions of people in need of food and medicines. It is so bad that people have begun to leave North Korea and seek refuge in China. You have heard about this situation no doubt?"

"Yes, I know about that. As I have mentioned before, I have joined the Friends of Unification. We are kept acquainted with what goes on in the North," I replied wondering why Kim was being so careful to explain something everyone knew about.

He went on. "The churches have for many years floated proposals to encourage reunification. Some individuals even broke the law and went to North Korea on their own. Well-known pastor, Moon Ik Whan, spent several years in prison because of his visit. None of these efforts came to fruition. We are now considering a new approach that may help the unification process. Under previous administrations this would not have been possible, but with the recent election of a non-military, democratic president, it might be acceptable.

"We, along with several other church organizations, have decided to send aid to a refugee camp in China. We will send contributions of rice from here in the South, and in addition we have contracted for supplies to come from abroad. We are expecting shipments to arrive through Dalian, China and Vladivostok that will then be trucked to the refugee camp near Dandong."

My bones began to shiver. Dandong was the Chinese city closest to my village, the one to which I had fled so many years before. With obvious agitation in my voice, I broke in before Kim could say anything else. "So why do you tell me these things? Why this special meeting? Please tell me what is going on."

"Brother Yun, we want you to be our representative in that refugee camp in Dandong."

I was plunged into a stupor of disbelief. Dandong! Back to where I had started so many years before. I had been picked up out of my remote village in North Korea; sent half way around the world and was now being restored to the very place from which I had started. From Dandong I could even arrange a visit to see my wife and children. It was too much. A mystery too deep for me to fathom. I sat in silence. No word of reply came from me.

Elder Han, as though reading my thoughts added, "If you are willing to undertake the job, however, you must promise that you will never attempt to enter North Korea. If you were to try such a thing, you would immediately be charged with treason and our whole refugee program would be put under suspicion. We hope that you will be able to gain news about your family, but you must promise not to go into North Korea. Now you know what is going on and what we want of you. What do you say?"

I avoided a direct reply. I had to get used to the question before I could come to an answer. Hope of going home was ruled out, but surely from Dandong I could send a letter or maybe even meet someone from home. At the very least I would be close to where I wanted to be. "What would my responsibilities be? Would the government authorities permit me to go?"

"That is something yet to be determined, but I think it is possible that the Special Ministry for Unification might give approval. Mr. Ko Young Bok, sitting next to you, is a close friend to the Minister in charge and is willing to broach the question to him. The recent election of a democratic administration might make this a possibility, but we want to be sure that it is done for the right purpose with the right attitude."

"I am not sure I know what you mean by that?

"What I mean," explained Mr. Ko, "is this. The new government policies may legally allow us to establish the refugee camp for North Koreans, but we want the work to be done with an attitude of brother-to-brother, not superior to inferior or capitalist to communist. We remember that the North sent rice to us in 1984 when bad rains washed out much of our harvest."

Elder Han then spoke again. "Here, Mr. Yun, is where you

come in. You are a North Korean who recently has come into the South. You are a symbol of possible reconciliation. You still love your homeland, yet live in peace and fellowship with us who are southerners. This symbolism of reconciliation is key to our undertaking. Feeding the refugees is important in itself, but we want it to also be a witness to peace and brotherhood.

"But we need to know your reply. Given the restriction on travel to North Korea, do you want to undertake the job? We need your answer now."

I paused only briefly before I gave my reply. "I cannot begin to understand my own life. For years I have fled from one place to another, not of my own choice. In each place I have suffered undeserved hardships, and received undeserved blessings. It is beyond me. I cannot understand. Now it seems like I may be coming to the end of my journey. I am honored that you would trust me to do such an important work. I gladly accept, and promise to be worthy of your trust."

Loud cheers and applause came from the others in the room. Each in turn shook my hand and promised support and prayers.

"Please say nothing to anyone else. It will take time for Mr. Ko to clear things with the Minister of Unification. Please continue your job with the construction crew, but in the evenings come to the church where we will have meetings with Reverend Whang to get you oriented to the work you will be asked to do." After those words, Elder Han offered a prayer of thanks to *Hannanim* asking for wisdom and guidance. Then the meeting was over. My premonitions of cataclysm had proven correct, but this time I sensed that the change would be for my good.

Six months later the Church's proposal to assign me to the refugee camp in Dandong was approved. The National Security Agency opposed the proposal, but the Ministry of Unification carried the day arguing that I was not only trustworthy, I was also a symbol of reconciliation between North and South. When the news came, Pastor Whang immediately notified Elder Han and me. We met at the church to make final arrangements.

Ko Young Bok gave a report of his negotiations with the government agencies. "Permission for this project is conditional. Many still carry strong hatred and fear of the North. They opposed the project. Permission was granted only on the basis that we perform strictly on the basis of charity. Any suggestion of political intercourse with the government or people of the North will mean the termination of approval."

"That, of course, is our thinking too," interceded Elder Han. Ours is to be a witness beyond the political-military intercourse that has heretofore dominated conversation between the two sides.

"Now let's do some planning. After the winter has passed, there is likely to be a large emigration of people out of the North. Their food supply is likely to be exhausted. Warmer weather will allow them to travel. So we plan to begin delivery of food, clothing and medicines to the camp in March and April."

"Therefore," interrupted the pastor, "brother Yun should prepare to arrive there soon after the first of the year to make certain that all is ready. We will have to make arrangements for his room and board and an assistant who can speak both Korean and Chinese."

After a few hours of discussion, Pastor Whang signaled that it was time to adjourn. He looked at me and asked, "Mr. Yun, do you have any final words before we close?"

"Yes, I would like to ask one favor. For several years now, I have lived among the followers of *Hannanim*. On several occasions they have saved my life. I cannot understand many of the teachings, but I do accept the teachings of Jesus of Nazareth as my guide for life. Indeed his Way seems to agree with the ideals and teachings that I received as a child. Before I undertake the job in China I would like to become part of your church. If you will accept me, I would like to be baptized."

The room was quiet for sometime before Pastor Whang

replied, "We would be overjoyed to accept you into the kingdom. Shall we do it the second Sunday of January at the New Year's celebration, just before you leave for Dandong? A new year, a new life and a new mission! Splendid!"

I arrived in Dandong the first day of February 1998. My assistant, a young Chinese-Korean man, met me at the airport and arranged for me to stay with one of the Korean-Chinese families in the city. The first day I walked the city trying to relive the few days I had been there, but much had changed. The market place was still there, but it was much more orderly. The wine house and the church were gone. I did, however, find the path where I had assaulted the old gentleman. I looked across the river. My home laid only a short journey away.

Officially, my first task was to call upon the local authorities. The Korean Church Consortium along with international refugee organizations had prepared the way. The Chinese officials were already aware of the plans and were willing to cooperate as long as the refugees and camp directors did not become involved in any political action or make any political statements.

That evening I met with representatives of the Korean-Chinese churches. Many of them were from families who had lived in China for three or four generations, but they were still Korean, still spoke the Korean language. I told them about my own background in North Korea, and something about my journeys. Then I introduced the purpose and goals behind the establishment of a refugee camp. "We cannot be sure how many people will seek refuge," I said, "but we will need many volunteers who can speak both Korean and Chinese to help them get adjusted to their new conditions. We cannot pay you anything, but if you can volunteer just a few hours a week, it will be a big help and also make our message of reconciliation all the more clear." Several men and quite a number of women agreed to work with us.

A small village of tents and wooden shacks able to house a

hundred people was ready by the middle of March, but by the end of March that proved to be inadequate. By the end of May, food and shelter for six hundred people were needed.

My major responsibility was to record names, origins and addresses, according to families, of all who came into the camp. From early morning to late at night I sat at a desk keeping the records and assigning the refugees to an appropriate section.

It happened in late June, just before I was to return to Seoul to make my first report to the church. A young man stood in front of me. He had come into the camp only that morning. A sense of the surreal crept through my bones. I was looking at a young version of myself.

"What is your name?" I asked, knowing the answer before I asked the question.

"My name is Yun Mo Dong. I come from the village of Sochun in the province of Pyung An Pukdo" Before the boy could finish, I interrupted. "Are your mother and sister with you?"

"Yes sir. They are, but how did you know?"

I asked my assistant to take over the desk, and led the boy to a far corner of the room. "Mo Dong, I am your father. Many years ago when you were only three I had to flee our village. But quick where is your mother? Is she in good health?"

Mo Dong was incredulous, but he looked closely at the face in front of him and realized it was true. "We thought you were dead. For years we cried and agonized. How did you get here? I don't understand! "

"It will take hours to explain, but first I must see your mother."

"Perhaps I'd best go ahead and forewarn her. If you suddenly appear, she may not be able to stand it. She is very frail. She has been starving herself to feed Young He and me. Let me go first, then I will come back for you." With this the young man left the room. It seemed like hours before he returned, but finally he came to the door and nodded his head for me to follow.

She was standing in front of a tent in section twelve—a small, haggard woman. She needed help from her daughter to stand erect. Her skin was taut against her skull, but her big round eyes shone brightly. "*Tangshin, Tangshin!*—my beloved, my beloved!— You are yet alive. I have waited. I have prayed. The happiness is too great. I am going to die. How can you be here? Are you a ghost? I shall certainly die!" She sank to her knees crying. I knelt on the earth in front of her. I embraced her and the two of us rocked back and forth wailing loudly as we gave vent to our happiness.

Through her tears and laments she choked out, "Where have you been? We thought you were dead? Why did you not come back?"

Bewildered by my wife's question, I replied, "You know why I left. I explained it to you. I knocked Pak Ju Won unconscious. For that I could have gone to prison, and you could have been sent into exile. Did you not denounce me?"

"But Father, it did not happen like that," interrupted my son. "Pak did go to the Party Chairman, but the Chairman called in your comrade, Kwan Ho Kyung, who worked with you that day. Kwan told the story from your side, and the chairman believed him. He had had many complaints about Pak. No charges were ever filed against you. For days the entire village searched for you in the mountains, but you had vanished."

The life went out of me. I fainted face down on the ground. For a long time I lay as still and silent as death. Then I heard deep, frightful moans escaped from my throat. "*Hannanim, Hannanim*, why has this suffering been put upon us? For years I have roamed as a homeless refugee. I've been ridiculed and beaten. My family has starved. Now we are together in a foreign land. No more, oh Lord. No more. Let us rest in peace."

A great silence descended upon us. No one spoke. Not a sound was heard. Young He, my daughter, fulfilled the silence.

She knelt down and gently lifted me to my feet. Without a word she led me to a nearby cot and laid me down. The first day ended that way. I lay on the cot. My wife sat next to me holding my hand tightly for fear I might again disappear.

Gradually our family became acquainted with each other in this strange, new environment. A routine took shape. With the help of women from the church, my wife and daughter began to peddle vegetables like onions, potatoes, cabbage and turnips in Dandong's big open market. A school was started for the camp children and Mo Dong helped with that in the morning. In the afternoons he worked alongside me, directing newcomers on how to get situated

One afternoon just before sundown a truck came lumbering in to the village and stopped in front of Mo Dong. The driver put his head out the window and said, "Son, do you know where I should unload my cargo? It is grain and medicine for the North Korean refugees. I have come all the way from Vladivostok. I need to talk to the man in charge."

"I do not know, but let me ask my father. He is inside."

Mo Dong walked up to the table where I was busy taking information from a new arrival. "Father a truck load of supplies has come from Vladivostok. The driver wants to talk with you. He says his name is Oh Ki Sop."

HOW LONG, O LORD?

This prayer was written in 1988 by a delegation of Christian leaders who met in Glion, Switzerland at the second historic meeting arranged by the world Council of Churches. It was known as the Prayer of Jubilee and used all over the world in 1995, which was the anniversary of 50 years of division of Korea.

O God, the Lord of History,
Who promised to nurture and sustain the earth and its life;
Who promised that justice would flow like a river, that slaves would be set free, that the hungry would be fed and that the covenant community would be created;
Who promised reconciliation between enemies and comfort for those separated from their loved ones;
Who promised to your people the realization of peace and unity;
Receive our thanks and praise.

The world still groans under the yoke of oppression;
War and hostility still ravage the people of many lands;
Hatred and division are the banners of a sinful world, O Lord.

We bring before you the cries (han) of the people of Korea,
Who have endured alien occupation and imperialism;
Who have suffered the devastation of a cruel, fratricidal war;
Who have been crucified by the division of their nation through no fault of their own.

-OGLE

O God of love,
How long will the people of North and South Korea regard each other as enemies?
How long will the ten million who have lost their family members be unable to find each other?
How long will their fate be determined by alien powers and ideologies?
How long will they be deprived of their human dignity as children of God?
How long will their rights and responsibilities to live with freedom and justice be abused?
Hear our cries and prayers, O Lord.

We cry out to you from the depths of despair over the division of Korea, which is the victim of a divided world.
You came to the world as the servant of peace.
You promised love and peace.
You commanded us to love each other.
We rejoice in your promises and recognize your blessings.

You have given us signs of hope in the midst of despair.
For more than 40 years you have sustained in the Korean people a hope and resilience that has fortified them in their struggle for justice, peace, and reunification.
You have set out a small light in a darkness that has lasted much too long.
You have opened up channels of communication between Chris-

tians of North and South Korea.

You continue to increase the number of those whose longing for reunification has been translated into concrete acts of reconciliation and hope.

Come, Holy Spirit.
Grant us the Gospel of Jubilee: the good news of liberation, freedom and unity;
Proclaim the release of the prisoners of division;
Recover the sight of those blinded by hatred, jealousy, greed and power;
Grant peace and freedom to the poor, oppressed and lost.

We pray that Your Kingdom come;
That your holy will of peace and unity come to the land of Korea and to the whole world.

Out of the depths of our hearts we cry to you, O Lord, united in prayer throughout the world, including both North and South Korea, in the name of Christ Jesus.

AMEN

ABOUT THE AUTHOR

George E. Ogle is a native of Pitcairn, Pennsylvania. After graduating from Maryville College and Duke Seminary he worked in South Korea from 1954 to 1974 as a United Methodist missionary. During the decade of the sixties, he along with his wife, Dorothy, and their four children lived in the industrial city of Inchun.

He and three Korean colleagues, pioneered in the work of Urban Industrial Mission (UIM). The three Korean pastors each took jobs as day laborers in one of Inchun's many factories. As a foreigner, Reverend Ogle could not gain employment, so he became an unofficial chaplain for a steel mill and a railroad car shop. Through sharing their hard labor and by being a pastor to those in need, UIM staff hoped to better understand the word of God for Inchun's industrial workers as they struggled for justice and respect in their work place.

During the 1960's Korea's Constitution permitted workers to organize and act collectively. Within this context UIM initiated a series of education programs, focusing on workers' rights under the labor law. Ogle and his colleagues also cooperated with Sokang University and Koryo University in Seoul, as these two institutions began their own industrial relations programs.

Unfortunately, however, toward the end of the 1960's President Pak Chung Hee (a former general in the military) decided to change the tone of Korean society. He established a military dictatorship with himself as perpetual ruler. From that time on the Korean Central Intelligence Agency (KCIA) began to intrude into all walks of life. UIM came under its surveillance.

UIM staff members were arrested, and participants in UIM programs were warned to stay away. The KCIA declared that UIM was a communist-front organization.

In 1971 Reverend Ogle returned to the United States where he completed his PhD in International Labor Relations at the University of Wisconsin. He received an invitation to teach at Seoul National University in 1973. In the following year, along with his duties at Seoul National University, he became a spokesperson for eight men who were unjustly sentenced to die by military courts. In December of 1974, the Pak Chung Hee government forcefully deported him from South Korea.

From 1975-1981 Dr. Ogle taught at Candler School of Theology at Emory University. From 1981 to 1991 he was the Director of the Department of Social and Economic Justice for the General Board of Church and Society of the United Methodist Church. After retiring from the Board of Church and Society he moved to Springfield, Illinois where he worked for the Illinois Conference of Churches as Director of Illinois Impact.

Since 1984 Dr. Ogle has returned to Korea on many occasions, and he visited North Korea once in 1995. He has published two books: *Liberty to the Captives* (1976), about the ministry of UIM, and *South Korea: Dissent within the Economic Miracle* (1990), a study focusing on Korea's labor unions in the period of 1987-1989. This new book," *How Long, O Lord?*" is his first book of fiction. Since retirement he has also focused on writing poetry, which has not yet been published.

BVG